D0108170

Kriti 2021

Dear Carrie-
Thank you so much for your support all along the way! You are a bookish superhero. I hope you enjoy this taste of sword-free fantasy!
- Dan

The Living Waters

Book 1 of the Weirdwater Confluence Duology

By Dan Fitzgerald

This is a work of fiction. Similarities to real people, places, or events are entirely coincidental.

THE LIVING WATERS

First edition. October 15, 2021.

Written by Dan Fitzgerald.

This book is dedicated to the memory of Phil Babiak, whose real-life adventures and joyous spirit will forever inspire me.

Table of Contents

Chapter One

Sylvan held perfectly still as Miki layered the sapphire blue onto his face, one steady brushstroke at a time. Miki was a true artist, angling his brush to cover every crevice and divot without ever touching an eyelash or tickling Sylvan's nose.

"I'm going to make such a mess of this on my own," Sylvan said while Miki was dipping his brush.

"That you are." Miki touched up the corners of his mouth and the bottom of his nose around his nostrils. "But where you're going, I doubt anyone's even seen a painted face before, so perhaps they won't even notice. Speaking of which, I've set out a few colors for you to choose from. I was thinking something in a ruddy beige might suit you." He stood back, checking both sides of Sylvan's face, and touched up the hairline above his left temple.

"I had my heart set on something a little darker, maybe a burnished bronze?"

"With your hair? Please. Anything south of slightly tan's going to be a stretch. Pucker."

Sylvan sighed and pushed out his lips. Miki dabbed them with black, tsk-tsking under his breath.

"You know you'll need a natural pinkish-purple for your lips as well."

"Yes, and some stinking rags to complete the ensemble. Let's worry about that tomorrow. I just want to look proper one last time before I go."

Miki stepped back, framed Sylvan's face with his golden-brown fingers, and smiled.

"You really are going to make a mess of yourself without me. I'm just glad I won't be there to see it."

Sylvan's father beamed with an irrepressible smirk in his gold-painted face as he stood and raised his glass, and the half-dozen conversations at the banquet table died out one by one. He scanned the table with his eyes and his smile grew more genuine as his gaze fell on Sylvan, who was glad for the blue on his cheeks to hide the blush.

"They say it is a negligent parent who does not wish a better life for their child. And though, my dear Sylvan, at twenty-five you are far too old to be called a child, I should wish for you a better life than the one I have enjoyed." Smiles hung expectantly on every face, knowing the twist was coming. With his father, nothing could be simply stated, no emotion laid bare without a solid coat of irony. "And yet, as I look around this table at the sons and daughters, partners and spouses here present, to say nothing of your dear mother, who condescended to accept my offer of marriage thirty-some years ago—" He paused to allow the polite laughter to run its course. "As I look around me, I cannot honestly say that I could wish for you anything better than the life the heavens have gifted me." He took a sip of his wine, set down the glass, and his face grew serious.

"But what I can wish for, what I do wish for, is your ability to choose your calling, to pursue it to your fullest, and to make the world a better place for your having lived in it. And now that you bear the title of Honorable Doctor of Life Sciences—" He raised his voice and his glass, and a dozen glasses joined his in the air. "There can be no doubt that you will contribute more to the honor and glory of this house than I ever have." Murmurs of assent mixed with clinking glass, and Sylvan drained every drop of his wine, his eyes swimming with unspent tears, which he dabbed away with his handkerchief so as not to smear his makeup. "In case anyone missed the announcement, after his roughabout, Doctor Sylvan Kirin will be joining the faculty at the Greater University of Anari as a full scholar, with his own cohort of undermasters to do his learned bidding."

The rest of dinner was a blur of wine and dish after decadent dish, and Sylvan drifted among conversational currents until at last tea was served and the group dispersed to the wide veranda overlooking the pond. Sylvan fell onto a chair at a table, cupping his hands around a lavender-scented candle, and stared out at the flotilla of water lilies, whose white flowers glowed in the moonlight.

"All alone at your own party? How very like you." Artemis slung himself into a chair opposite Sylvan, sliding his teacup onto the table.

"Intruding on my peaceful solitude? How very like you, Art."

Artemis raised his teacup, took a sip, and sat back, staring out at the pond, his copper-painted face shining in the reflected moonlight. "What are brothers for?"

"What indeed." Sylvan held his hand above the candle's flame, searching for the perfect height where the heat was uncomfortable but would not burn his skin.

"What's this I hear about a riverboat?" Artemis

leaned forward, both hands wrapped around his cup.

"It's called a shantyboat, apparently. It's basically a cabin on top of a raft with great sweeps for steering."

"How charming!"

"And we have to help build it."

Artemis almost choked on his tea. "You're going to come back with lumberjack muscles. You'll have to be fitted with all new clothes."

"Such are the sacrifices we make in pursuit of the truth."

"And tell me, what truth do you hope to find in that filthy river? That waterborne parasites are real? That there truly is a life out there more miserable than the outer circles of Anari?"

"I'm sure there's a lot more out there than we know. And they say once we get past the big cities, it's wild and beautiful, and there are no people for miles around. Just think of the research possibilities, fish, creatures, and plants I've only read about—things I haven't even read about because no one's ever written them down, or maybe even seen them!"

"Sounds like my idea of paradise." Sylvan's mother hovered over his shoulder, and he craned his head back to smile at her.

"Come sit, mother."

She slid into a chair between him and Artemis, holding a lacquered box in her lap, a self-satisfied smile on her burnt-orange painted face. Artemis rubbed his hands together, his bright eyes flitting from his mother to Sylvan.

"Well come on, the suspense is killing me!" Artemis looked down to his mother's lap, then back up at Sylvan.

"Well I don't know, now that I think of it, maybe he'd rather wait until after his roughabout? It would give him something to look forward to." Her eyes twinkled in the candlelight, her smile warming Sylvan to his core.

“That sounds perfect, actually,” said Sylvan, playing along, though his heart fluttered with anticipation. “As I lie there dying of some exotic disease, I can entertain myself with thoughts of what might possibly have been in that pretty box my mother showed me at my lifting off.”

“The diseases people die of downriver are rarely so exotic. Dysentery, oxbow fever, mudworm, Ulver’s cough—” She stopped, a serene smile growing on her face. “But you’ll be in good hands. Your minder is an accredited herbalist. You’re more likely to be devoured by needleteeth than succumb to anything as prosaic as a petty disease.” She gave a slow blink, breathed out through her nose, and lifted the box onto the table.

It was one of the more elaborate book boxes Sylvan had ever seen. Its edges were carved into the shape of curling waves, and the surface of the box showed images of fish, snakes, turtles, and more fantastical aquatic creatures, in wood of varying colors interlaid with gold and silver filament. The hinges and clasp were of brass so polished they appeared to give off their own light. Sylvan’s mother slid the box toward him, turning it so the clasp faced him, then withdrew her hands slowly, letting them settle on her lap. She sat up straight, her deep eyes full of loving pride.

“We had the box special made, triple-lacquered and seam-sealed so it will float, and keep the book dry through flood and storm.”

Sylvan fumbled with the clasp, his fingers trembling as he sorted out the unusual interlocking brass pieces. This box wasn’t going to pop open by accident. He looked up at his mother and brother’s expectant faces, closed his eyes, and opened the box. He kept his eyes closed for a moment as he inhaled deeply, the tang of fresh-dyed leather mixing with the musty odor of centuries-old vellum. When at last he opened his eyes, his breath caught in his throat as he stared at the cover, rich blue calfskin with letters set in elegant swirls of mother-of-pearl.

The Living Waters

L. G. Servais

"Mom, gods, it's incredible, I—" Sylvan opened the cover and flipped the book open with delicate fingers. Though the cover was new, the handwriting and illustrations were from the late classical period, around the time the book was written, though many copies had been made even in Servais' time. But the marginalia were something else entirely, fine pre-modern penmanship with tiny letters, but with an urgent, almost aggressive quality. Next to a clever drawing of a fish with long spines running the length of its back was a note that read: *The spines are half this length, it has no teeth to speak of, and the description of its diet is entirely inaccurate. It has been proven to be herbivorous.*

"You read it in study, I presume?" his mother asked.

"Yes, in second year, but the student edition was abridged, and certainly had no marginalia. Who wrote these notes anyway?"

His mother turned her palms up, feathering her fingers in the air. "The antiquarian said they were the work of an anonymous scholar, whose handwriting has not been identified elsewhere. The book's provenance is not entirely certain, as it surely changed hands during the war, but he assures me it's a first edition, and he knows what would happen if he were caught in a lie."

"It's the most incredible gift anyone's ever given me!" He leaned over the table and gave her the least awkward hug his angle would allow.

"I figure it'll give you something to occupy yourself with while you float. And who knows? Maybe you'll stumble across the Living Waters themselves. The writer of the marginalia implied he had been there, and that Servais had not. If you do, you can add your own marginalia."

"Let's not give in to the fantastical, mother." As a child, he had devoured the stories of this legendary place, said to hold wonders that defied the imagination, though modern scholarship had all but proven it did not exist. "Besides, I could never desecrate a work of art such as this, but rest assured I will bring back copious notes of whatever I may find."

"And I'll make sure they get published," she said, sticking a finger in the air, "if the quality is there."

"I will endeavor not to underwhelm you."

"Well speaking of underwhelming, my gift might look a bit less glamorous, but I hope it will prove equally useful." Artemis retrieved a knife in a black leather sheath from the pocket of his robe and thumped it down on the table. Sylvan slid the knife from its sheath and held it up to the candle to study it. The hilt was wrapped with fine braided wire, wound tightly, and lacquered smooth. The blade was just short of a hand's length, straight on one side and roughly serrated on the other, as for cutting rope, though it might be useful for scaling fish as well. It felt light and sturdy in his hand, and he smiled at his brother as he tested the sharp point on his finger.

"Thank you, so much. This will definitely come in handy." He reached out and took his brother's hand.

"Wait, you haven't seen the best part." Artemis let go of his hand and took the knife from him, turned the hilt toward himself, and unscrewed the end, revealing a set of fine pincers built into the butt. "For sampling those little critters you're sure to run across." He squeezed the pincers as he said it, then handed them to Sylvan and slid the knife across the table.

Sylvan put his hands over his heart, then reached them out, one to his mother's hand, the other to his brother's.

"I'm going to miss the hell out of you two."

Artemis squeezed his hand. "Just make sure you

come back to us in one piece, brother."

His mother closed her eyes for a moment as she smiled. "And please, mind your paint. It wouldn't do to have you get sunburned."

Chapter Two

Temi stood in her black robe in the dressing cubicle, the cloying sweetness of the lilies overpowering even at this distance. The murmured voices died out as the temple door closed with a muffled thud. The bell rang one time, its tiny, clear voice resonating against the marble walls. Temi slipped out of her robe and hung it on the hook, staring down at her body, whose whiteness was all the starker since the hair above her sex had been shaved off just before the ceremony. She tried to take a few calming breaths as she was taught, then she shook her head and let the anger flow; perhaps a little flush would darken her a shade. The bell rang a second time, and she shivered as the marble drained the warmth from her feet. When the bell sounded again, she swung the door open and entered the tunnel.

As she stepped into the blinding brightness, she felt like a child again, frightened and alone as she crossed the first line, staring at her pale feet, which glowed against the creamy yellowish floor. A slipper scuffed and she sensed the assessor's presence beyond the slit in the marble to her left. The bell's ring pierced the tunnel, and she stepped across the second line, a paler shade, but her feet still shone, and the bell rang again. With each step, each line crossed, each ring of the bell, her chest grew tighter as her feet seemed to fade into the increasing whiteness of the marble beneath. When the sixth bell chimed she was almost surprised, as she could hardly discern her toes from the ghostly pale stone. Her breath grew short, and she clenched her fists with rage as she crossed into the seventh circle, where all she could see of her feet against the marble were the pink shapes of her toenails. This was where it would end. This was where it always ended.

She looked up to the lilies at the end of the tunnel, their smell creeping down her throat like perfume from an open coffin. The deeper voice of the big bell hit her like a punch to the back of her neck, and she felt again the old wrack of shame, embedded so deeply she could not root it out, no matter how much her conscious mind railed against it.

She exhaled a long breath and padded forward through the increasingly stark whiteness of the final three rings, trying as always to summon a vision of Queen Endriana, the only one to have ever reached the tenth circle. She pulled seven lilies from the vase, one by one, and the three that remained slumped awkwardly without the support of their sisters. Her mother's drawn smile greeted her as she exited the tunnel, and Temi offered her the flowers, which she took with a gentle blink. Her mother had worn silver paint for the occasion, an extravagance she surely couldn't afford, but she always found a way to keep up appearances. Her eyes ran up and down Temi's body, and her expression of tempered approval, acceptance of slight imperfection, burned Temi's stomach, though her mother had always been a shade six.

"I was worried your exercises this morning would bring you down a shade."

"I had hoped as much, but we can't all get what we want."

Her mother's tight smile belied the hurt in her eyes. "Your wit cannot keep our home from crumbling into ruin, but your skin just might, if you manage to keep it. Not everyone gets to choose, Temi."

Temi swallowed, staring down again at her body, which looked almost dirty white in the shadows. She wanted to spit, to wash the taste of bile rising in her throat at the thought of trading her body to keep her family's crumbling estate afloat. She forced her eyes back up to meet her mother's.

"I know, mother."

Her mother held her gaze for long enough Temi was worried she might suss out her true designs.

Temi returned to the dressing cubicle and donned the white ceremonial dress that had been her mother's. The fabric was frail from repeated soakings in lye and sour milk to maintain its whiteness, and it did no wonders for her figure, not that it mattered. The quality of her dress would not affect her prospects for marriage, but there were a half-dozen shade sevens in Anari without large debts attached to their houses. She sank the wide-brimmed hat low on her head and arranged the triple-layered veil so she could more or less see through it, then stepped out the side door, where her mother awaited her.

They walked arm in arm out into the punishing midday sun, making their way through the crowds, on foot, like commoners. Temi's mother guided her around the mud and horse droppings, holding her arm with a gentle grip, to avoid putting any undue pressure on her skin, which flowered purplish yellow with the slightest bruise.

Her mother wrestled with the ornery lock on the

gate, which finally conceded with a rusty shriek, and they passed through the tidy courtyard into the airy parlor.

"Why don't you go get changed and put your face back on." Her mother slid open the cold box and stood staring into it with vacant eyes. "I'll find us something to eat."

Temi painted her face yellow, the color a bit faded she noticed as she touched up around her ears, but beggars couldn't be choosers. She'd had to add cooking oil to an old tin she'd found, as their credit had dried up like the paint in the back of her mother's vanity drawers. She found some green lipstick that didn't clash too badly and did a passable job with it, good enough her mother wouldn't say anything but not so good she wouldn't give her a look. Come tomorrow, she would be wearing a light tan on her face and lips, and no one on the roughabout would notice or care if it wasn't applied just right.

Her uncle had sent her a fresh sketchbook and a fine set of pencils, which she hadn't dared touch. She'd had to withdraw from art school to help hand-paint the ceramics that were her family's only remaining source of income, and which were falling out of favor with the fad of exotics from the far West. She still hadn't figured out how her mother had paid for the roughabout, but she wasn't going to turn down a chance to make a break for her freedom. She hoped to slip away and find her way downstream to Rontaia, where she was sure to find work as a calligrapher or illustrator. Though her mother always insisted she had no obligation to accept any offer of marriage that didn't please her, Temi couldn't imagine one that did. The notion of love made as little sense to her as religion, a blind faith in something no one could prove existed, but everyone seemed to cling to it, though it seldom brought them much joy. If she stayed in Anari, the noose would slowly tighten around her neck, and she didn't intend to wait around until someone decided her pallor outweighed her family's debt.

Temi kissed the air around her mother's cheeks four times, wishing she could just hug her like when she was a girl. Time and misfortune had sapped the joy from her mother's face, and the tears she dabbed from her eyes as she waved at Temi through the carriage window were surely not for Temi alone.

She sat back in the creaky carriage as it lumbered through the streets, stopping at the bottlenecks made by the line of carriages filling out paperwork at the third and fourth ring gates. Even where the side streets were walled up past the fourth ring, traffic was impossible; it was market day, and vendors' wagons competed with carriages and commoners schlepping bulky sacks of provisions. It took close to an hour to escape from Center City to Port Road, which was bustling, but wide enough that her carriage kept clop-clopping along until it pulled up in the semicircle just outside the port's stone gate. She pulled a two-lep coin out of the pocket in her dress and dropped it in the driver's tip bag as if it were the most natural thing in the world, though the gesture depleted her meager reserves, leaving her little room for error. She shrugged off the porters vying to carry her bag and slung it over her shoulder. She knew it would leave a bruise if she carried it too long, so she stopped periodically to switch it to the other shoulder, then carried its awkward weight in one hand, then the other, until at last, she found a free bench in the shade by the old watchtower.

She pulled the brim of her hat low against the river's glare and studied the boats at the dock. She hadn't been on a boat since her father's funeral, and she had spent the trip studying the myriad lines and billowing cloth of the sails, marveling at the practiced skill of the sailors who handled the ropes like artists drawing lines with a quill. A warm breeze brought the smell of dead fish and rotting moss to her nose, which she wrinkled, then opened fully, letting the pungent funk wash over her. She was going to be spending the next month surrounded by these smells and worse, and she tried to embrace it and stifle the instinct to breathe only through her mouth.

"Temithea Yskan?" The voice was firm but gentle, and the woman who stood before her wore pants, leather sandals, and a rolled-up shirt that showed her muscled bronze arms and neck.

"Yes, you must be Ms. Harkoven." Temi stood and inclined her head.

"Gilea." The woman held out her hand, rough and square-fingered. Temi took it gently, and Gilea's mouth turned up at the corners as she gave Temi's hand a light squeeze. "Your bag," she said. Temi lifted the heavy bag, which Gilea shouldered as if it were full of feathers. Temi had expected her minder to be primmer, more severe, more like a tutor than a sailor.

"The ship leaves within the hour." Gilea gestured with her head as she turned and started walking, and it took Temi a few steps to find her stride in the ridiculous shoes her mother had insisted she wear. *Until you're on the ship, you represent our house,* she'd said. *After that, no one should know who you are.*

Chapter Three

Gilea looked over her shoulder to make sure Temi was behind her. Painted faces tended to walk slowly, but Temi managed to keep up with her pace, despite her impractical shoes. Hopefully, this roughabout wasn't going to be as rough as the last one, an island-hop off the southern coast in the middle of typhoon season. Leo had promised safer travels and greater wonders on this trip, but he was ever one to paint the sky with the colors of his heart.

When they got on board, Sylvan sat hunched over a book in the shade of the dining deck, dressed in faded work clothes and sporting a fairly convincing reddish-tan makeup job. If it weren't for the book, he could have almost passed for a nobody, except for the fact that he was wearing gloves and a wide hat in the shade on a hot summer day. He stared at the book, oblivious to their approach, until Gilea scuffed her sandal on the deck, and he looked up with a start, slamming the book shut.

"Hello Gilea, and you must be Temithea." He stood up, bowing deeply, the book clutched to his chest. Its cover was a rather vibrant blue, inlaid with mother-of-pearl letters Gilea couldn't see enough of to read.

"Temi." She bowed in return, looking around anxiously.

"I was just going to show Temi her quarters, so she can freshen up before our trip."

"Yes, of course, I—" Sylvan's smile widened and he bowed again. "It's nice to meet you, Temi."

Gilea surveyed the other passengers for signs of anything unusual, but they were mostly center-ring folks off visiting their families in the provinces on holiday. The ship had an all-female crew, a solid-enough-looking bunch: six deckhands, a mate, and the captain, a dark woman whose face bore a long pink scar running from her forehead between her eyes and across her nose. She flashed Gilea the knowing smile shared by sisters-at-sea, and Gilea's shoulders relaxed a little. She was in good hands.

Temi emerged from her cabin just as the ship was pushed off the dock and the oars began digging through the water. Her face was painted in uneven layers of a tannish beige that would convince exactly no one. Her mouth was stuck in a bitter half-smirk, which eased somewhat as they reached open water and the sails were raised and began filling with the warm, steady breeze. Temi stood just inside the open dining cabin and stared off across the wide river, her back to Sylvan, whose eyes never lifted above the pages of his book. Gilea knew they wouldn't have been paired for the roughabout if they were romantically compatible, but she hadn't yet figured out the details, and pairing mistakes were not unheard of. It was hard to read their faces beneath their ridiculous wide-brimmed hats, so she would have to keep an eye out.

The ship slowed as the wind turned, but the crew made the most of what push they had, and they moved downriver at a steady clip. The Agra was wide enough for most of its course that they could move on sail power much of the time, as long as the wind was favorable. Gilea could feel the sails' tension in her bones, and she sank into it, using the regular slap of the little waves against the prow to measure her breath. She began to form a picture of all the crew and passengers, her mind assigning a unique shape and color to each so she would not lose track of them as they moved around the boat. She kept large, bright spots for her charges in the front of her mind, blue for Sylvan and yellow for Temi, according to the paint they had worn when they came aboard. Sylvan's shape took on a mellow, rounded character, while Temi's was hard around the edges but fragile as ripe fruit beneath.

By midafternoon, Temi had moved to sit near Sylvan, evidently drawn in by the book, and they exchanged words, tepid at first, growing warmer with the passing hours. By dinnertime they were sitting with their legs almost touching, their voices rising in quiet laughter as they pointed out things in the book, turning it this way and that to examine what looked to be drawings of fish and other aquatic creatures. Gilea had a moment of panic when she saw their closeness, but as she studied their movements, the casual comfort of their body language, she soon realized she had nothing to worry about. Their colors merged into a soft green in her mind, and she allowed the harsh cries of the gulls and the hum of the sail lines to create a frame of chaos over stability, with her resting in the middle as the shapes and colors of the passengers and crew moved in increasingly predictable ways. If anything came out of order, she would notice in an instant.

Gilea sat with Captain Olin long after her charges had retired to their quarters. They talked about storms they had weathered, exotic creatures they had eaten, and oceans they dreamed of sailing. Gilea sipped her whisky, while Olin drank with abandon, her eyes glossy in the lantern light, her taut, muscled body leaning toward Gilea. In a tavern between jobs, there was no doubt the conversation would have ended in tangled sheets, and Olin was four shots to the breeze and clearly ready to throw down. Gilea stayed engaged but kept just enough distance to make her position clear, and Olin settled back with a wry smile on her face.

"So you're taking them to Freburr, and then what?"

Gilea shook her head, moving her glass in a circle on the table. "You know we can't talk about that stuff."

"Oh right, the code of silence, the gilded chains that bind you." Olin touched her wrists together, and Gilea smiled, feeling she must have known Olin in a previous life.

"It beats the hell out of hemp rope."

"Touché." Olin raised her glass and dumped it down her throat. "But the way I figure, if you're going to Freburr, there's not much inland there, no mountains or great wild spaces, just industry and a rough city center, then ring after ring of increasing squalor. Not much of a place for a roughabout." Gilea smiled but did not answer. "I've got this all figured out. You'll set out from Freburr, or someplace just downstream, on a boat, something simple, primitive, and make them hunt and fish for their dinner while the suckflies and the mudworms feast on their tender skin."

"You make it sound so glamorous."

Olin shook her head gently. "People who've got it hard looking for a way to make life easy, that I can see. But this..." Olin's hands waved and flapped about. "Why go out of your way to make things more difficult?"

"Greener grass, I suppose." Gilea downed her glass

at last and slid it towards Olin. "You run this route regularly?"

Olin smiled with her eyes first, and her mouth followed, strong teeth flashing between soft lips. "My contract goes another six months, in case you come back before then. I might even let you ride for free."

Clouds and drizzle tamped down the heat the next day, and Sylvan and Temi seemed more relaxed, even taking off their hats as they sat in the crowded dining deck. Sylvan continued studying his book, which Gilea got a better look at. The cover was new, but the pages were old, like some of the books she had seen as a child in Wulif's library. Her mother had cured Wulif of a terrible skin disease, and he let Gilea come to his house in the Bluffs from time to time and look through his books once he was convinced she would be gentle with them. Gilea was never much for reading, but she had always been fascinated by the script in the old books, and especially the artwork, which ranged from minutely detailed to fantastical and whimsical. She'd even snuck a peek at the more exotic books in his collection, often shocking in their explicitness. As a child, she had studied the drawings of anatomy and sexual positions, not really understanding what they were about, but feeling they were important somehow, part of an adult world that was more mysterious to her than any remedy or ritual of her mother's practice.

Olin pressed her case again that night, and again Gilea turned her down, with great regret. She was going to be stuck on a raft with Leo and two grown children for the next month or more. Olin was just her type, and she badly needed the release, but she needed the money more. Two roughabouts a year was a small price to pay for complete freedom the rest of the time, and her reputation for consistency and control kept her from having to work the kind of grind Olin was stuck in. Though as she watched Olin stand the next morning, hand at the wheel, barking orders at the crew, she could see the appeal.

They arrived in Freburr at midday, and she shepherded her charges through the chaos of the port, south toward the public riverfront. Temi was intent on carrying her own bag, and Sylvan followed her example, which was a good thing, as they had almost two leagues' walk ahead of them, and Leo had insisted they come on foot, "So they get a little taste of what's coming." Gilea was not opposed, though as she watched Temi and Sylvan constantly readjusting their bags in the first few minutes of their march, she almost broke down and hired a carriage.

When they arrived, Gilea saw the raft was almost completely built. It was about thirty feet long, with a deck made of long tree trunks lashed together and a partially built cabin on one end. The cabin's roof looked spotty, and it lacked walls, but it was farther along than she had expected. Leo was nowhere to be seen, but Sea Wolf sat back on his haunches, staring up into a tall tree whose branches hung high over the water. A rope danced and dangled beneath the branches, and a nut-brown figure inchwormed his way out on a narrow limb, which bowed slightly beneath his weight. He held a rope in his mouth, and he let go with his hands and swung upside down by his knees from the branch, revealing his nudity, which was thankfully vague from this distance. He made several deft loops in the rope and secured it to the branch. Leo swung on the rope for a moment, bouncing as if testing the knot, waved at the group, then launched himself down like a spear into the water, where he made hardly a splash.

Gilea smiled as she heard Temi and Sylvan gasp on

cue, then again when Leo surfaced, blowing water like a breathfin, his smile showing every one of his teeth. He went under and did not surface again for more than a minute.

"Where did he..." Sylvan dropped his bag, putting his hand above his eyes, even below his hat, to scan the sepia-colored water.

Temi glanced at Sylvan, then pointed to the raft, a self-satisfied little smile on her face.

"There."

Leo pulled himself out of the water, which rushed down between the logs on the raft. He stood for a moment, naked and dripping, as if to prove how little his nakedness bothered him. He finally picked up a towel, and as he dried and dressed, Sylvan looked away, while Temi watched with laughter in her eyes.

Leo strode out with short pants and no shirt, stray drops of water scattered across his wiry physique. He strode right up to Sylvan and stretched out his hand.

"Sylvan Kirin, I'm honored to meet you. I'm Captain Leo." He shook Sylvan's hand, then turned and gestured toward the raft with both hands as if displaying a great treasure. "And this is the Aelefthi."

"It's a pleasure Captain. Your reputation precedes you, and the honor is mine." Sylvan bowed deeply, and Leo beamed a smile back at him.

"Temithea Yskan, but I bet you go by Temi." He shook Temi's hand, rather roughly from the look of it, but Temi did not falter. "Welcome aboard."

"It's bigger than I expected." Temi let go of his hand. "How does it move? I don't..."

"Sweeps, Temi. Long poles with boards attached. Like giant oars."

"Oh, of course, that makes—"

"And we need to get working on those, so come drop your bags in the cabin and let's get to it."

Sylvan and Temi looked at each other, then to Gilea, who closed her eyes and smiled.

"We just walked two leagues, Leo," Gilea said. "Mind if we catch a breather and maybe a drink of water before we jump right into the manual labor?"

Chapter Four

Leo fed Sea Wolf a two-finger dollop of the butter, which he'd gotten from a farmer in exchange for the leg-sized whisker he'd caught on his trotline. The butter would last another day at the most in the water cooler, and there was no way the group could eat it all before it spoiled.

"You like that, don't you, Wolfie, yes you do." He scratched the dog's head with the other hand as Sea Wolf licked his fingers clean. Leo stuck his fingers into the butter again and scooped out a lump for himself, which he stuck in his mouth, sucking on his fingers as the richness exploded on his tongue. It was almost enough to make him gag, but it was energy to burn. He noticed the new charges staring at him and shrugged.

"Can't let it go to waste." He held out the bowl to them, giggling when they waved it away with polite gestures of their gloved hands. He tousled Sea Wolf's ears, returned to the boat, and put the bowl back into the cooler, which he'd made from an enormous turtle shell he'd found washed up. The water was running warm with the summer's heat, but it still extended the life of perishables somewhat.

"All right, who's ready to do some sawing?"

Temi and Sylvan looked at each other, and Temi stood up first. She seemed hardy enough, though it would take a few weeks to work the softness out of her. Painted faces always had some athletic training, so they were never as weak as they seemed, but many of them lacked real toughness. Sylvan stood up more slowly, stretching to the sky and shaking his legs. Leo bet he'd never walked two whole leagues in his entire life. He might take a little longer to become useful.

They spent the rest of the day cutting wood for the sweeps and mounts from the junked rowboat he'd found a couple of leagues downstream. It had taken him two days to paddle upstream towing it, but the wood was mostly useable, and the oarlocks were of soft enough iron he'd been able to widen them so they would just work in the mounts he'd planned. When they'd finished for the day, Temi sat on a stump, her arms draped over her knees, while Sylvan lay flat on his back, his arms splayed above him like a fallen soldier. Sylvan fought off Sea Wolf's licking and sat up with a groan.

"You had said something about dinner?"

Leo grinned, held out his hand, and hauled Sylvan to his feet.

"For today, I've already caught it. Tomorrow, that's on you." He walked to the boat, turning his head to make sure Sylvan and Temi were following him, which they were, albeit slowly.

"Nothing like fresh whiskers." Leo hauled up the rope with the two smaller fish from the night's trotline, still more than enough for dinner and breakfast, and maybe lunch, depending on how well the painted faces ate. He could never tell with the new ones; sometimes they wolfed everything down like they'd never seen food before, but often they picked at their food for the first day or so, having never eaten river fish. The muddy taste took a little getting used to. He untied the rope and held it out, and Temi took it, her face serious beneath her sweat-streaked makeup. Sylvan leaned in to get a closer look at the fish, studying them from all angles, his face inches away from them.

"Is this one a spotted whisker?"

Leo nodded, feeling a smile grow on his face. Sylvan might be fun to have around. "Yeah, that's a spotter."

"And this other one, with the pointy nose, I think might be a unicorn whisker?"

"Close. It's a pointed whisker, what we call a pointer. Some say it tastes a bit sweeter, but I don't really see the difference."

"These vertical lines on the pointer are amazing." Sylvan traced his finger along the fish's body without touching the vibrant blue-green stripe on the silver-gray body. "And this tail, built for power, much wider than the spotted...the spotter." Leo could see he was going to like this painted man-child, whose curiosity was not unlike his own.

Temi swung the rope over to Sylvan so he had to dodge out of the way to avoid being hit in the face by the fish.

"Are we going to cut these up or have an anatomy lesson?"

Leo laughed as Sylvan took the rope gingerly, holding it far from his body. Leo pointed to the cutting block, which still had traces of blood from previous cleanings.

"Let me see that knife you've got." He gestured toward the knife on Sylvan's belt, which was shiny and clean, surely new.

Sylvan laid the fish on the block, pulled out the knife, and held the handle toward Leo. The hilt was wrapped in fine braided wire, and the blade was one-sided, with sharp serrations near the hilt on the blunt side that would be useful for cutting rope. The end of the hilt was rounded, and as Leo examined it, he saw that it screwed off.

"You mind?" Leo made a twisting gesture, and Sylvan nodded, hiding a smile behind his gloved hand. Leo unscrewed the cap, and attached to it was a pair of thin pincers, too flimsy to be useful as a fishing tool. He squeezed them together with his fingers, and they closed gently. He cocked his eye at Sylvan.

"For retrieving and examining specimens."

Leo stared at him for a moment, then looked down at the pincers. They looked delicate enough to pick up a dragonfly without killing it.

"You're a scientist, right?"

"Life scientist. Just made Doctor a week ago. I study fish and other aquatic life. It's why I chose this roughabout."

"Well, you'll surely learn a lot on this trip. Starting with how to clean fish for cooking. I don't guess you've ever done that before?"

Sylvan's head bobbled, half nod, half shake. "I've dissected a few, but only for study."

"And you didn't eat them?"

Sylvan shook his head, frowning. "Gods no. Not that...I mean, I don't know what they did with them after."

"Someone ate them, you can bet on that."

Sylvan furrowed his brow, studying the fish on the rope he was holding.

Leo went to screw the cap back on, and as he did, he saw that inside the wire, the hilt was made of soft-looking wood. He pressed his fingernail against it, and it left an indentation.

"Huh! Cork handle, so it will float. It's a nice knife." It was custom-made and had probably cost as much as Leo would make on the entire trip. He screwed the cap on, flipped it high in the air, and caught it by the blade, staring into Sylvan's eyes the whole time. Sylvan gave a start, then smiled and took the handle, studying it.

"Thanks, I didn't even know about the handle. My brother never told me."

"Well, for cleaning a fish, a long, thin knife like this would be better." Leo pulled out his filleting knife, showed it to Sylvan, then sheathed it. "But you brought that beautiful piece of equipment all this way, so you might as well give it a try. I'll work on the fire while you get those whiskers cleaned up."

Leo tossed a pinch of everyspice on the fish and cattail roots, smearing the mix around with his fingers and placing a piece of each into his mouth, chewing slowly. He resisted the urge to devour the entire plate without stopping since he knew from long experience it would not satisfy his hunger. Not that anything ever did, except when he was lucky enough to get his hands on a loaf of seed bread, which was rare, given his lifestyle. Sylvan struggled to pull the fish off the bones, spending half his time picking things out of his mouth and tucking them into the corner of his plate. Temi devoured her food like a winter-starved wolf but did not fill her plate again once she had cleaned it down to a set of perfectly intact bones. Her hands glowed ghostly white in the firelight, though her fingers were swollen and red from the day's labor. The gloves she had worn during the sunlight hours were thin and well used, and they would not last more than a week or two of river life. Leo hoped she had a spare pair.

Sylvan peppered him with questions about fish and

other creatures they might see, and Leo entertained him as long as he could bear, then stood up, running his finger across his tin plate and licking the last muddy essence of the meal before leaning the plate next to the fire to be sanitized. He was already feeling crowded, penned in, not just by the new passengers, but by this spot in the public riverfront where he'd spent the last two weeks. There was nothing new to see here, and he longed to be floating again, scanning the horizon for the next batch of swirls.

He'd seen a few just past Smelting Row, which puzzled him, since he'd only ever noticed them before in cleaner water, far from the waste and detritus of human settlements. He walked down to stand on the foredeck, staring out at the moonlit water, watching for them, but all he saw was an occasional fish splashing and a pair of *chukin* swimming downstream, giving the raft a wide berth before hewing close to the bank again. He heard Gilea sharing a few calming words with her charges, who soon went quiet, though it was a while before they stopped rustling around on their reed mattresses.

"What do you think. Will they make it?" Gilea stood next to him, staring out across the water.

"They usually do. Temi has some spirit, I guess. And Sylvan, well." Leo pursed his lips. "He might stick around just to see the fish downstream from Endulai, where the water clears up a bit."

Gilea stood silent, but Leo could hear the change in her breathing as she exhaled through her nose, which she only did when she had grave doubts. She made that sound a lot.

"What, you worried about some ghost stories?"

Gilea turned to stare at him, her eyes dark and hard in the moonlight. "I'm not worried about ghosts. I'm worried about pirates. You heard about the ink boat."

Leo felt his smile drop. A boat carrying valuable ink had been waylaid a few months back en route to

Rontaia, just downstream from Endulai. Its wreckage had been discovered by another cargo ship, but they found no survivors.

Leo nodded, hands behind his back. "You have a point. But it's not like we have any real money, or anything else of value."

"Do you have any idea what Sylvan's family is worth?" Gilea hissed. She paused, collected her breath, and continued in a stage whisper. "We'll be sitting ducks out there. And we don't need to go all the way down. It will take us two weeks or so to get to Endulai, and we can take it a little slow, explore some of the sloughs and bayous along the way, have a couple little adventures, and then reward them with a few days of meditation and relaxation before we head back upland."

"You think Endulai will have them? Two nobles from the heart of the problem?"

"Into Endulai proper? Certainly not." Gilea paused, staring out at the water. "But the sanctuary gardens outside have tents that can be used, given the proper donations."

Leo shook his head. He wasn't prepared to use their slush fund to pay for a pleasure camp, though it did have its appeal. He had joined Gilea in some of her meditations, which borrowed from the Endulian tradition, and it did bring him some measure of peace. This must have been why she was so keen on ending the trip there, rather than fear of pirates, if such a thing were even possible on the most traveled riverway in the continent.

"We'll see how things play out," was all he said. Gilea's nose-breathing did the talking for her, but she could breathe as she liked. He was the captain of the shantyboat and the leader of the roughabout, and unless there was a verifiable threat, she had no authority over him. Not that she'd ever tried to pull a legal on him, but he knew the rules as well as she did. And he intended to explore downstream from Endulai, among the bladegrass fields, where the stories told that the Living Waters would be located. He figured it was just a series of wetlands, but there should be clear water there, which might give him another chance to see more swirls. His eyes danced with visions of the wobbling circles of water, with nothing beneath them, no visible source of their movement. His chest tightened at the thought, and he could tell he would know no peace until he saw them again.

Chapter Five

Sylvan's hands burned with every stroke of the paddle, even through the gloves. His palms were raw from the morning's work sawing and hauling wood for the raft, but Temi showed no signs of letting up, so he gritted his teeth against the pain. Gilea sat between them, scanning the water and the riverbank as if on high alert, though Sylvan didn't see what harm could come to them in a canoe in the sleepy Agra River off the outer rings of Freburr. They steered clear of the warren of thatched roofs and steaming chimneys Gilea called Smelting Row, but even from a hundred yards out, all sorts of unnatural odors wafted their way.

"He's going to beat us." Gilea pointed, and Sylvan could just make out a shape moving through the water at unbelievable speed toward the wide creek mouth a quarter-mile downstream.

"Does he have fins?" Sylvan griped, pushing his paddle a little deeper.

“They’re called muscles,” Temi called over her shoulder.

Sylvan snorted. No aspect of Leo’s anatomy was unknown to them since an hour before, when he had stood up, stripped off his pants, and launched himself into the brown water fully naked. He’d come up facing them, treading water, his grin a little wider and wilder than usual.

“I’m going to swim across to the other side, then swim back and meet you down at Ink Creek. If you beat me there, I’ll clean the fish for dinner tonight.” He’d gone under and emerged a few seconds later in a powerful crawl, heading out toward the middle of the river, which was so wide Sylvan couldn’t see the other side.

Sylvan knew the Agra was two miles wide in spots, and he couldn’t imagine swimming all the way across it, let alone back, and certainly not naked, especially with swarms of needleteeth patrolling its waters. But Leo’s nudity, for all his hair and lovely muscles and deeply tanned skin, did not shock Sylvan as much as he would have expected. Leo’s lack of self-consciousness about his body was as complete and natural as a child’s. When they arrived at the mouth of Ink Creek, he was reclined on a tree limb ten feet over the water, a leafy branch held over his privates, the same toothy grin filling his face.

“What took you so long?” he asked as he rolled off the branch and dived into the water, emerging beside the canoe and pulling up to hold onto the gunwale.

“They wanted to stroke your insatiable ego,” Gilea said, prying his fingers off the gunwale one by one. “I trust they succeeded?”

Leo pushed off the boat and floated backward, belly up, his privates cresting on the water’s surface. Sylvan looked away, and his eyes fell on Temi, who was watching Leo with a genuine smile on her face. Leo kicked in circles around the canoe as they turned into the creek, and he motioned them over to a fallen log, where he got in and slipped his pants back on without even rocking the boat.

They paddled up the lazy creek, all crammed together into the canoe. Leo stood just in front of Gilea, scanning the water ahead with his eyes.

"Shhh—" He crouched and made a gesture, and they stopped paddling. He pointed ahead in the creek, where the water was swirling in several spots, though there didn't seem to be enough current to move the water like that. The swirls moved downstream towards them, side by side, pausing when they came to within ten feet of the canoe, two almost identical swirls of water, each as wide as a barrel top. They began moving again, one passing on each side of the boat. Sylvan watched the one to his right, hoping to see what fish or other crcature was responsible. He saw nothing but the swirl on the surface, which rejoined the other behind the canoe and continued down toward the river.

"What the hell was that?" Temi stared at the water behind them, her eyes narrowing as she moved her gaze to Sylvan, who shrugged, then to Leo and Gilea.

Gilea pursed her lips and blinked at Leo, whose smile was a bit darker and less toothy than usual.

"They're just called swirls. You don't usually see them this close to urban areas." He looked out at the river, then turned to look back up the creek, staring in silence for a long moment.

"What makes them?" Temi's voice mixed wonder with concern.

Leo shook his head. "No one really knows. I've seen them in clear water a couple of times, and there's no animal or fish or anything beneath them." He turned back toward Sylvan, his eyes deep, almost pleading. "I wonder if there's something in that book of yours."

Sylvan wiggled his jaw, trying to recall anything like that from when he'd read it in study. He'd only reread the first twenty pages thus far on the trip, as he was trying to savor the handwriting, the delicate line drawings, and the curious marginalia.

"I think there is a short section on myths and legends. I remember a drawing of a mermaid that some of the other students found titillating."

"Well, I guess you have your homework once we get back to the raft. In the meantime, I need to catch something for dinner, so you can clean it. Paddle up around this bend, nice and slow, and when I say stop, keep quiet and don't move."

Leo picked up a well-worn bow and an arrow attached to a coil of thin cord. He moved to stand just behind Temi, shading his eyes with one hand as he scanned the water ahead. As they neared the bend in the creek, he motioned for them to stop, and they lifted their paddles out of the water. The canoe drifted upstream against the slow current, the front end pulling sideways, and Leo put down his bow and took the paddle from Temi's hand, turning the boat back toward the bend with a few quiet strokes. He crouched with the bow in his hand, and Sylvan could see the muscles in his arms, legs, and back tense as he raised himself up in a slow, fluid motion, pulled back the arrow, and shot it into the riverbank.

A squeal erupted, and a ball of brown fur and flying blood tumbled into the water. It looked like a giant rat, the size of a small dog. Its body twisted and flailed in the water, its legs paddling in vain against the cord as Leo jerked it back to the canoe, looping the cord in the bottom of the boat with each pull. He maneuvered the creature to the side of the boat, and its legs moved feebly, its jaw opening and closing mechanically, more and more slowly with each breath, as a stream of blood flowed from the arrow lodged in its chest. Leo walked the cord past Gilea and handed it to Sylvan, who held it limply, staring into the poor creature's terrified black eyes.

"Use your knife to finish it off," Leo said softly. "Just at the base of the neck." He made a stabbing motion, and Sylvan felt sick as he unsheathed his knife, pulling the creature close to the canoe, which almost tipped as he leaned toward it. He spread out his body to balance the boat, lifting the creature's head to the gunwale. He knew exactly where to plunge the knife, having studied the anatomy of many such creatures. He was pretty sure this was a *chukin*, a common river rat, used by the working classes for their fur. And, apparently, their meat.

"Any time," Leo said.

Sylvan looked the creature in the eyes once more, angled the cord so its neck dangled before him, then jabbed the knife just above its shoulder blades. It went limp, as did Sylvan.

Sylvan hurried through dinner, not that he had much appetite for river rat and fire lily tubers, especially after the gory task of scraping the stringy muscles from the creature's bones and tendons. Leo had insisted Temi bait the trotline with the leftover bits of the *chukin* carcass, and while she worked, Sylvan brought his book close to the fire, picking delicately through the pages until he found the section he remembered: *Of myths and legends concerning beasts of the Living Waters.* Servais always capitalized the words, which was unusual, as classical writers didn't usually even capitalize names.

He saw the drawing of the mermaid with the copious breasts, which many of his classmates had found inexplicably fascinating. There were depictions of snakelike fish swallowing boats, a beautiful naiad bathing naked under a waterfall, her long hair miraculously covering her nudity, and an assortment of creatures mixing one animal and another, usually a fish of some kind with something else, none of them scientifically plausible.

But nothing that looked like a swirl. The light was too low for him to easily read the text, but he could see that this section was particularly loaded with marginalia, filling almost every available inch of space in the scant four pages the book devoted to these imaginary creatures. He tilted the book farther toward the fire, turning it sideways to read what appeared to be a continuous passage of tight, almost aggressively small lettering spanning the height of the last page.

> *Servais' disdain for the unexplained shows he has never spent time in the Living Waters. A real scientist would find the source of the tales and reveal the truth that lies beneath. The things he does not mention reveal more than those he does. Where are the ipsis, the sitri, the duni? One might forgive his inaccuracies regarding the anatomy and diet of the more commonly known creatures, but to make no mention of these phenomena shows him to be a charlatan.*

Sylvan's heart fluttered at the certainty of the unknown scholar. They wrote like a true scientist, critiquing Servais' work and demanding greater accuracy. But they also wrote as if the Living Waters were a real place, rather than a fictional construct, a symbol for the pristine nature that existed before the rise of human civilization. Though he had always been fascinated by the legend, this idea that it had a basis in concrete reality sparked his scientific mind even as it dredged up the fantasies of his childhood.

"Did you find what you were looking for?" Gilea lit a cheroot that stank of rotten flowers, inhaled deeply, and held it out to Sylvan, who waved it away.

"Not really. Servais writes about mermaids and naiads and the like, but only as legends. There's nothing about any random swirls of water. Unless..." He turned back down to the book, studying the marginalia once again. There was something about the names that was vaguely familiar. *ipsis. sitri. duni.* The names were reminiscent of old Enduli, which he'd only sampled in study. He looked up at Gilea, who caressed Sea Wolf's ears as the dog leaned his head on her lap.

"Unless?"

Sylvan shook his head. "Unless I can summon the knowledge of an ancient language I never knew very well. Do the words *ipsis, sitri,* or *duni* mean anything to you?"

Gilea's head shook almost imperceptibly. "I only know the Anari and Rontai dialects, and a little Enduli, mostly meditation terms."

Sylvan gave a start. "How did you learn Enduli? Have you been to Endulai?" It was said that few were allowed to enter the holy city, and the dialect was not spoken outside Endulai and the temples scattered across the continent. Gilea shook her head, her eyes crinkling as her mouth formed a pained smile. He gestured toward the cheroot, which she passed him. He inhaled the acrid smoke, held it, and blew it out, then passed it back, marveling at the rich bronze color of her hand next to the pallor of his own.

Gilea set the half-smoked cheroot on a rock and looked down into Sea Wolf's adoring eyes, rubbing the top of his head with both thumbs.

"I never have, but there was an Endulian temple in my neighborhood in Rontaia. I used to go there when I was a kid, while my mother was working and I was kicked out of the apartment. I'd sit in the back and practice imitating the master, repeating the words and imagining what he was saying. In time I picked up a few things, and I had a girlfriend once who practiced, in her way." Gilea went silent and turned toward the river, and Sylvan followed her eyes.

He could see the little waves forming and dissipating, over and over, in exquisite detail. Hear them lapping at the shore, slapping the logs of the raft. Here and there the water roiled with a surfacing fish, and the v-shaped wakes of *chukin* gave geometric complexity to the otherwise fluid shapes of the waves. But as long as he looked, as hard as he stared, he could not see anything that looked like a swirl of water, moving on its own, without any visible force beneath it.

Temi rubbed the thin lather over her stinging hands until she couldn't take it anymore, then rinsed them in the brown river water, pulling them out quickly, in case the movement might attract needleteeth. Leo had assured them the fish posed no danger, and his naked swim across the filthy river showed he believed it, but Temi wasn't entirely convinced. She held her hands up to the candle, cringing as she examined the blisters, some swollen yellowish bubbles, others pink ovals where the skin had been rubbed away. Her gloves were all but useless, and if Sylvan offered her his spare pair one more time she might just take him up on it. She applied the minty balm Gilea had given her, which stung even worse, but the last thing she needed was an infected wound on her hand, and the waters of the Agra were surely tainted with human waste, especially below a city like Freburr.

She lifted her hand to her nose and recoiled in

disgust, as the musk of the river rat had permeated beyond the reach of any soap or balm. She imagined what her mother would say if she could see her now, the dirt, the scratches, her makeup, which was no doubt smeared and streaked. She sat down on her bunk and slid the sketchbook from her bag, running her hands over the thin leather cover before opening it to the first, blank page. Though the candle gave off but feeble light, it was just enough to shave the tip of the pencil sharp and draw that first oval, almost round enough to be a circle, but the uneven shape gave it a feeling of movement. She penned in concentric smaller ovals beneath it, which became tiny circles near the bottom before tapering off in a thinning line. She held it at arm's length, pulled it in to add a few more lines of detail, then held it out again.

A smile spread on her face, then a shiver overtook her. Whatever had caused the swirls in the water was invisible, but also intelligent on some level. The swirls had paused, then split around the canoe before continuing together out into the river. She was no naturalist, but it didn't seem like something fish would do, nor any mammal she had heard of. Most animals were afraid of humans, and rightly so, but something in the way the swirls moved suggested curiosity perhaps, but certainly not fear. She sharpened her pencil to a flat tip and used her best calligraphy to write *Swirls* beneath the drawing, highlighting the word with a curved line with two neat slashes through it. It wasn't her most accurate drawing, as the circles made it look too deep, but it had a pleasing symmetry. At least it was a start, and she got the feeling she would have ample opportunity to study the swirls and make all the drawings she wanted as they drifted down the Agra.

Temi heard the crash as she was nailing a salvaged board on the almost completed cabin wall. It sounded far away, but the noise had heft to it. She looked to Sylvan, who held a board against his thigh, looking off in the direction of the sound. Gilea pivoted toward the noise too, her serene face sharpening.

"What in the world was that?" Sylvan's eyes showed curiosity, mixed with a little fear.

"It sounded like a building collapsing," Gilea said. "In the direction of Smelting Row. Maybe there's been a fire."

Temi scanned the treetops and the sky. "But there's no smoke."

Gilea's jaw clenched and unclenched, and she looked toward the river. Temi knew Leo had gone off downstream at dawn to try to scavenge some more wood, as they had stripped the old rowboat and were a few boards short. After a moment, Gilea turned back toward them and shrugged, though her face remained tense.

"We'll find out soon enough."

Temi and Sylvan used up the remaining wood and completed three of the walls, leaving wide, slightly uneven window holes in two of them, which could be covered with additional boards from the inside in inclement weather. They had left small gaps between the boards, as Leo had shown them, to let a little more air in while still keeping the creatures and the weather out. Sylvan collapsed onto his bunk, arms spread out like a dead man, sweat piercing his makeup as he let out a sigh that seemed to last for an hour.

"I just can't help thinking, how is building this boat going to prepare me to be a better scientist?" He shucked his gloves and stared at his hands. His fingers were blazing pink but his wrists showed lily-white where his sleeves slid down. Temi guessed he was a shade six, though it was hard to tell, as the morning's exertion made it impossible to see his true color. With his wealth and education, he might be able to pull a shade eight bride. She sensed from the way he looked at her, and how he had averted his eyes when Leo stripped down, that he was not interested in women, but that wouldn't keep him from taking a wife, who might give him children of shade seven or even eight if he were lucky. Temi, with her family's troubles, would be lucky to find a six willing to take her. Not that she wanted to be taken, bred for her unhealthy pallor like *Gimni* dogs with no fur and pink skin, but she could not easily shed the guilt that had been woven into her psyche. *Your shade is your inheritance,* her mother often said. *Mind you don't squander it.*

She looked through the window at Gilea, who stood on the foredeck, her bronze skin shining in the sun, staring downriver for Leo's return. She wondered what it would be like to just stand there, arms, neck, and face uncovered as the sun bore down on her. On sunny winter days when her mother wasn't around, Temi would sometimes sit in a corner of the courtyard, remove her gloves and hat, and let the feeble sun warm her cheeks and the backs of her hands, just for a moment. She would imagine she was on a sailboat on the Southern Seas, soaking up the fierce sun, both from above and from the glare off the water. She envied Gilea, and especially Leo, who felt free to do with his body as he wished, to expose it to the sun and the water and the eyes of anyone who might care to look. Though she supposed he was attractive in his way, she wasn't compelled by his body so much as in awe of his freedom, his pure delight in becoming one with the world, with nothing between him and the elements. Like a child.

When Leo returned, Temi and Sylvan had already cleaned the fish from the trotline and had the fire ready to cook. Sylvan had gotten excited about one of the fish, a long one with silver scales and milky white discs where its eyes should have been. He called it a thinkfin, and he had a great deal to say about the origin of its name, the thin tendrils that ran along the top and bottom of the fish, and about how it used its other senses to make up for the lack of eyes. Though Temi wasn't especially interested in what he was saying, his passion made her smile and gave her something to think about other than the depressing reality she'd left behind and the miserable one they now shared.

Leo's face was grim, but with a fierceness that shone like the moon. He tied off the canoe and stepped onto the raft, dropping a heavy brown furry carcass on the deck. It was twice the size of the *chukin*, and it had a flat tail with tiny spikes radiating out around it. Sylvan laid down his book and hurried over to examine the creature, pulling the little tongs from his knife hilt to prod at the tail and lift the lips to study its huge yellow front teeth.

"It's a *dimura*, right?"

Leo nodded, staring at Gilea, who moved toward him from the fire as if summoned.

"This tail, they whack it against the water to warn off predators," Sylvan said, turning to Temi. "And if that doesn't work, it's got these spikes, and if I recall correctly, they have some kind of mild toxin—"

"The Inkworks have been destroyed." Leo turned sideways so he could see them all.

"By what?" Gilea's tone was flat, as if she wasn't asking a question.

Leo rubbed his face and nodded, then shook his head, his teeth showing in a reluctant grin.

"They said it was a huge wave that rushed in out of the creek, some sort of freakish flash flood or something. I started paddling upstream when I heard the sound, and the rush of water almost capsized me. The creek was running red with ink, and there was a lot of good debris floating too, but I didn't get too close. We'll go out tomorrow morning to salvage some."

They all stood watching him, and he blew out a deep breath, wringing his hands.

"The thing is...The creek was full of swirls. I mean, full of them, like, bank to bank, and some of them were going upstream, and some were going downstream, most of them small like the ones we saw, but I saw one wider than my canoe."

Up to this point, Temi had seen Leo as someone incapable of fear. The look in his eyes told her something had changed.

The boards they salvaged the next morning were tinted pink from the ink, which tinged the muddy water as well. They filled every empty space in the canoe until it sat low in the water, and paddling back upstream was easily the hardest physical labor Temi had ever done. They saw a handful of swirls heading downstream from the creek, with a reddish tint. They moved in clusters of two and three, in sync, though they occasionally swapped positions. One pair, in particular, moved in a kind of dance, side to side, then one in front of the other, then circling around each other. No one said anything about them, but their eyes were all watching, studying the swirls' movements. When they returned to the raft, Temi slouched forward, resting her forehead on her paddle, which she lay across the gunwale.

"We can unload the boards after lunch," Leo said. "I'm going to get started pitching the roof while you rest, as those clouds look ready to cause us some mischief."

Temi lay flat on her back in the grass next to Sylvan, who quickly fell asleep with his hat over his face. Temi was exhausted, but she stared up at the gray sky, looking for swirling patterns in the clouds that rolled in. It was nice to leave her hat off for a while, though she had to squint despite the darkening color of the sky. She hauled herself to her feet, shaking her hands, which were so sore she could barely grasp the waterskin. She kicked Sylvan's foot, and he let out a gentle groan, removing his hat from his face and shielding his eyes from the light, then rolled over onto his side and pushed himself slowly up to a seated position.

Gilea brought over a smoked fish from the night before, the thinkfin, whose silver scales were yellow from the smoke. She peeled back the skin with a few deft strokes of her knife, a long, thin blade like the one Leo carried. Temi took a pinch of everyspice from the plate, sprinkled it on the fish, and began sliding chunks of it off the bones. She was used to the muddy taste, as her mother often bought cheaper fish at the river market, but Sylvan's expression showed he was accustomed to eating clearwater fish, like most painted faces.

"Is this going to be our life for the next two months? Eating mucky fish and river rat three meals a day?"

"Tonight you get to try *dimura* tail," Gilea commented, sliding a chunk of fish into her mouth with practiced ease. "It's considered a delicacy."

"By whom, exactly?"

Gilea gave a pained smile, shaking her head gently. "By people who live on the river and can't afford better."

Sylvan grimaced, and Temi could almost see him blush beneath the paint. "I'm sorry, I didn't mean..."

"It's fine. I expect that's why they send you on these roughabouts." She smiled and nudged him with her foot. "Now if only they would send me on a layabout, where we could live in your villa and be served fine wine and cheese all day long."

Temi giggled. "That does sound nice, actually. Can I come and stay at your house for a while when we get back, Sylvan? My mother only breaks out the good stuff on holidays. The rest of the time it's sheep cheese and rough reds for us."

"You are both welcome in my house any time."

Temi and Gilea exchanged a glance and a little smile as they continued chewing the fish and pulling out the little bones.

Chapter Seven

Gilea sat crosslegged on the floor, sinking into the sounds of the rain pattering on the roof, Sylvan and Temi's restless tossing and turning, and Leo's rhythmic snoring. She closed her eyes and rushed past the noises like a diver outswimming the bubbles in her wake, until she floated, calm, supported by equal pressure from all sides. In her mind's eye she saw the surface of the water, where a circle formed, spinning around until another, deeper circle joined it, and her face floated up to the middle of the swirl. Her nose and mouth poked above the surface, sucking in a breath of clean air, then she sank below again, watching the swirl hover and spin, wobbling slightly like an errant top. Another joined it, and another, dozens and scores and hundreds filled her vision, and she watched, entranced by the shimmers of light they threw in all directions. Then her feet felt a draft of cold water, and her body was pulled forward as the swirls before her peeled off to make way for the largest one of all, which swallowed them, growing bigger and bigger until the surface above her was one huge swirling bowl of water, sucking her into its orbit. She started to spin with the swirl, sinking, pulled below, past any hope or desire to return to the surface, to the world she'd once called home. The dark depths called to her, and she answered them with closed eyes and open heart.

The rain stopped by mid-morning, but more clouds loomed to the west, and Leo set to work on the sweep mounts, barking orders at Sylvan and Temi as sweat rolled off his face. Gilea had been through plenty of weather with Leo, and if he was worried, she needed to be too. She chipped in as much as she could, tweaking a couple of spots in the roof that had leaked the night before, while they finished lashing the sweeps to the mounts. They were unwieldy paddles, close to ten feet long, with wide double-board heads on the end, and would require two people to fully power them, though she doubted Sylvan and Temi combined could match Leo's strength. At best, the sweeps could help them avoid objects they saw from a distance, but the raft was too big and lacked a proper hull, so the sweeps would be useless for quick changes of direction. The river began to rise, a torrent of milky brown water rushing hard along the bank, overflow from a creek upstream, ripe with the stench of washed-out gutters and latrines. The ropes strained to hold the raft in place and it thumped against the shore as the current battered it. Leo untied the downstream rope and tossed it on the deck, then unwrapped the upstream rope from the tree, leaving only one loop to hold the raft from careening down toward a logjam just downstream.

"We're going to get beat to hell against the bank," he shouted. "She may not hold together." He squinted at the approaching storm, shaking his head. "I don't see any lightning. We're going to try and ride this one out in the open. We just need to get away from the bank. Be ready with the poles!" He gave everyone a toothy little smile as he hopped onto the raft and made for the foredeck. He tucked the downstream rope between his teeth and dove out into the churning brown river.

Sylvan and Temi pushed off with long poles as Gilea released the rope and hopped onto the raft, picking up her own pole and pushing with all her strength. Between their poles and Leo's pulling, they barely cleared the tangle of branches from overhanging trees along the bank, which scraped the cabin, dislodging one of the roof boards. While Gilea was fishing it out of the water with her pole, Leo popped up over the side of the raft, flopping the rope onto the deck and taking hold of one of the new sweeps. He gestured impatiently toward the other sweep, and Sylvan and Temi rushed over, swinging the sweep awkwardly and pushing along with Leo. Gilea tidied up the ropes and poles to the sound of Leo yelling at the painted faces.

Sylvan and Temi found a rhythm with Leo just in time to clear the edge of the logjam, and before long they were floating with the steadier current of the main river, a safe distance away from the bank. They were alone on the water, apart from a few small fishing boats hurrying toward shore before the storm arrived. Leo clambered onto the roof and reaffixed the roof board, then went to work applying pitch around it and some other boards in need of attention. He paused on occasion to shout orders to Temi and Sylvan, who would push one of the sweeps to rotate the raft, or both to move it, though they couldn't do much with just the two of them.

Gilea's contract specified she was there to watch and protect them, and only engage in physical labor when it was necessary for their immediate safety, though Leo put little stock in contracts, and often expected her to do more. But he wasn't the one whose neck would be on the line if something happened to the painted faces.

She let him push one sweep while her charges powered the other, and she sat on the roof, keeping watch on the storm rolling toward them. As Leo had said, there appeared to be no lightning, and the wind was pushing straight upriver, which tempered their speed, though the raft bucked uncomfortably in the opposing forces of wind and current. The wind slowed as they hit the curtain of driving rain, and they scurried inside the cabin as the raft drifted down the center of the river. Leo sat down and smiled, wiping the water from his face.

"The river runs straight for the next five miles at least, by which time we should pass through the storm and we can look for another place to land." He took a huge slug from a waterskin, then corked it and leaned his head back against the wall, closing his eyes.

Sylvan sat studying his book with the intensity of one starved for reading. Since he had arrived on the raft, Leo had kept him and Temi moving, and Gilea had noticed him eyeing the book with longing on more than one occasion. She knew he was a newly minted doctor of natural science, but not a medical doctor; he seemed to have devoted his life to the study of living things, aquatic ones in particular. She marveled at the privilege of his life; his job, as far as he could be said to have one, appeared to be reading books, learning about plants and animals, and presumably teaching and writing about them. He held the book this way and that, angling it to catch the faint light peeking through the reed curtain Leo had installed over the doorway to the foredeck. Temi sat close to him, reading over his shoulder, though she spent quite a bit of time staring at the rain through the curtain. As Temi ran a hand through her hair, Gilea was drawn to the shocking whiteness of her wrist, like fresh goat milk.

Gilea turned her eyes toward the curtain, where the sun behind the quick-hitting storm was already coming into view. The line of black clouds was speeding past them, but the rain battered the cabin harder than ever, sending little sprays of mist through the reeds. The raft rocked a bit with the waves, and Gilea relaxed into the rhythm. Her charges were safe, almost happy, and Leo's eyes were barely slitted open, his mouth turned up in a little smile.

"Gods, look at this, Temi," Sylvan burst out, quieting toward the end of his sentence. Temi leaned over the book and her mouth dropped open. She cocked her head sideways, running her finger along the vertical edge of the page, her eyebrows furrowed with confusion, then snapped back to the place where Sylvan's finger was pointing. Gilea wanted to move over and have a look, but she kept her distance.

"The swirls," Temi whispered. "Is that right? I can barely read it—is that Old Southish?"

"The text is, although the marginalia are more like Middle High Southish, but yes, it's a bit different. It says," at which point he squinted, leaning closer to the text and angling his head sideways, "The...*duni*, as the Endulians call them, appear as swirls on the surface of the water, and as Servais neglects to mention them at all, one must conclude that he either never traveled the Living Waters, as I suspect, or that he did travel there, was aware of their existence, and chose to leave it out of his book for reasons unknown." Sylvan sat back, his face animated.

"So what, like a conspiracy of silence or something?" Temi smirked her disbelief.

"I know it sounds strange, but have you ever heard of anything like these swirls?"

Temi shook her head. Sylvan looked to Gilea, who blinked no, but she was pretty sure Leo knew more about them than he had let on. She was also fairly certain Leo had plans to drag her charges off looking for the swirls, and she wasn't sure if she could stop him. Gilea glanced over at Leo to see if he was asleep, but it was impossible to be sure.

"Right, and neither have I, and get this—I've literally spent the last eight years studying the various aquatic plants and animals of the world, or whatever can be learned in books and at the fish market, plus the occasional private fishing charter. And never have I heard or read anything about them."

"Well, you've never floated down the sewage-choked waters of the Agra, have you?" Temi said.

Sylvan shook his head impatiently. "No, see, once you get past the big cities, past Endulai, there are a few smaller towns here and there, for a while, but beyond that, there's almost nothing until you get close to Rontaia. I've seen a map, and it's...a couple hundred miles at least. I've read that the water runs clear there, as there's no agriculture and no industry, and it's clean water and aquatic grasses as far as the eye can see." Gilea could see that Sylvan had fallen under the spell of his book, the same spell as Leo: the lure of the Living Waters, or the idea they represented.

"It sounds lovely," Temi said. "I can only hope we make it that far."

When Gilea awoke for her morning meditation, Leo and the canoe were gone. She climbed up onto the roof and scanned the horizon, but saw nothing in the dim light of dawn. Leo often disappeared before daybreak, so she was hardly surprised, but she felt a little vulnerable alone on the boat with her charges. They were moored in a slough, where the trees broke the wind and the current was negligible. The air was light, almost cool, and she breathed deeply, in through her nose and out through her mouth, over and over, her eyes half-closed against the growing light of the sun, which illuminated the treetops across the slough. Familiar lines crossed the water: snake, *chukin*, and *dimura*, and the occasional splash of a fish sent rings out into the open water, where they dissipated quickly in the light chop.

Quiet voices sounded from the cabin below, and she rounded out her breath cycle, then climbed down, pushed aside the curtain, and saw Temi wiping her face with a rag. Temi turned away, and Gilea averted her eyes and stepped back onto the foredeck, but she could not erase what she had seen. Temi's forehead and cheeks glowed white in the darkness like a bleached skull, and her face was pained, her eyes sad, flickering to shame as she saw Gilea looking at her. Gilea's heart sank. She had seen the unpainted faces of previous charges before, by accident, once or twice, and it was like seeing someone's nakedness when they didn't know they were being watched, but it felt like a greater intrusion somehow.

Temi gave her a shy nod as she passed through the curtain onto the foredeck, her tan makeup hastily applied. She avoided eye contact as she skirted around to the aft deck. When she returned, she smiled, squinting against the sun, though it shone only on the trees opposite them.

"Looks like the clouds have all moved on." Temi's voice sank as she spoke. It took Gilea a moment to figure out why that was a bad thing. It made sense, given her sensitivity to the sun, but it felt odd to hear it. She was glad, at least, that the awkwardness of their accidental encounter seemed to have passed.

"Yes, and the wind's pretty steady out on the river. We'll see if Leo feels like we should float today."

Temi nodded, shading her eyes as she looked out over the river. "You've worked with him before?"

Gilea chuckled. "Plenty of times. Mostly on the Southern Seas, as that's more popular. Everyone wants to see the great *falin*."

"Are they really as big as they say?"

Gilea opened her mouth, and Sylvan poked his freshly painted face through the curtain.

"Did someone say *falin*?"

He was soft, but she couldn't help liking him.

"Yes," she said with a smile. "And yes, they really are that big."

"As long as a full galleon?" Sylvan asked, putting up both hands to shield his eyes.

"Not that long. But I was on a caravel, seventy-odd feet, and one swam beside us, longer than the boat and just as wide."

Sylvan's smile nearly reached his ears, and Temi erupted in a giggle as she looked at him, covering her face with her hand. Something in her gesture sent Gilea's heart fluttering, and she clenched her jaw and sucked in a slow breath to fight the awkward feeling.

Chapter Eight

Leo stood atop the cabin, shielding his eyes against the sun as the raft floated down the river, with a troublesome upstream wind pushing them toward the left bank. Sylvan and Temi were working in tandem on the sweeps, but Leo had to hop down and help them from time to time, powering one sweep while they combined on the other. Both of the painted faces were weak, but Temi at least had some grit in her soul. Sylvan's only strength seemed to lay in his mind, which Leo grudgingly admitted might come in handy somewhere along the way.

Just as he was about to jump down onto the foredeck to help push the raft back toward the center of the river, he saw them. Three swirls, moving in triangle formation about thirty yards to the right. He had to strain his eyes to get a better look because of the sun's glare, but the swirls seemed to have a reddish tint to them. He stared at the swirls as he worked the inside of his cheek with his tongue. The water below the Inkworks had run red after the incident, so all the swirls had looked red in that area. But here in the middle of the river, miles downstream, even with the muddy water, he could see the red. It had to mean something.

"Don't you think you should help them? It rather looks like we're going to be pushed into that bank of marsh grass." Gilea's voice was calm and quiet, and she showed no signs of moving from her cross-legged position. Leo swung his legs over the ladder, giving her a hard glare on his way down, which she greeted with her usual serene half-smile.

By the time they had horsed the raft out of harm's way with little room to spare, he could no longer see the swirls. He sent the painted faces in from the sun, and he heard them collapse onto their bunks while he stood on the roof of the cabin, scanning the horizon in vain for swirls, red or otherwise. Nothing more than the occasional branch or current shift stirred the surface of the water. His knuckle found his front teeth, and he bit down, hard enough to hurt but not quite enough to break the skin. He needed to see the swirls again, needed for them to be there, even if just beyond reach. In their absence, his chest tightened, compressing his lungs, and his breath came shallower and more ragged. When he couldn't take it any longer, he stripped off his pants and dove off the raft into the muddy water, which rushed past his ears, drowning out the sound of Gilea's near-silent sigh.

They floated past huge farms, whose neat fields of green and gold stretched on beyond the limits of their eyes, pasture land with black and white cows, oxbow lakes dotted with houses, and dense swaths of forest, which became rarer as they approached Tralum. Toward evening, they passed the great industrial city, where the smoke from innumerable chimneys pooled in the sky like a low-hanging storm cloud. They maneuvered to a slack spot just around the bend from one of the city's outer rings, next to a rough encampment of shanties lining the dry area above a wide bank of stinking mud. They tied the raft to a massive logjam in the shallows, where a half-dozen children were fighting a pitched battle with sticks. The children scampered to the far end of the sprawling mess of half-rotted trees, eyeing the raft and its occupants warily. Leo watched with a smile as Gilea stepped off the raft and glided along the trunks and branches toward the children, her movements smooth and unhurried. He saw the children's faces go slack as she stopped and spoke with them, and one by one they hopped off into the shallow water and waded back to the shore in a straight line, peering over their shoulders as they scurried along a path of well-placed driftwood through the mud and disappeared into the shantytown. Her powers of persuasion were uncanny, and he briefly wondered if she'd ever used them on him without his knowing.

"The whole place will be talking about us," Gilea said with a tight smile when she returned to the raft. "We're in their crosshairs now."

"You make them sound like hunters, Gil." Leo touched her arm, and she flinched just a little. "They're curious, that's all. And so am I! Aren't you?" He let her go, turning toward the settlement, most of whose inhabitants continued about their business, but more than a few stood watching the raft.

"You're not taking my charges into that slum. They'll be eaten alive."

"I most definitely am taking *my* charges into that collection of dwellings over there so they can meet some people, some real people, people they would never have met if they'd stayed in their protected little bubble." Leo's anger raised the hackles on his neck, and he noticed Sylvan and Temi's heads swivel toward them. He lowered his voice a little. "You think they came all the way out here just to eat *chukin*?" He shook his head. "I hope you'll be there to, what is it you do now? To *mind* them?"

Gilea closed her eyes, bit her lip, and nodded. "Okay. Okay!" She raised her hands in the air and turned away, then stopped, turning her head back around. "But I just want to go on the record as saying, you're kind of a fucking idiot." She side-eyed him, clambered up the ladder, and swung herself into a seated position on the roof, staring out at the river. No doubt she was trying to clear her mind using those Endulian techniques of hers, but what she needed was to fill it up a bit. Sometimes Leo couldn't help but see her as another one of his charges, in need of a little rough living to wisen her up some.

"Wolfie, you stay here and guard the boat."

Sea Wolf lowered his head onto his paws, his wide eyes showing hurt.

"Hey." Leo squatted down to grab the dog playfully by the snout. "I'm trusting you to keep this place safe. To keep our home safe. That's a big deal."

Sea Wolf licked his hand, settled back on his haunches, and perked up his ears.

"I promise I'll bring you a treat."

He slung the string of whiskers over his shoulder and stepped down onto a log that was a bit slimy, but mushy enough the painted faces probably wouldn't slip off. He hopped and stepped his way to the end of the last tree, then jumped down into the knee-high water, his feet sinking so deep in the mud the water came up almost to his waist, releasing a torrent of bubbles that nearly overwhelmed him with their fetid odor. He turned to see Temi jump down into the water, cursing under her breath as the mud pulled her feet down. She held out a hand for Sylvan, who took it, stepping gingerly off the edge and making a horrified face as he sank down, clutching Temi, whose eyes almost rolled through the roof of her head. Gilea followed, wading impassively through the muddy water.

When he had crossed the driftwood path onto more or less dry land, Leo looked around at the many faces watching him, raised the fish, and flashed his biggest smile.

"Anybody got a fire?"

Dimit poured their tea with panache, dipping the spout in each cup and raising it up as the thin stream churned bubbles into the steaming liquid. He set the pot back down on the table, rested his hands in his lap, and looked expectantly at Leo and the others. Dimit's son had begged Leo to come to their shack, and Dimit had welcomed them like honored guests. Leo picked up his cup, closing his eyes as the peppery steam awoke his sense of smell. He sipped carefully, trying not to slurp, and his mouth filled with a spicy, almost numbing sensation, with an aftertaste like the musky fruits on the islands in the Southern Seas.

"It was my wife's recipe," Dimit said, wincing. He took a slow sip, then lay his cup on the table without a sound. "She passed two years ago. Ulver's cough."

"To her name." Leo put his hand on his heart, and Dimit blinked his appreciation.

"To her name." Dimit took a small sip of his tea, his face drawn with sadness. "We have become accustomed to her absence, but the pepper tea is a small comfort."

"It's really good," Sylvan said. "What gives it that tingling sensation?"

Dimit flashed a narrow smile. "That's a secret I will take to the grave. After all, it's our ticket inside the rings."

"How many rings are there in Tralum?" Temi asked, leaning toward Dimit.

"Six, though the sixth ring is worse than outside, if you want my opinion. I'm saving up for a place in the fifth, or maybe the fourth if I can get my brother-in-law to go in with me."

Temi leaned back slowly, and Leo could see a spot behind her ear where her makeup had smudged, and the white shone through. He wondered if she had ever been to the outer rings of Anari, which were said to be as miserable as the inner rings were pristine.

"And how will this mystery tea get you in?" Sylvan asked.

"I sell tea at the scholars' lounge of the university library. That's second ring, by the way, and they line up for it. One of these days I'm hoping to get picked up as a tea curator for one of the painted faces, which half the scholars are anyway."

Sylvan cocked his head, and Leo could have sworn he could see the blush through his ruddy beige paint.

"Did I say something wrong? I hope..." Dimit covered his mouth as he looked at Sylvan's face, then Temi's. "Oh, gods, I'm so sorry, I didn't—"

"It's fine," Gilea said, breaking the tension with her even tone. "Dr. Kirin is a scholar himself."

"Oh really, wow, I am so honored, Doctor. Would it be irretrievably rude if I asked your discipline?"

Sylvan barked a genuine laugh. "Not at all, it's life science, with a specialty in aquatic life forms, especially fish. And please, call me Sylvan."

"That's so amazing!" Dimit's eyes sparkled. "I serve tea in the lounge of the science building here. You're from Anari? As in, the Great University?"

Sylvan nodded, his face growing animated. "Yes, I was fortunate enough to..."

Leo excused himself with a gesture and slipped

outside to suck in great lungfuls of air redolent of river mud and roasting whiskers. His eyes were wet and his head was spinning. It was becoming harder and harder for him to spend time indoors, crammed in with other people. He had started sleeping on the roof of the raft when the weather allowed and making excuses for going off by himself in the canoe. But once he was alone for long enough, he found himself paddling desperately back to the raft, to Gilea and the painted faces. The sweet spot between belonging and isolation had evaporated, and the only thing that gave him a feeling of peace was the pursuit of the swirls, of the mystery they represented. Though he couldn't explain it, even to himself, Leo felt drawn to them, with a singlemindedness extreme even by his obsessive standards. And he was convinced that the key to understanding the swirls was to find the Living Waters, which his mind had transformed from a fanciful notion into a sure reality.

Leo noticed that the group of kids had resumed their swordfight on the logjam. They seemed to be divided into two teams, one occupying each end, a few of them making brief forays into the opposing territory for a quick skirmish before skittering back with a giggle. Sea Wolf stood at full attention, watching them with calm but steady eyes, and the children avoided the part of the jam closest to the raft. Leo kicked at a piece of drift wood, bleached white and sucked of its weight by the sun. He picked it up, flipped it to grip to the opposite end, which had a Y-shaped crook that could serve as a cross guard. It was a good length, longer than the sticks most of the kids were wielding. He waded out through the shit-brown water, circling around to the opposite side of the raft as the deep mud swallowed his feet and the water came up to his neck. Sea Wolf ran over to sniff him when he climbed out, river water cascading off him and splashing onto the logs. He followed the dog to the foredeck, leaped onto the closest log, and let out a little roar.

"Who dares to invade the territory of the Lost Man of the River, a pirate so lonely and so fierce that none have ever seen him—and lived!" He used his best villain voice, and finished with a big smile, brandishing his stick like a cutlass.

The children's heads all swiveled toward him, a few moving away from him, but some creeping closer. An older girl, nearly a teenager, flashed a smile and swished her stick through the air in an X shape.

"Listen, Lost Man of the River, if you even are who you say you are, this island belongs to us." She spoke loud and clear, like a theater actor. "And we will brook no foreign powers setting foot on our land without they pay the ultimate price."

She gestured with her head, and four of the older children moved forward to join her, while the others closed in to watch.

"And who's going to stop me? The likes of you? Ha!" He leaped to the next log, then stood with his stick out, the silliest smile he could conjure on his face. The children charged, whacking his stick and his legs with theirs, while he put up only the mildest resistance. Sea Wolf rushed in to shoo the children away, but he knew it was a game, and he kept his cool. Leo took a step back and lowered his stick, holding up his other hand and showing his palm.

"You fight fiercely, and you have superior numbers, so I propose a truce," he said in his most piratical voice. "You may occupy that side of the island, and we will content ourselves with this little corner. Do we have a deal?"

The girl spat into the water between the logs and nodded. "We have a deal. For now." She furrowed her brow and turned away, waving the other children along. They followed like rats after a flute and soon busied themselves in their wargames on the other end of the logjam.

“We showed ‘em, didn’t we, Wolfie.” Leo knelt on one knee and ran his hands over the dog’s head.

Sea Wolf answered by jabbing his nose into Leo’s cheek and sloppily licking his mouth. Leo grabbed hold of the dog’s ears and licked him right back.

Chapter Nine

Sylvan sat cross-legged on his bunk trying to read his book by the dim lamplight, but between the bugs and the incessant itching of his feet, he could hardly concentrate. He noticed Temi scratching the soles of her feet, twisting her ankles upward to examine them. They were swollen and covered in tiny red dots, mostly on the soles but some on the tops of her feet and ankles as well. Sylvan looked down at his own feet and could see the same thing, between the red streaks left by his scratching. He bent his ankle to get a glimpse of his soles and saw scores of the tiny red dots. As he stared, he thought he could feel each of the dots pulsing, as if from the inside.

"You've got them too." Temi leaned over to inspect his feet. "Gods, they look awful!"

"What the hell is this?"

"You're the life scientist. Some kind of bug bite maybe?"

Sylvan's face broke out in a sweat, and his feet tingled all over. He looked up at Temi, who sat up straight and frowned.

"I think..." He looked down at her feet, which were easier to study, and he thought he saw movement just under the skin. "Wait, let me get my magnifying glass." He moved the lamp closer, dug it out of his bag, and leaned in close to Temi's feet. Just as he had suspected, there were tiny movements beneath each of the red dots. He handed her the glass, feeling short of breath, and she leaned over and studied his feet.

"Gods, there's something...moving underneath the skin." She looked suddenly queasy, and sweat beaded through her tan makeup.

"It must be some kind of parasite. I...I mostly know the larger creatures, but I've read about tiny worms so small you can't see them—"

"Mudworms," said Gilea, leaning down over her bunk. "I got a couple too. I'll have to burn them out tomorrow. Sorry, I forgot to check when we got out. It's... Holy shit!" She climbed down from her bunk, staring down at Sylvan's feet and covering her mouth with her hand for a moment. When she moved her hand away, her face returned to its normal serene expression, but there was a tell in her eyes.

"Is it bad?" Temi asked.

Gilea nodded, glancing at Temi's feet, then quickly turned her eyes up to meet Sylvan's.

"I've never seen more than five or six at a time. They live in the mud, in places where sanitation is lacking."

"And you said you have to...burn them out?" Sylvan's heart raced, and Gilea shook her head.

"Normally that's what you do when it's just a few. But this..." She stroked her chin, staring at the wall for a moment. "I'll have to find an herbalist. We could go into Tralum, but with any luck, there will be someone in the encampment who has what we need."

Sylvan sat up, his scientific interest piqued. "What do we need?"

"There are some plants that are toxic to mudworms, and if you get to them fast enough, you can kill them by soaking your feet in a solution of their sap, mixed with salt and water."

"And if you don't get to them fast enough?" Temi looked ready to faint, and Sylvan felt his stomach rising in his throat.

Gilea looked away. "I'll go out at first light and find someone. In the meantime, get some rest, and try not to put your weight on them more than you have to."

Sylvan's feet were red and swollen in the morning, and when he went to the back of the raft to relieve himself it was like walking across a bed of needles. He collapsed onto his bunk, and Temi stood up and disappeared for a couple of minutes, returning and sliding onto her thin reed mattress without a word, but her face showed she felt the same anguish as he. Leo and Gilea had gone off in the canoe before Sylvan was up, so he rolled over and tried to go back to sleep, but he could feel the mud-worms wriggling and pulsing under his skin. He sat up, leaned over to pick up his book, and tried to read by the light of the open window, in the hope of distracting himself.

Temi watched him for a while, then got out her sketchbook and pencils and stared at the blank page for a long time. She flashed him a smile when she noticed him watching her, then leaned toward him, her eyes on his book.

"I guess we've got the morning off," she said, scooch-ing closer.

"I'd say more than just the morning." Sylvan gestured toward her feet, which were even more swollen than his.

“I’m sure Gilea will take care of us. She’s an accredited herbalist, and this is a major city. She’ll find what she needs.”

Sylvan nodded, gazing blankly at the pages before him. “They must get these things all the time, living here.” He pictured the children swordfighting on the logjam, splashing carefree through the muddy water. He’d tried to give Gilea a few coins, to buy extra for Dimit and his son, but she’d refused, saying it wouldn’t be appropriate. He was still trying to wrap his mind around that. How could it not be appropriate to give medicine to someone who needed it?

“I bet their feet are a lot tougher than ours,” Temi said. “And I bet they know to check right away.”

“I guess.” Sylvan’s feet squirmed, and his heart with them. He shook his head and leaned in toward the book. “There’s nothing in here about them. Servais doesn’t talk about anything smaller than a water beetle.” Temi shot him a quizzical look. “The writer. He wrote The Living Waters six hundred years ago, and students like me have been studying it ever since. There are modern books that are more accurate and more exhaustive, but it’s a seminal text.”

“Have you found anything else interesting in the marginalia?” Temi rubbed the soles of her feet together, breathing out deeply.

“I’ve been too tired to read much, but I guess we have time today.”

Temi nodded and opened her sketchbook. “I’m going to work on some drawings of some of the fish. I think they might be a good decoration for our plates.”

“Oh right, I almost forgot! We have an old set my mother brings out on holidays, with the little birds wrapping laurels around the lampposts.” Yskan pottery had been all the rage when he was younger, but hardly anyone used it these days, with all the exotics from the western traders.

Temi huffed a small laugh. "Yeah, that old-school stuff doesn't sell anymore, so I'm hoping to get some inspiration for a new line."

"You should totally do the thinkfins! With those blank eyes and all the scales, that would be amazing!"

Temi cocked her head, looking out the window. "Not a bad idea. Are they in your book?"

Sylvan nodded, flipping delicately through the pages until he found the section for the scaled fishes. There was a drawing of the thinkfin, but it was all wrong—the fish was too fat, and the mouth too narrow. Temi leaned in to get a better look.

"Here it is. Not very accurate, I'm afraid. You'd want to make it longer, more sinuous, and the mouth should definitely be wider. And with those weird little serrated teeth. And the fins—gods, how did they draw this fish with only two lateral fins?"

"Did Ser..."

"Servais."

"Did Servais do the original drawings himself?"

"We think so. No one knows for sure, but they were all done by the same artist, at any rate, so either him or someone he worked closely with. You know how meticulous art copyists are, so you can bet this is very close to the original."

"And the...lateral fins—how many should there be?"

Sylvan studied the marginalia in the myths and legends section, which was filled with the unknown scholar's caustic commentary about Servais' depictions of the creatures. Other than the mentions of the *duni*, which he now knew was what the swirls were called, and whatever *ipsis* and *sitri* were, there wasn't much new to him, though he had come to believe that the author of the marginalia was talking about real things they had actually seen. He began scanning the margins of the other sections, to keep his mind off his throbbing feet, and he was just starting to feel drowsy enough he might be able to fall back asleep when the word *ipsis* caught his eye. It was in the margins of the section on aquatic plants, which was not his favorite topic, so he had hardly glanced over it before. Servais wrote of fields of bladegrass taller than a man, and sharp enough to slice through flesh. In the margins, in tiny script, Sylvan read:

> *Servais exaggerates as usual. The points of bladegrass are sharp enough to draw blood, but the edges leave only scratches. And how does he not mention the ipsis, who tend the bladegrass in the Living Waters to filter the water and alter its flow, so no craft larger than a canoe can pass unimpeded?*

"What is it?" Temi looked up from her drawing, a remarkably lifelike impression of a thinkfin, though its dorsal fin was much too small.

"What? Oh, nothing, just..." Sylvan felt embarrassed to be so obsessed with these details, though he didn't know why, since Temi seemed to find them as fascinating as he did. Her eyes stayed with his until he continued. "The marginalia say there are these people, or creatures, called *ipsis*, who tend the bladegrass in the Living Waters."

"Like farmers?"

"I guess; it doesn't say. But whoever wrote these marginalia makes it sound like they spent significant time in the Living Waters. And they also mentioned the *duni* there, which is what they call the swirls. And there's something else called a *sitri,* but I have no idea what that is."

"You think it really exists then?"

Sylvan shrugged. He had to admit to himself that he did, though he was unwilling to say it out loud. It went against everything he had learned in the past decade studying the science of living creatures, but what science could explain swirls in the water with no physical force causing them?

Temi gazed out the curtain thoughtfully. "I doubt we'll even get that far anyway. I kind of got the impression Gilea was trying to get Leo to take us to Endulai. Which would be so amazing. I've always been curious. Haven't you?"

Sylvan bobbled his head. "Sure, I mean, I guess it would be pretty unique, but I heard you're not really allowed to talk there? Which doesn't exactly seem like my scene."

Temi giggled, biting her nail, then held out her sketchbook. "What do you think of my thinkfin?"

"I think plates with that design are going to be on every table this time next year." He knew Temi's family had run on hard times, and he genuinely hoped it was true.

Sylvan heard Leo and Gilea arguing as the canoe approached.

"It's going to take at least two days to get their feet in working order, and I'm not contracted to push sweeps for two days unless our lives are in danger." Gilea's voice was not raised, but her speech rang clear across the water.

"Fuck your contract, Gilea. You've gone soft with all that time off. We're not even going to make Endulai if we spend two days tied to shore every time they get a boo-boo."

"Well, they wouldn't have feet full of mudworms if you hadn't insisted on stopping in the shit-infested slums just so you can give the painted faces a touching little moment with the common folk."

"You're the herbalist and their minder. Aren't you supposed to know to check them for parasites after a dip in unknown waters?"

Gilea didn't answer, and the canoe pulled alongside the raft moments later. Leo's head poked through the curtain, his wide smile showing all his teeth.

"How're your feet?"

"Positively wriggling with mudworms," Sylvan said. "Please tell us you've got good news?"

Leo's head disappeared, and Gilea slid through the curtain, holding a bundle of what looked like dried onions in her hand.

"We found some pullweed roots at a market in the fourth ring. Sorry it took us so long; the lines to get past the fifth were atrocious." She turned and called over her shoulder: "Leo, be a dear and get the pot boiling."

"On it," Leo called. Sylvan could hear him scraping out the firepit on the front of the raft.

"Now let me see those feet," Gilea said, putting the pullweeds on the bunk and sitting down between Sylvan and Temi. Sylvan pushed his feet toward her, and her face remained calm as she gently twisted them sideways to examine the soles. He winced, as even the slightest touch set his feet wriggling.

"I've never seen...honestly I've never even heard of anything like this. I'm really sorry I didn't check as soon as we got back to the raft." She looked over at Temi's feet, but she did not touch them.

"The pullweed, will it get them out?" Temi asked in a small voice.

Gilea nodded, frowning. "It will. But I'm not going to lie to you. It's going to hurt like hell."

Chapter Ten

Temi sat with her feet in the scalding footbath Gilea had prepared, which smelled like fetid onions cooked with rotten fish. Her feet felt like they were on fire, and sweat ran in rivulets down her back and armpits and beaded through her paint, which was surely streaking. She mopped it delicately with her handkerchief, already stained dirty tan from the endeavor, and wondered how much of her face was showing through. Leo was out in his canoe again, so she didn't need to worry about him seeing her, and Sylvan would understand, though his paint was surely of the best quality, and remained intact through the sweat. It was Gilea she worried about, not because she felt judged, but because Gilea had been acting strange around her of late, ever since she'd seen Temi's face without her paint. Gilea seemed to avoid meeting her gaze, and Temi felt guilty somehow, as if her pale face had offended Gilea, though she knew it was ridiculous.

"You okay?" she asked Sylvan, whose face was clenched with pain.

"Couldn't be better," he grunted. "You enjoying our little spa time?"

"I keep thinking the water will cool off a bit before long, or that my feet will become numb to it, but..." Temi breathed out through her nose, willing her feet to stay in the bucket. "Tell me about some fish or something."

"You want to know about fish?"

"Distract me. Tell me about...tell me about the one fish you most hope to see if we ever get to the Living Waters. If it really exists."

Sylvan's face relaxed for a moment, his eyes fixed on the curtain. "It's not a fish exactly, but have you ever heard of a lavender breathfin?"

Temi smiled and shook her head. "I've seen breathfins once, on a trip with my father to Rontaia, but they were gray. We spent a couple of days on one of those islands off the southern coast, and we saw breathfins every day from the beach. But I thought they were only in saltwater?"

"Well, Servais describes them living in the Agra, though it's surely a lot more polluted than it was back then. But if the water runs clear there, maybe? It's one of the cool things about the lavender breathfin. Not only do they live in freshwater—and they're not the only ones, by the way; there are two other known species of freshwater breathfins—they also have some unique social features you won't find in any other mammals..."

By the time he had finished, the water had cooled enough it no longer made Temi want to scream. There was a knock on the doorframe, and Temi touched her face with her fingers, but there wasn't time to do anything about the mess.

"Come in!" Sylvan called, and Gilea ducked through the curtain.

"I'm glad to see you've still got your feet in. How are we feeling?" She glanced at Temi, then her eyes shot to Sylvan.

"A bit better, now that the water has dipped below the boiling point."

Gilea pulled the curtain aside to let in more light, and Temi and Sylvan squinted at the same time. "Sorry, I need to get a look here." She opened the window and knelt next to Sylvan's bucket, lifted his foot out, and inspected it from all angles. "Looks like most of them are out." She stared into the bucket, and Temi leaned over to look into her own bucket. The surface of the water was covered in tiny inert squiggles. Temi put her hand to her mouth and leaned back against the wall, fighting the urge to throw up.

"Wow, yours have really come out." Gilea moved over by Temi, lifting her foot delicately and looking it over. Temi's foot glowed pink against the warm bronze of Gilea's hand. Gilea lowered Temi's foot back into the bucket and looked up at her. "I know it's gross, but believe me, it's a lot more so if you let them get comfortable. It's a good thing we got them in time." She stood up and flashed a tepid smile, then closed the window. "One more good soak and you should be in the clear. I'll go set the pot going again." She hovered for a moment, then turned and walked out of the cabin, pulling the curtain back across the door as she left.

By the end of the day, Temi and Sylvan sat cooling their feet in buckets of clean water, which Leo had brought back from somewhere in his canoe. Temi's feet had almost returned to normal, perhaps a shade five, though they were still a bit swollen and tender. Leo had brought back a soft-shelled turtle, which he made into a stew, along with some sort of tuber, and nettle leaves tossed in near the end. Though it had the same muddy aftertaste as most of their meals, Gilea had bought a zesty spice mix in Tralum to liven it up, which was a nice change of pace from the monotony of Leo's beloved everyspice.

After they had eaten, Leo and Gilea cleaned up, as Temi and Sylvan's feet were still too sore to stand for extended periods. Temi heard them talking in low tones as they washed, with less of their usual pugnacious banter. Afterward, they all sat on the foredeck as the sun set, drinking the tongue-numbing tea Dimit had gifted them and waving away suckflies. They did not speak much; even Sylvan seemed lost in thought. Temi stared downriver, wondering how long it would take her to get to Rontaia. She hoped she had enough money to book passage on a boat like the one they'd taken to Freburr; if worse came to worse, she could maybe offer to wash dishes or something to offset some of the fee.

Gilea sat cross-legged on the raft's logs, staring out across the water, taking small sips of her tea at regular intervals. Leo stood looking out at the river, then turned toward the bank, sat, stood up again, played with Sea Wolf for a while, then finally put down his cup and cleared his throat. Gilea turned away from the river and looked up at Leo, then at Sylvan and Temi, her eyes set with worry.

"I think we can get started again tomorrow, and Gilea has agreed to help with the sweeps if your feet are still recovering. I've been talking to a few folks on land and studying my river map, and I have a plan, which I'm going to share, and I want your input."

Sylvan sat up straight, side-eyeing Temi, then turned back to face Leo like a student about to hear the answers to a test in advance.

"We will reach Guluch in a couple of days, and I don't plan on stopping there unless we have to." Temi's stomach lurched at the name; Guluch was an industrial town where they made bricks and cheap metal and was reputed to have the highest number of brothels, bars, and soma dens in any city south of the Silver Hills. Her mother would always warn her she'd end up in Guluch as a slop girl if she didn't mind her manners. "From there, it's about three days to Endulai, then another day or two to where a large swath of wetlands branches off from the main channel." The unusual gravity of his voice had everyone watching him carefully. Even Sea Wolf stared up at him with deep, attentive eyes.

"My plan is we tie the raft up on shore, out of sight somewhere, near the wetlands, and go on in the canoe to explore for a few days. Some folks say..." Leo hesitated, looking each of them in the eyes. "Well, one guy said those wetlands are the basis for the legend of the Living Waters." Temi heard Sylvan's sharp intake of breath at the words, which filled her with an odd sense of dread. "The water is supposed to be much cleaner and clearer there, and calmer, so it should be an easy paddle, and we might find some things you'd never have a chance to see again."

"I love this plan," Sylvan blurted out, his hands clenched together. When he turned to Temi, his eyes were so bright and eager she couldn't help smiling, despite her deep misgivings. She blinked at him, took a deep breath, then turned to Leo.

"You hear all sorts of things about the Living Waters. Are you sure it's safe?" Temi didn't want to put a damper on anyone's passion project, but she wanted to see his reaction.

Leo swallowed and looked down for a moment, and a curious smile bloomed on his face.

"No." He squatted and ran his hands over Sea Wolf's ears. "I'm not sure of anything." He stared out at the river, then stood up again. "And we won't do this if either of you is uncomfortable with it. We can always stop off at Endulai, if they'll have us, and do a few days of meditation, or float for another week to Pilachis, where we'll hire a carriage or a boat to bring you back to Anari.

That's the return plan, regardless of what we do."

Temi felt Sylvan's stare burning into the side of her face.

"You said you're not sure it's safe, but do you *think* it is?" Sylvan's voice was strained with panic and hope.

Leo's smile broadened. "I do. I've been to a lot of places and seen a lot of things, and I've never come across a situation I couldn't handle."

"There's always a first time for everything," Gilea said, then turned to look Temi in the eyes. "But I've been with Leo on many a trip, and I trust him to know when to keep going, and when to turn around and go back." Her tone became more pointed toward the end of her sentence.

Sylvan turned to Temi, his eyes pleading. "Tem, think of it. Clear water, passages in the tall grass, flowers and birds in every color of the rainbow—when are you going to have a chance like this again?"

Temi shook out a little shiver creeping up her neck, then forced a smile. "If Gilea is okay with it, I'm in." Sylvan's sigh of relief was almost like a moan of pleasure. "You only get one roughabout in your life, right Sylvan?"

Temi sat filling a page of her sketchbook with swirls, some trying to capture the exact details of what she had seen, others more fanciful, the kind of thing that might look good on a teacup or spoonrest. She still planned to flee before the return trip, but it kept her occupied, and she needed to keep her skills sharp if she was going to make a go of it in Rontaia. She only vaguely remembered it from a childhood visit, but from what she'd heard, it seemed so lively and free compared to the stifling life she led in Anari. When Gilea returned from her nightly meditation on the roof, she glanced at Temi's sketchbook as she climbed up to her bunk.

"You still thinking about the swirls?" Gilea stopped halfway up, and Temi opened the sketchbook to show her.

"I'm working on some designs for my family's pottery."

"I like that one, with the wobbly edges." Gilea pointed to one of the more basic sketches, which did have a nice feel of movement to it.

"Thanks. I'm still not sure if I want to go simpler, or more elaborate." Temi pointed to a pair of swirls connected with flowery lines, which she thought might sell well in the higher-end lines.

"I like the simpler ones, but I'm not a very good judge." Gilea climbed the rest of the way up, and Temi closed her sketchbook.

"You're from Rontaia, right?"

Gilea leaned her head over the bunk. "Yes. I grew up there, then moved away for my apprenticeship. I've been back a few times, but it's been a while."

"What's it like? I went there as a kid, but I don't really remember much. I picture all these artists and musicians and the like, and seafood of course, but..."

Gilea smiled, then frowned. "All of that is true, but when I think of it..." she trailed off for a moment, staring at the lamp. "When I was a kid, I would roam the streets while my mom worked. I'd go down by the docks, watch them load and unload boats, listen to the shouts and laughter of the dockers. And the little bars where they went for their lunch, the smell of mussels and ale and smoke. That's what I think about. I never saw the big art factories, which were up the hill from where we lived."

"How many rings does it have?"

Gilea smiled. "Rontaia doesn't have rings. It's more of a cluster, or a cluster of clusters. There are places you're not really welcome if you don't look right, but there are no walls and no checks."

Temi smiled, staring down at her sketchbook. No walls, no rings, and no checks. No way to find someone who didn't want to be found. Now all she had to do was figure out how to get there.

Chapter Eleven

Gilea pitched in with Leo at the sweeps until around noon, when Temi walked out across the raft's logs, her face steeled against the pain, and gave her a little smile.

"I'm ready to take over. I can't bear sitting in that cabin for another day."

Gilea looked down at Temi's feet, which were shod in sandals, her skin smeared with the same tan paint she wore on her face, with thin stripes of blinding white peeking out beneath the straps. No doubt her feet were still too swollen to fit into her shoes. Gilea stepped back and offered the sweep with a flourish of her hand. "I'll be on the roof if you need a break."

Gilea watched Leo sweeping with one arm while Temi pushed with her whole body, gritting her teeth with the effort. She smiled at Temi's determination, the strength behind her fragile exterior. Sylvan emerged from the cabin just as they had maneuvered out of the way of a cargo vessel with three sails full of wind shoving it down the river. Leo relinquished the sweep, slipped out of his pants, and dove into the water as Sylvan averted his eyes. Gilea smiled and turned her attention toward the river, where the hazy brown of the water sparkled with flashes of yellow sunlight. She pressed her fingertips together, pushed her thumbs into the space between the fingers, cupped her hands, and held them up so she could look through the tiny diamond between her ring and pinky fingers.

As her focus shrank to this minuscule point in space, her mind expanded outward, filling the edges of her vision with waves of darkness and light, washing over one another to the rhythm of the water slapping the raft's logs. In this state she could sense the emotions the others were projecting, to make sure nothing was too far out of line. She could feel Leo's urgent movement through the water, his need to flee and then return, to be unbound, yet connected, and the mirage of the swirls and the Living Waters, pulling him downstream. Sylvan gave off a vibe of longing, of curiosity, of wonder, all interlaced with the fear of someone who had never felt his life in danger, even for an instant. But Temi's energy kept nagging at her, drawing her in and repelling her at the same time.

She had sensed this before, but it came clearer now. Temi's mind was fixed on something beyond the raft and the roughabout. It didn't feel like homesick energy, or anything related to Anari, which was too refined for what Temi was projecting. It wasn't Endulai either; there was chaos and noise, rather than peace and silence. Temi was hiding something that threatened to burst through her fragile shell, which Gilea could have pierced easily enough, but she blew out a deep breath and let her hands fall into her lap. Whatever was going on in Temi's mind, it didn't feel dangerous, and Gilea felt a little dirty for reading as much as she had. But Temi was so unlike most of the painted faces it was hard to resist.

Gilea had always seen them as pampered adult children with no real worries or problems. Their lives were so easy they had to go on roughabouts, just so once in their life, they could experience the same struggles that were the daily lot of most people. Some painted faces found the challenge so unbearable they quit within the first week. Every roughabout had an early bail-out option built in for this reason. But most were able to adapt to the physical and mental challenges, and perhaps even grow a little as a result. Sylvan fit that mold pretty well; though he was not a natural at physical labor, he did his part, and his complaints were more self-deprecating than genuine. With Temi, there was something else.

Temi accepted each challenge as it came, and did her part with the diligence of one accustomed to hard work, though perhaps not of the physical kind. She did not complain, but neither did she seem to take the perverse joy many painted faces showed when they were "roughing it," knowing within weeks they would be sitting in a cushioned chair, having wine delivered by one servant while another painted their faces in extravagant colors. Gilea did not get any of the usual vibes from Temi. She got a single-minded determination, a will to endure and persist, to go beyond, which was rare enough in the general population, but unheard of among the painted faces. Temi was running, but to what, or from what, she could not have said. Gilea's heart stirred; she hoped she could help Temi find whatever she was looking for.

Leo came back from his morning outing a little later than usual, out of breath and with a huge smile on his face that could only mean trouble. He chugged two cups of water and crammed some leftover roast tubers in his mouth as everyone watched him with expectant faces. He did not appear to have brought back any animal carcasses, scrap wood, or edible plants, and Gilea braced herself when he swallowed the last of his food, downed another cup of water, and spoke.

"I got us an invitation to dinner tonight."

"Where, in Guluch?" Sylvan looked like he was going to throw up, and Gilea had to look away to hide her smile.

"No, a little upstream from there, with some friends I made. Nice folk. You'll love them."

"Will there be mudworms?" Temi's voice was flat but her eyes twinkled.

Leo gave a little chuckle. "The bank is all sand there. There will probably be sand flies, but they just take a little bite from the surface and go about their business. As long as you stay covered up, you'll be fine."

They floated most of the day under an overcast sky, which seemed to lift the painted faces' spirits. In late afternoon, they maneuvered the raft to a sandy bank littered with driftwood, where they all got out and stretched their legs.

Leo stood gazing at the dense forest, his bow slung over his shoulder. "I'm going to go inland to try and find some nice nettle, or some *dimsha* root, and maybe shoot something if I can. Sylvan, Temi, you want to set up the trotline? I left one of the small whiskers from yesterday trailing behind the raft. You should be able to get a dozen or so baits from it. Toss it out over there by that rock, where there's an underwater dropoff. I'd like to bring a little something for the pot if we can."

Gilea stepped toward Leo, and he turned his head in her direction, though his body was facing the forest.

"These...friends you speak of..."

"Oh, they're fine. Totally safe, nothing to worry about. Two brothers. Nice folks, and I'm sure they have some good stories to tell."

Gilea gave him a stern look, which he deflected with

a smile. She blinked at him, and he turned and padded into the forest, unshouldering his bow and ducking into a narrow game trail. Leo was always finding these random 'friends' and dragging his charges off to meet them. And though it always gave Gilea pause, they had done it scores of times over the years, and only once had the situation required her intervention. She had to admit, even visiting the shantytown had been a good idea; it was her fault for not checking for mudworms after. Leo had good instincts, even if he was a bit too trusting for Gilea's comfort. She turned back to see Temi toss the whisker carcass toward Sylvan, who jumped back a little and stood with his hands on his hips for a moment before drawing his knife and kneeling on the sand.

Gilea kept her awareness on the forest as she watched her charges bait and throw out the trotline, then wash their pale hands several times, sniffing between applications of the harsh soap Leo kept on the raft. She had seen the blisters, scrapes, and scratches, especially on Temi's hands, which were painful to look at. It seemed that, in addition to being unhealthily pale, her skin was also particularly fragile, like tissue paper. Gilea caught her mind drifting to imagine Temi's body, delicate as a freshly bloomed lily. She cupped her hands over her eyes to block out the image and inhaled deeply, letting the dead-fish smell of the river and the sappy richness of the forest's many perfumes wash away the thoughts she could not allow to flourish.

Sylvan cried out, and Gilea snapped to attention as she saw him pointing toward the trotline, which was bowing the sapling they had tied it to. She breathed out as she watched him dash over to seize the rope and pull up the line. A large whisker with a flat head and a bright orange tail flopped and splashed in the shallows, and Temi stood watching as Sylvan danced around the fish, reaching down to grab it and then jumping back again each time it flipped. Gilea heard pounding footsteps from the forest, which she immediately recognized as

Leo's. She turned to see him emerge from the game trail with a broad smile and a sack overflowing with greens in his hand.

"Nice coppertail!" he called, dropping his sack and bow and bounding across the beach. Gilea followed him, and they stood for a while watching Sylvan's attempts to pick up the fish. After a while Leo swooped in, slid his fingers inside the fish's gill slits, and held it up, the muscles in his arm bulging with the effort.

"I thought that was a clearwater fish," Sylvan said, leaning in close to study the fish's tail.

"Big ones like this, usually, but nature does love to surprise you. Our friends are going to be thrilled with this one."

"Tell us about these friends," Temi said.

"Well, they should be here before long. They wanted to see the raft, so I told them where we would be landing."

"You paddled all the way down here and back just this morning?" Sylvan backed up as Leo swung the fish toward him.

"Yes. Just stick your pointer and middle fingers in one gill and your ring finger and pinky in the other. It takes the fight right out of them. You have to hold on real tight because she's heavy as hell."

Sylvan glanced at Temi, took a deep breath, then slid his fingers into the fish's gills, taking it from Leo. The fish gave a little flip, and Sylvan staggered but held on, smiling and holding it up just above his waist.

"So, what do we do now?"

"Tie it on the back of the raft, sit back, and wait."

Gilea cocked her ear at an odd sound coming from downstream. When she looked, she saw a strange boat plodding upstream toward them.

"Looks like we won't be waiting long," she said.

There were two men in the boat, one in front and the

other behind, and their arms moved in an unusual way, as if they were punching the air. A steady splashing noise emanated from the boat, and the water frothed along the sides of the craft. As it approached, she saw that the men were each holding onto curved metal rods, which they cranked with their hands to turn wheels on both sides of the boat equipped with many small round paddles. Leo waded out to grab the prow as they pulled up close, and dragged the boat partway up onto the sand. The men lifted the curved rods out of the deep grooves and laid them in small indentations next to the grooves on the gunwales, lifting the paddlewheels out of the water enough to avoid scraping in the sand.

"Max! Zander! I see you found us all right."

"You were right where you said you'd be," said one of the men, perhaps fifty years old with ruddy tan skin, hopping out into the shallow water and shaking Leo's hand. He turned back to the boat and held out his hand to help the other man down, who looked a bit younger, and who moved a bit more slowly, as if afraid he would lose his balance.

"Your boat is amazing!" Leo exclaimed after shaking the younger one's hand. "Your arms must be tired though."

"Truth be told, my arms are a little tired," said the older man, gazing at the raft. "I bet your whole body gets tired pushing those big sweeps too."

"For sure. It's not the most efficient, but it gets us out of the way of the big ships."

"Well, efficiency isn't really what ours is about either. Anyone can paddle or row a boat, but where's the fun in that, right Max?"

"What'll you do with it?" The younger man stared at the raft with troubled eyes, and Gilea felt his discomfort with the social interaction, combined with a deep curiosity about the raft.

"Beg pardon?" Leo said.

"When you get to where you're going. What'll you do with your raft?"

"Well, I'm not sure, Max. I was thinking of selling it or trading it. Somebody might want to live on it for a while, don't you think?"

Max nodded, his mouth open in a half-smile that showed his crooked teeth. "You could make a tent over the front, for sitting in any kind of weather." He walked toward the raft, and the older man called after him.

"Max, come meet our friends before we go invading their privacy."

"It's fine, Zander," Leo said, following Max. "Go ahead, Max. Let me show you around." Gilea smiled at Leo's gentleness.

Zander shook his head and flashed an apologetic smile. "My brother does love his boats."

Chapter Twelve

Leo walked with Max along the sandy bank where the boats were tethered, just downstream from Max and Zander's encampment. There was a rowboat fitted with a sail, a giant canoe that looked to have been made of two canoes spliced together, a sort of pontoon with a seat perched on a wooden lattice above two connected logs, and a small flatboat with a rectangular cut-out in the back, with a half-built waterwheel laid across the deck. Leo leaned over to study the last boat, which had a high seat, with two foot-sized boards beneath it, linked with iron bars that curved underneath the seat toward the back of the boat.

"We need to find more boards for the wheel and iron for the cranks, but she's gonna go someday." Max spoke without looking at Leo.

"So you sit up here, and push these with your feet, and it turns the wheel?" Leo was impressed with the ingenuity of it, more so because it was built with washed-up parts. Whatever his social challenges, Max clearly had a deep understanding of mechanics.

Max nodded. “The iron is the hard part. Boards wash up all the time. Sometimes they have good nails in them, but iron doesn’t float.”

“How do you work the iron, when you find it?”

Max sucked his teeth. “There’s a guy in Guluch with a little forge. He helps us sometimes. We bring him fish.” He turned as Zander called out and waved them over. “Dinner is ready.” His eyes met Leo’s for a moment and a nervous smile flashed on his lips. “I’m glad you brought that big coppertail. They taste sweeter than candy.”

They sat on stumps around a terra cotta stove that had been cracked and repaired several times. Max served them stew made with the coppertail, some kind of dried meat, turnips, and the nettle Leo had brought. Max walked slowly and handed out bowls with careful gestures. The stew was badly lacking in salt, and Leo wished for a healthy dash of everyspice, but after Zander passed around a jug of fiery liquor a couple of times, it didn’t seem to matter so much.

Leo joined Sylvan making small talk with Zander about the fish in the river, and they tried to pull Max into the conversation, but Max said little, staring at Sylvan and Temi intently, seeming to grow agitated as the evening wore on. As Sylvan was in the middle of telling the story of the coppertail, Max blurted out:

“You two are painted faces, aren’t you?”

“Maximilian!” Zander barked. “Show some common decency. These people are our guests!”

Max looked down, chastised, and Temi reached out her hand toward him, though she did not touch him.

“It’s fine, and yes, Max, we are. Sylvan and I, that is.” Leo appreciated Temi’s gentle way with Max, so unlike most of the painted faces he had known.

Max looked up at her for a moment, then back

down. "I could tell you were, but with him, I wasn't sure at first."

"We don't see a lot of city folk out here." Zander's tone was apologetic and embarrassed. "And manners aren't my brother's forte."

Max side-eyed Zander, then looked back up at Temi, squinting, as if in pain. "Is it true your skin burns real quick in the sun? Is that why you wear it? That's what I heard." He looked back down as he finished.

Temi smiled. "Well we don't catch fire or anything, but it turns red really fast, and it hurts."

Zander stood up slowly, stretching out his back. "Well, I don't know about you folks, but I think it's about time for some tea. Max, you want to get the tea ready? The red box, since we have company."

Max flashed a sudden smile and made his way to their boat, which wasn't much different than the raft. It had a bigger cabin, and a proper hull instead of just logs, though it looked to be badly in need of pitch. It had no sweeps or oars that Leo could see, so he assumed they didn't move it around. It had no doubt been put together of pieces salvaged from the riverbanks, like their other boats, like Leo's raft. Leo admired the brothers' lifestyle, as hard as it was, the simplicity of it, the oneness with the river. He didn't know if he could stay anchored in one place like them, but if he were ever going to settle down, it would have to be along a river, whose changing face would never grow stale.

Max returned with a large clay teapot, which he placed carefully on the stove, then collected their bowls and returned them to the boat. As they sat waiting for the tea to boil, Leo asked Zander about Guluch.

"It's not bad, as long as the sun is up. After dark, it gets a little dicey. I go there once a week to a tavern by the north docks and play my lao for a few coins, which come in handy for the things we can't get from the river or trade for."

"You have a lao? Can I see it?" Leo couldn't imagine an instrument as delicate as the lao being kept in tune in such a humid environment, but the brothers clearly had skill with wood.

"After tea, I'll play for you, if you like."

The kettle poured steam, and a peppery fragrance filled the air. Max poured tea into handmade wooden cups, and as Leo held it under his nose, he felt a tingling, almost numbing sensation in his nostrils.

"This reminds me of the tea we were served a little upstream, in a little settlement just below Tralum."

"It's made from pepper root and sky chili. I got it in trade for a canoe we'd found and repaired."

"The canoe was too heavy," Max said, blowing on his tea. "Made of ironwood. Tough as rocks, and just as heavy. We have a better one, made of featherpine. Lighter and faster. But we have to seal it up twice a year."

"I bet you do." Leo had heard of boats made of featherpine, but it wasn't very practical, as the woodworms would turn it to lace in a matter of months if it stayed wet. "Did you build it yourselves?"

Zander chuckled. "It washed up after a storm, with a picnic basket inside, with a good dry sausage and some sheep cheese. I figure it floated down from one of the pleasure camps upstream." He glanced up at Sylvan and Temi as he said it. Leo had worked at a pleasure camp as a teenager, which gave the painted faces a little taste of the outdoors, without any work, or risk.

"It could be," Sylvan said, with a remarkable lack of self-consciousness. "They had featherpine canoes at Ivy when I was there." He looked to Temi, who stared down into her tea. "I don't recall any sheep cheese or dried sausages though. Mostly a lot of specklefish, as I remember."

"Don't get specklefish around here," Max said. "Too muddy. There's a couple of clearwater streams around, but they don't let you fish there. You have to go a ways downstream to find speckles."

"Yes, I've heard the water runs clear at Endulai," Gilea said, speaking up for the first time all evening.

"Clearer than here," Zander said. "But you'd need to go a lot further before it clears up enough for speckles."

"Not much further," Max said into his tea. Something in his tone snapped Leo to attention.

"You're talking about the wetlands past Endulai?" Leo asked, leaning forward on his stump.

Max looked at Zander, who shook his head and shrugged.

"That's right," Max said. "It's a whole other branch of the river, and it runs clear as air."

"You've been there?" Sylvan asked.

Max set down his cup and blew out through pursed lips.

"He got lost there once," Zander said, a little nervously. "He—"

"Dammit, Zander, let me tell it!" Max's voice rose and cracked, and Zander held up both hands. Max poured more tea into his cup, set down the pot, and sat rotating the cup in his hands. He said nothing for a good minute before opening his mouth again.

"When I was a kid, we used to live in Tralum. Fifth circle, not too bad. Before mom and dad died." He shook his head and slurped his hot tea. "Me and Zander, we would go out fishing along the river, and one time we found this rowboat, kind of busted but we spent the summer fixing it up. Not a bad little boat, we called it the Fish Hawk, didn't we, Zan?"

Zander smiled and closed his eyes. "We did at that, and a fine boat it was."

"Well this one time, Zander was sick with Ulver's cough, what later took mom and dad, so I went out by myself, to catch some whiskers and whatever. Zander told me not to do anything stupid, not to take the Fish Hawk out by myself, but I didn't listen. I never listened if he wasn't around."

"Still don't." Zander smiled over his cup. Leo was moved by Zander's big-brotherly affection for Max.

"So I got out there, and the next thing the wind whips up, and there's this big storm, and I'm out there in the middle of the river, and one of the oars jumps the lock and goes into the river, so I'm trying to paddle with this one big oar, but I was just a kid, see? And the water started getting fast, so I just curled up in the bottom of the boat and prayed it didn't sink."

Only crickets and the low crackle of the fire broke the silence while Max paused.

"When I woke up, the storm had passed, and I was stuck in a field of bladegrass, taller than you or me." Leo's fingers tightened around his cup. This was the exact same detail he'd heard from the fisherman he'd spoken with in Tralum when he'd asked about the Living Waters. "I started pushing with my oar, trying to find my way through, when I heard these noises, like someone wading through the water. I hunkered down in the bottom of the boat, and it got closer, and the grass moved, and there was this face looking down at me, this tall man, tall and thin, the tallest man I ever saw." Max stood up, ran his hands through his tangled hair. "His face was...different, longer somehow, like out to here." He held his hand six inches from his face. "He smiled, or at least I think he did, and then he grabs my boat and starts pulling me through the grass. After a while, I sat up, and then the grass opened up, and it was like a big lake, with grass on all sides."

Leo looked to Zander, whose smile was strained, and to Sylvan, who listened, rapt.

"He takes me around the edge, and I can see things in the water, speckles, snakes, thinkfins, and there's these swirls everywhere, only the water was clear, and there was nothing moving under them." He shook his head, and Leo stood up, unable to contain his excitement any longer.

"Have you seen these swirls around here?" he asked in a near whisper.

Max nodded and stood up too. "Sometimes. A bunch of them a couple days ago, in fact. But there, they were everywhere, some small, some wider than my boat. There were other things in the water, things I couldn't quite see, but moving, flashing, like a bunch of invisible snakes swimming together." He gave Zander a sheepish look. "Everyone thinks I made it all up, cause I like to tell myself stories, but I didn't. I saw it all."

"What else did you see? Were there any breathfins?" Sylvan asked in an excited voice.

Max cocked his head at Sylvan. "There were, and they were kind of purple-gray, about this long." He held his arms about three feet apart. "I've only seen one once up here, but there were a bunch of them, puffing mist when they came up and everything." He sat back down, holding his face in his hands. "But let me finish. This tall man, he pulls me a long way, through these channels in the grass, then it opened up again, then more channels. There were more men like him, tall, so tall, and they talked, but I couldn't understand them, and finally, he takes me to this one place, like a big lake, with an island in the middle, and then he says something to me, only I couldn't understand what he said. And then this big canoe comes out from behind the island, like it was made of a whole tree trunk, paddled by two more of those...whatever they were."

Zander reached over and put a hand on Max's shoulder. Everyone kept silent as Max caught his breath and continued.

"They paddled me over to the island, and they point to this tunnel, and I'm scared but I go through it, cause what choice did I have? It leads me to this pond in the middle of the island, with a little channel pouring out down one side, and there's this stone bench next to the pool, so I go and sit down. There's a gourd full of water and a wooden cup, and I'm so thirsty, so I pour a cup, smell it, and drink it down." He closed his eyes for a moment. "Let me tell you it's the best water I ever tasted. So clean it like washed the whole thing away, the storm, losing the oar, getting lost, even the tall men. I drank another cup, and when I look out into the pool there's this guy rising up out of the water." He turned and shrugged Zander's hand off his shoulder.

"This man, I knew right away, it was the Lost Man of the River, the pirate ghost, you know the story?" Leo nodded, but the painted faces looked confused. Evidently, that legend hadn't made it up as far as Anari. "He was kind of glowy, silvery in a way. I can't explain it. He was a person, but he wasn't a person, not really. He didn't have a face or anything, but he was shaped like a person, only...He was made of water." Max shook his head, picked up his empty cup, and tilted it back, his eyes wet in his pained face.

"And that's where the story always ends," said Zander, putting his hand on Max's knee.

"I made him a promise," Max said to the fire, and everyone remained silent for a moment.

"How did you get back?" Leo asked.

Max shook his head.

"He showed up in the boat," Zander said. "Pulled up on shore, with both oars intact. He was sound asleep, and he slept for two days. Everybody figured it was oxbow fever, and he just passed out in the boat and dreamed it all."

"It wasn't a dream," Max grumbled. "I know the difference."

Leo stared into the fire, images of swirls rushing through his mind, rising up into watery men. The Living Waters were real. And he was going to find them.

Chapter Thirteen

Sylvan lay awake in his bunk, replaying Max's story in his head. The detail of the tall men Max had described kept circling his consciousness like a fly buzzing just out of reach. His fingers found the lacquered cover of his book box, and he wished he could light the lamp again to reread the marginalia. Apart from the lack of creature comforts, the food, the cramped living quarters, and the parasites, the thing that bothered him the most on the roughabout was his inability to read late into the night as he was used to. He took a few deep breaths, closed his eyes, and tried to picture the text in his mind. The unknown scholar who'd written the marginalia had mentioned three creatures, or phenomena, with names that felt vaguely Endulian. One was the *duni*, and he was sure they were the swirls. The other was *ipsos*, *sipsos*...It came to him after a moment: *ipsis*. He had studied ancient Enduli, though he was by no means an expert, and he knew a little bit of modern

Enduli too. The word was familiar but twisted somehow. The word swirled around in his mind until at last, he had it: it felt like the word for tall. So the tall men were called *ipsis*. Not that it helped much, but it meant the names definitely had an Endulian origin. He fell asleep puzzling over the word *sitri,* with images of tall men with long faces pulling him in a boat through fields of bladegrass, into a lake where lavender breathfins spouted and frolicked in the sun.

They set out early the next morning, exchanging waves with Zander and Max as they floated past their encampment with its odd assortment of salvaged boats. After another hour, they saw Guluch rise on the riverbank like fungus on a rotting log. Ramshackle docks and rough warehouses along the water rose to misshapen, time-stained buildings, ring after ring, with a castle of yellowed stone in the center. Cargo boats rowed upstream, fishing boats and canoes crisscrossed the waters, and scores of somber figures hauled and carried along the docks. Great plumes of smoke belched from chimneys on the downstream end of the waterfront, which stretched for more than a mile past the main city. Besides crime and debauchery, Guluch was known for making bricks and forging iron and tin, and acrid fumes drifted across the water. Sylvan and Temi sat inside the cabin, watching through the window, holding handkerchiefs over their mouths to stop themselves from coughing. As they passed the last of the larger docks, Sylvan saw scores of smaller huts and docks downstream. He heard Leo clamber down the ladder, calling "To the sweeps!"

Sylvan followed Temi out onto the deck, and Leo gestured them toward the left sweep while he powered the right.

"We need to get to the left bank as fast as possible. Give it everything you've got!" His neck strained and his arms bulged as he powered the sweep with a force Sylvan and Temi could not match combined.

"What's wrong?" Gilea called from the roof, scanning the river all around.

"Swirls," Leo grunted as he lifted the sweep out of the water and swung it toward the front again. "By the docks. We need to land and get the canoe in the water right away!"

Sylvan pushed as hard as he could, angling his head to see what Leo was talking about. He could see some disturbance in the water around one of the huts, but as curious as he was about the swirls, he wondered if it was a good idea to get in a canoe with them in the water. The swirls hadn't seemed hostile in Ink Creek, or in Max's story, but he found himself less than eager to get a closer look. It took a while to get the raft maneuvered toward shore, and they eased toward a muddy bank a half-mile downstream from the last of the smaller docks.

When they reached the shore, Leo untied the canoe and shouted "Who's coming with me? I need one person in the canoe, and the other two can tie up the raft." Sylvan and Temi looked at each other as Gilea grabbed a pole and steadied the raft against the shore.

"Sylvan, come on then," Leo called from the canoe. "Come on!" he shouted, and Sylvan shrugged at Temi, hurried over, and hopped in. They paddled upstream, Leo's powerful strokes propelling the canoe, while Sylvan tried hard to stay in sync. His heart pounded and his mind spun as he saw the size and commotion of the disturbance ahead. A pair of swirls floated downstream past them, almost silvery in the morning sun, then a trio, and another pair, until soon the water was filled with swirls. Most of them were about the size of a barrel top, with a few smaller and a few larger. A woman stood on one of the docks, a ratty broom in her hand, watching the swirls, paying almost no mind to Sylvan and Leo. A couple more of the neighboring huts' inhabitants stood staring into the water, their faces transfixed. Sylvan could see a huge group of swirls roiling the water around one of the docks ahead.

"There," Sylvan called, looking over his shoulder and pointing with his finger still on the paddle.

"Okay, ease up," Leo said, steering them outside the now steady stream of swirls moving downstream. Leo turned them back toward the dock, and Sylvan saw one swirl, wider than the canoe, spinning in place just upstream from the dock, while the others spun and flashed in the water. Sylvan's jaw hung open as he stared into the huge swirl, wondering what caused it, and what made it different than the others, which flashed silvery in the sepia water.

"Do these look shiny to you?" he asked Leo.

"They do." The canoe was drifting downstream, and they paddled back around, just upstream from the dock, and floated slowly past it again. Though the water was stained and muddy, the swirls glimmered as they floated away from the hut. Leo held the boat steady as they watched for another pass, and as they turned to reposition themselves again, the stream of swirls thinned, then the water went calm, except for the largest swirl, which moved slowly toward the canoe.

"Don't move," Leo whispered.

"Not a problem," Sylvan managed as the swirl approached, spinning with a slow, steady pulse. It was close to eight feet wide, and its center was a couple of feet below the surface. It did not shine silver like the smaller ones, and it stopped less than five feet from the canoe, spinning ominously for a few moments, then moved slowly away, following the rest of the swirls downstream. Sylvan let out a long, slow breath as the swirls grew distant. Was it their leader somehow, their guard, or their shepherd? He heard footsteps on the dock and looked up to see a diminutive woman with dark skin and gray braids pulled back in a thick ponytail. She held her hands out in front of her, looking into the water, then downstream, then up at Sylvan.

"They're gone?" she stage-whispered.

"They..." Sylvan mumbled, not sure how much to tell.

"The swirls, idiot! Are they gone?" Her voice rose in anger, or sarcasm, or both.

Sylvan's gasp turned into a nervous giggle. "Yes, they're gone." He pointed downstream.

"Why were they here?" Leo asked, paddling the boat closer to her. The woman crouched and took hold of the front end of the canoe, guiding it alongside the dock, which was soaking wet as if it had just rained. She offered Leo a hand and helped him out of the boat, then hauled Sylvan up onto the dock with unexpected strength.

"They were after my quicksilver, I think." Sylvan's focus narrowed at the mention of quicksilver, which suggested alchemy. She looked down into the water on both sides of the dock as Leo tied up the canoe. "I guess they got it all."

"They did have a kind of silvery look to them," Sylvan said. It all made sense now. Except for why the swirls would have taken it, or how.

She shook her head. "I've seen them red before, but never silver." She walked back to her hut, standing in the doorway with her hands on her hips. "And now I have no quicksilver." She put her hand to her chest, huffing in anger. "What the hell am I supposed to do with no...fucking...quicksilver?" Her voice rose into a shout, and she kicked something inside the hut, and a racket of thuds and splashes and clangs followed. She turned around, her eyes red, her face drawn with rage. "What the hell—" She stopped, dropped her hands to her sides, and slid down the doorframe. "I'm ruined," she whispered, fumbling in her pocket for a flask, which she opened and took a long pull. She held it out toward Sylvan, who waved it politely away, but Leo accepted the flask, lowered to sit on the wet dock next to her, and took a swig. Sylvan followed Leo's lead, sitting down and taking a tiny sip of a liquid so fiery and foul he nearly coughed himself into the water.

The woman barked a laugh, then took the flask back. "Like hot lava down your gullet, isn't it?" She turned the flask up, and drops ran down her chin as she gulped down the remaining contents and pounded the dock with her fist three times.

"Patia." She held out her hand to Leo, who shook it.

"I'm Leo, and this here is Sylvan." Sylvan shook her extended hand. "We have a raft just downstream."

"And you just came paddling up here when you saw the swirls swarming around my dock?"

Leo's smile broadened, and Patia's lips curled up just a bit at the edges.

"I've been seeing them a lot," Leo said, "and I have to admit I'm curious."

"Curiosity strangled the cat, as they say." She noticed Sylvan peeking inside the hut and kicked the door shut. She pushed herself up to her feet and dusted off her robe. Before the door closed, Sylvan had seen a copper pot, a clay stove, and a strangely shaped glass container that might have been an alembic.

"You practice the Good Works?" he asked. The alembic, combined with the quicksilver, removed any doubt that she was an alchemist. He'd learned about it in study, and he hoped using the name preferred by its practitioners would get her to talk. Patia gave him a long, searching look, then looked to Leo before turning back to Sylvan.

"What do you know about the craft?" She stood towering over him, and as he stood up and looked down on her, her neck craned back so her eyes stayed locked on his.

"Not much," he admitted. "We studied it in the history of chemistry, but just an overview, really. But when you mentioned the quicksilver..."

She squinted at him, studying his face, his hands, his feet. She must have known he was a painted face, but she didn't say anything.

"What's your discipline?" she asked, her posture relaxing. "I studied natural philosophy down in Rontaia until the money ran out, then I kind of struck out on my own." She gestured vaguely toward her hut.

"Life science, aquatic animals, mostly." *I just received my doctorate,* he stopped himself from saying.

"You got any theories about these swirls then?"

Sylvan shook his head. "They don't seem to be made by any animal, not a visible one anyway. But they're not exactly natural phenomena, are they?" He'd been so focused on the other creatures mentioned by the writer of the marginalia he had hardly begun to think about the swirls' origin.

"Well whatever they are, they came up and made a mess of my shop. Come on, I'll show you." She opened the door, then pushed open a shutter to let in more light.

The shack's floor was an extension of the dock, with a square hole cut in the center, with twisted hinges that had been partially ripped out. Next to the hole lay the cover, with splintering where the hinges had been attached, and a buckled latch hanging off the edge. Water stained the floor and much of the walls, and various pots and kettles were scattered around an overturned table. Near the hole in the floor was a curious cylindrical furnace or kiln with several small metal doors at different heights, and a lid with a looped steel handle. Sylvan had seen pictures of such devices in textbooks, but this was the first time he'd seen one in real life. A sturdy shelf high on the rear wall held the alembic and other glassware, the only things in the hut that did not appear to have been disturbed. A cot with a filthy blanket sat in the corner near the rear entrance.

"See! They cleaned me out entirely." Patia squatted

next to a copper pot with a latched lid, which lay open. "There's not a drop left, and they somehow managed to undo the latch without breaking it, gods know how." She held the pot, staring into it for a while, then closed the lid, latched it, popped the latch, and repeated the procedure. "You ever see water with fingers before?" Her bloodshot eyes stared up into Sylvan's.

He shook his head as he squatted next to her, holding his hand out for the pot, which she passed to him. He unlatched it, which required a hard push of his thumb, and looked inside. It was completely empty, with nothing but a tiny bit of water in the bottom, and there was no way the lid could have come open on its own. "I wonder what they want with quicksilver," he murmured.

"It's the cosmic womb, the gateway between this world and the next." Patia paused, staring out the window in the direction the swirls had gone. "Neither solid nor liquid, it exists in flux, and as such it is an agent of change."

"And without quicksilver—"

"I am ruined," she said, taking the pot back and hugging it to her chest.

Chapter Fourteen

Temi sat on her bunk sketching the hut and the water around it roiling with swirls. She'd only caught a glimpse of the scene while leaning into the sweep, but her fingers moved of their own accord, and her mind followed. Below the hut, which had a pleasing asymmetry to it, she'd drawn a huge swirl, with scores of smaller swirls flowing out of it toward the dock, filling the water and overflowing like milk left on the stove two seconds too long. *Below Guluch,* she wrote in practiced flowing letters beneath the drawing. She coughed, raising her handkerchief to cover her mouth. Ever since the smoke from Guluch, her throat had been raw and her chest congested.

The curtain parted a tiny bit, and Gilea's hand poked through.

"Safe to enter?"

Temi slapped the sketchbook shut and crossed her legs on the bunk. "Sure thing." She wanted to go outside, but she had been trying to limit her exposure. She had been skimping on her paint, which was running out faster than expected; the paint at the bottom had hardened, and she hadn't been able to get it to mix in with the rest. She could probably borrow some from Sylvan, though the color would be all wrong. Not that Gilea or Leo would have cared, or even Sylvan, but she had her pride.

Gilea slid through the curtain without letting in too much light, though the sun was partially obscured by the clouds, so it wasn't too bright out anyway. Temi smiled at the considerate gesture.

"They still up at the dock?" Temi asked.

"I think they went inside the hut. Maybe Leo'll get some answers." Gilea eyed the sketchbook. "What've you been up to?"

"Just a little sketching. Nothing serious." She noticed Gilea's eyes fall to her hands, and she buried them instinctively in her lap, then brought them back out. It was infuriating how hard it was to break the habit of hiding her skin. "You've been meditating?"

"Sort of." Gilea sat down on the supply crate, leaning her elbows on her knees. "Trying to keep an eye on the boys too."

"How can you do both at the same time?"

Gilea looked down, smiling, then back up. "Have you ever looked at something and sketched it at the same time?"

"I have to keep looking back and forth, but yeah."

"You ever seen someone who can do it without looking down?" Temi nodded. "Well, it's a bit like that. I've been practicing for a long time."

"And you learned that in Rontaia, right?"

"At first, yes. And other places. But mostly on my own now."

"Is that why you want to go to Endulai?"

Gilea leaned back and closed her eyes. "It's always been a dream of mine." She paused, and Temi wanted to ask, but Gilea's distant look kept her mouth shut. "Also I know someone who I think is there. An old friend." She sat forward after a moment, looking at Temi's feet, at her hands, then at her face, and Temi had a sudden urge to check her paint.

"I've heard it's beautiful," Temi said. "I met a woman once who studied there—I'm not sure if study is the right word, but anyway she was there for a whole year. She didn't talk very much about what she did there, but she described the buildings, and the stone gardens, and the flowers. She said she'd never seen so many flowers in one place, not even in the Royal Gardens in Anari."

"I've been told it's the most beautiful place in the world."

"Then why haven't you gone before?"

Gilea shook her head. "It's not that simple. Not just anyone can enter the holy city. The outer city is open to anyone, but to get inside the walls? You have to..." She stared down at her fingers, which were curled up like a flower. "I hope I'm ready."

"With all that meditation you do? I bet they'll be glad to have you."

Gilea smiled and shook her head as if to clear it. "I wish it were that simple. They have...protocols."

"Gods, that sounds worse than Anari."

Gilea laughed. "Anari is locked down pretty tight. One time a family asked me to come meet them in their home before taking me on as a minder, and they had to pull all kinds of strings just to get me past the third ring. And even then, the paperwork took almost an hour."

Temi let out a giggle that turned into a small cough. Paperwork was considered an art form in Anari, and half of her artistic training had involved different registers of calligraphy.

"How are your feet?" Gilea glanced down for a moment, then quickly back up. Temi stuck her legs straight off the bunk toward her, and Gilea pushed open the shutter to let in a bit more light. She leaned forward and studied the tops of Temi's feet for a long time.

"You mind...?" She gestured with her hands.

"Of course!" Temi said, unsure if she should be offended that Gilea was so hesitant, or if it was something else.

Gilea pulled Temi's toes up with gentle fingers, leaning forward to study her soles, then slowly released her toes and repeated the process on the other foot. She then held Temi's heels in her palms and studied the tops of her feet, her brow furrowed. She sat back, and when she looked into Temi's eyes, there was a cool intensity in her gaze that made Temi want to look away.

"You've healed up nicely from the mudworms, but I'm worried about your sun exposure. That's a pretty thin coat of paint you've got on there, and it looks like you might have some burning around your sandal straps."

Temi felt her face flush beneath her paint, imagining what her mother would say if she heard this conversation. "I've only worn them for two days, so hopefully it will fade."

Gilea nodded, turning her eyes to Temi's hands. Temi held them out, and her breath caught as she saw the tiny faint freckles that had started to form where her gloves had worn thin. Gilea leaned forward and put her hands under Temi's, lifting them up with the slightest touch of her fingertips. Temi's heart tingled at the delicacy of Gilea's gesture, so unlike the frank touch of most doctors or healers.

"You don't have a spare pair of gloves?" Temi shook her head, looking down for a moment, then back up into Gilea's eyes. "Look, I'm not your mother, but I do work for her, and for you. I have some cream I can give you, if you want, that will help those fade, and you can use it on your feet as well. And I can send Leo to Guluch to get you some gloves." She lowered her hands and leaned back, her face unusually tense. "If that's what you want."

"I don't want to be any trouble." Temi mostly didn't want to admit she didn't have any money. Or rather, she had just enough to get to Rontaia, with any luck, so she couldn't afford to spend any on gloves or paint or anything else.

"Well if you don't want to be any trouble, you might try not coming back covered in freckles." Gilea gestured at Temi's hands. "Nothing wrong with freckles, they can be kind of cute, but..."

"Yeah." Temi stared at her hands, wondering what they would look like if she spent more time out of doors. How many freckles would she have? Would her hands be covered in tiny dots like specklefish? She pictured her mother's face, the expression of disappointment mixing with her disdain for those who didn't take precautions. She half wanted to see that face, to stare into her mother's eyes and dare her to say anything.

"I guess I should get some gloves." She rummaged through her bag and fished out her purse, but Gilea put out a hand to stop her.

"No need. Leo will pay for it. We build in a little slush fund for things like this. Though he's a cheap enough bastard he'd probably take your money if he were here." Gilea must have sensed Temi was low on funds. Endulian practitioners were said to have uncanny powers of perception, but it felt like she was reading Temi's mind.

"If you're sure..." Gilea nodded, and Temi put her purse back in her bag.

Gilea stood up, opened the supply crate, and retrieved a box made of lacquered dark wood, worn with age but well maintained. She pulled out a small jar, unscrewed the lid, and handed it to Temi.

"Put this on your hands and feet, anywhere that's been exposed, first thing in the morning before you apply your paint and last thing before bed. Leo will get you some gloves, and you might want to start wearing your shoes again if they'll fit." She glanced down at Temi's feet, which were no longer swollen.

"Thanks," Temi said, sniffing the cream, which smelled of yeast and lavender, and coughing a bit as the scent flooded her nose and throat. She put a dab on the back of her hand and started rubbing it in.

"About double that amount." Gilea was watching Temi's hands intently. "Don't worry, I brought more."

When Temi started putting it on her feet, Gilea looked away and stood up.

"I'd better go check on Leo and Sylvan, see they don't get too comfortable. I'll send Leo back straightaway." Gilea stepped toward the curtain, stopping when Temi spoke.

"Gilea, if you don't mind, don't mention this to Sylvan." She gestured at her hands and feet. "I'm sure he wouldn't care, it's just..."

Gilea blinked her assent. "I get it," she said, then slipped back through the curtains.

Temi heard the splash of the paddles as she finished applying the cream to her hands and feet. She waited until she heard Gilea ask Leo to go get the gloves. There was some discussion; Leo tried to convince her to let Sylvan come with him, but Gilea shut it down, and she heard Leo paddle off just as Sylvan came bursting through the curtain.

"Tem! You'll never believe what we saw!"

The gloves Leo had gotten her were a little too big, but they were made of supple leather, and her hands hurt quite a bit less after a day of pushing the sweeps. They ate grilled eel and some kind of chewy, nutty greens for dinner, and Temi almost didn't notice the eel's muddy flavor. Sylvan choked his down with obvious distaste, but he ate every bite. After dinner, they sat on a sandy bank on logs Leo had dragged from the woods and enjoyed a soft breeze that kept the suckflies somewhat at bay. Temi had learned to keep her dress tucked around her ankles to reduce exposure, and her veil kept them off her face.

Leo joined Gilea in her meditation, sitting cross-legged on the sand, facing the water. Their arms moved in slow, fluid motions, their hands coming to center in a variety of shapes at the end of each cycle. Sylvan pored over his book, leaning in close as the last of the sun dipped below the horizon. Temi stepped into the cabin, removed her gloves and shoes, and re-applied Gilea's cream, soothing the dry places on her hands and feet where the sun and weather had taken their toll. The cream had a very oily consistency, and she opened her tin of paint, scraped off a bit of the crusty bottom, and rubbed it around in her palm with a bit of the cream. The paint softened to a smooth consistency, perfect for spreading. She scooped out a fingerful of the cream into the tin and used the little spoon to scrape more off the bottom, mixing it with the cream. If she did this a little each day, she might be able to make the tin of paint last. She sighed, and a cough rumbled up from deep in her chest. She had been coughing more than usual, and she had been eager to write it off as nothing more than the aftereffects of the smog around Guluch, but this time felt different, more like the long illnesses she'd had as a child. Her heart wrenched with the thought of what might be wrong with her.

A soft, tender note echoed in through the window, followed by more, a slow, haunting melody on what sounded like a flute. She peeked out the curtain and saw Leo sitting on a log, flute pressed to his mouth, sending beautiful strings of notes into the dusk. Gilea stood facing the river with her palms together in front of her chest, and Sylvan held his book closed, watching. Temi went and lowered herself onto the log next to Sylvan, who gave her a gentle bump with his shoulder. Leo's melody rose and fell in an oddly circular pattern, spiraling up a few notes, then down partway, then up a bit higher. Temi half-closed her eyes and imagined swirls rising like smoke rings into the purple sky until at last Leo hit a high note and held it for a long time, and the vision dissipated. When the last of the sound had been subsumed by the night insects, he laid the flute on his lap and leaned forward, taking his face in his hands.

Chapter Fifteen

Gilea lay awake in her bunk, listening to Temi coughing in her sleep. She struggled to shut down her mind's swirling chatter, her worries for Temi, her fear of rejection at Endulai, her doubts about where they were headed, and random thoughts that flitted by before she could even see what they were. She slowed her breath, curving her mind to funnel her thoughts so they slid down into a ball like dew on a lotus leaf. But try as she might, she could not make that ball roll off into the water. It shone with a crystalline intensity, and she had no choice but to sink into it, to see what was at the core of her mind's disturbance.

As she flowed through the smooth surface of her mind, she saw Temi's hands, her fingers curling up toward each other, pale and delicate as water lilies. Her slender feet, glowing in the moonlight. Her quiet smile when she caught a joke the others had missed. Gilea's heart lurched as it dawned on her that the curiosity and warmth she felt for Temi had morphed into something more, something with the power to undermine the basic foundations of her mental discipline. Her blood surged through her veins, hammering in her ears, warming her face, her neck, spreading down through her body in a flood of desire. Her breath grew shallow and fast, and she wrapped her arms tightly around her chest as she jammed her eyelids shut, but she could not make it stop. She slipped out from under her sheet, climbed down with shaking limbs, and tiptoed through the curtain out into the night.

She climbed up to the roof of the raft and stood with arms stretched wide, tilting her head back to stare up into the sky, thick with gauzy stars behind a veil of haze. Her chest opened to the river, and with time, the stars and the air and the stretch helped her bring her breath under control, and her pulse slowed. She lowered to a cross-legged seat, curving her fingers to touch at the tips like a ball, pressing together with the muscles in her arms and back, which helped release the tension in her chest. She let her hands fall to her knees and allowed her thoughts to bloom again, but with a cultivated dispassion. She could not deny her attraction to Temi, nor could she allow it to control her. Gilea was Temi's minder, and there was no question of her acting on her feelings, even if the social and other barriers between them did not make the notion preposterous.

Gilea had never fallen for one of her charges before, and it was more than a little disconcerting. It wasn't her age; Temi was young, but they were only ten years apart, and Gilea had slept with women a decade older or younger more than once. It was her role as minder that made any such thoughts inconceivable. Protecting her charges, protecting Temi, was her sworn duty, and she couldn't do that if she let her emotions get the best of her. Her objectivity and control were a point of pride, one she had made her reputation on, and she was not about to let that change.

In truth, the painted faces tended to be so inured to their own privilege they had little empathy for others, so she rarely found them attractive. And though she had been with fair-skinned women before, she liked her women strong, and she usually found the fragility of the painted faces unappealing. But Temi's fragility was only skin deep; the strength beneath it, her resolve, drew Gilea to her. As her body sank deeper into the seated position, her hips lowering and her legs pressing down on the roof of the raft, Gilea's mind opened to the sky. Temi's resolve floated in her mind like a cloud, and as she studied the shape and hue of it, Gilea could see clearly what should have been obvious all along. Temi's questions, her attitude toward Anari, her fierce silence, all came into focus. Temi was planning to flee the raft and make her way to Rontaia.

As outlandish as the plan was, given the distance, her frailty, and her inexperience, it made perfect sense. Temi was a rare shade seven, but her relative poverty was obvious, despite her status. Gilea did not understand all the complexities of the painted faces' social hierarchy, but she knew skin tone alone did not determine their position. Sylvan was a shade six, but his wealth and privilege were undeniably higher than Temi's. Gilea had met Temi's mother, who carried herself with the wounded pride of those who felt they deserved much better than their station. Perhaps their family had fallen on hard times and were struggling to maintain their lifestyle. The roughabout would have been a financial strain, costing more than what most regular people could expect to make in several years of hard work. Temi would no doubt be expected to marry someone wealthier than herself, using her skin tone as currency. Gilea couldn't imagine Temi wanting to marry the kind of man who sought a bride for her physical attributes, and the very thought twisted Gilea's insides into a knot.

Gilea had always been puzzled by the outdated social norms of the nobility. Regular people had the freedom to love and marry whomever they wanted, but the wealthier one became, the more restricted their lives. And while pale skin tones were considered a liability in most of the world, in the inner rings of Anari and the other major cities it was the opposite. Rontaia was the one outlier; while there were painted faces in Rontaia, they tended to live on the outskirts of the city, and they were seldom seen in the city proper, except in transit to their enclaves. They were viewed with a kind of patronizing disdain, relics of a corrupt system that had evolved beyond reason.

Temi could not have known any of this, of course, and she had shown great interest when Gilea had told her the city had no rings. She probably saw it as a sign that she would be free there. And perhaps there was some truth in that. Given Rontaia's robust arts industry, Temi would surely be able to find work, if she could get there in one piece, though whether she was ready for the rigors of Rontaian poverty was another question.

Gilea stayed on the roof meditating until she could conjure the image of Temi's hands and feet without losing her center. She herded her desire into the space she kept for hunger, thirst, and fatigue, hoping to use the same techniques to keep it at bay until she could find a way to assuage it. With any luck, when the roughabout was over she would be able to find Captain Olin again and take her up on the offer of a free ride. She put Olin's sharp eyes and strong hands in the center of her mind and let herself be carried away with thoughts of stretching against Olin's taut body to the rhythm of waves slapping against the boat.

The next few days brought calm weather and only a light breeze, which meant they did more floating than sweeping, and everyone seemed to settle into a quiet routine. Sylvan and Temi spent most of the daylight hours in the cabin, Sylvan poring over his book and Temi filling pages in her sketchbook with drawings of swirls and fish. Leo would stand on the roof, scanning the horizon for swirls, occasionally diving into the water when he thought he had seen them. He would swim off furiously, then return a few minutes later at a slow crawl, his ever-present smile dimming slightly as he shook his head at Gilea's questioning look. Gilea spent much of her time on the roof, doing poses to keep her muscles active and to distract her from thoughts of Temi, and of Endulai, which they would be passing before long.

As a child, she had spent hours studying a painting of Endulai that hung on the wall of Wulif's library. The painting showed a harmonious assemblage of white stone buildings in flowing, organic shapes, highlighted against a backdrop of tumultuous black clouds. At the center was a dome, its center open to the sky, and light seemed to pour out from the opening, illuminating the bottoms of the clouds. When she closed her eyes, Gilea could see the painting in perfect detail, and even when her eyes were open, the image lay over her consciousness like a veil. Endulai, or the idea of Endulai, tugged at her mind.

Most Endulian practitioners followed the Temple Way, honing their awareness within the confines of one of the temples, under the direction of the masters. Only a very few ascended to a high enough level of practice to make it to Endulai. Gilea had chosen the Lonely Way, or perhaps it had chosen her, and it was even rarer to reach Endulai following this path, but it was not impossible. She worked every day to maintain and expand her practice on her own, with hopes of one day visiting the holy city, and perhaps even joining the Caravan. It was said that Endulian masters could use it to travel with their minds to the far corners of the continent, and communicate with whoever was at another one of the crossroads. The cradle in Rontaia, which was on display one day a year, was an elaborate wooden structure with a shining copper ring for the traveler's head, but she had heard the cradles in most cities were made of gold or other precious metals. It was those cradles she imagined as a child in Wulif's library, losing herself in the painting of Endulai and flying across rainbow bridges to places of breathtaking beauty and peace. Even now, those childhood visions were part of what had helped her maintain her practice.

She worked hard to keep these thoughts at bay. Perhaps after the roughabout was over, she would set her mind right and pay a visit to the holy city, but not now. She knew even if she could reach Endulai, her mind was in no shape to accept what it had to offer. The distractions of a roughabout were already taxing, and her struggle to keep thoughts of Temi out of her mind fragmented her consciousness further. In her current state, there was no way they would let her in.

Toward evening of the second day, Leo steered the raft toward a pebbled bank just downstream from where a clear-running stream ran through a field of cattails into the muddy river. Once they had tied down the raft, Leo took the canoe off to explore the stream, and came back wet and smiling.

"Anyone fancy a clearwater bath?"

Sylvan nearly leaped into the canoe, and Temi followed, an amused smile on her lips.

"You might want to grab a change of clothes and a towel," Gilea reminded them, and they returned to the cabin and retrieved their things.

Leo steered the canoe along the pebbled bank for ten minutes, then made a wide turn as they approached the stream. A circle of clear water marked the place where the stream poured in, and they could see fish darting and shimmying around the edges of the current.

"Look! Speckles!" Sylvan called, standing halfway

up and pointing, then sitting down hard as he lost his balance.

"I know," Leo said. "We're going to eat well tonight." He steered them to an eddy, hopped out, and tied the canoe to an overhanging branch. A pair of five-foot-tall white marble pillars bracketed the spot where the stream entered the river, property signs for whoever owned the stream.

"Technically, we're not supposed to go past the pillars," Leo said, "but I paddled a little ways up and didn't see any sign of a house or anything. There's a little pool fifty yards in, and it's shallow and sandy along the banks, so no mudworms to worry about. Gilea, you take Temi up to that pool, and I'll keep watch while Sylvan bathes here."

Sylvan shot Temi a curious glance, and she blinked back at him. Gilea had noticed Sylvan's modesty around Leo, which was funny because Leo took no more notice of nakedness than an animal would. Gilea stepped out of the canoe into the soft sand of the stream, gesturing to Temi to follow her up past the pillars. She was a little uncomfortable trespassing, but she figured if the owners found them, she could persuade them to let it go. And besides, she really needed a bath herself.

They waded in the shallow edge of the stream, which ran through a stand of tall, thin featherpines. The forest floor was all pine needles and ferns, a contrast to the lush vegetation along most of the river. Temi walked close behind her and grabbed Gilea's arm when a long green snake unfurled itself and slid into the water just in front of them.

"It's just an emerald worm," Gilea reassured her. "Completely harmless."

Temi let go of her arm but stayed close enough Gilea could feel her breath on the back of her neck. They arrived at the pool, which was no more than five feet deep in the center, with a large flat rock on the deep side of the pool. Minnows darted around the edges, while small specklefish patrolled the little dropoff. Gilea turned to Temi, who eyed the pool nervously.

"Give me your bag. I'll sit on that rock and watch the forest, so you won't have to worry about your privacy." She took Temi's bag and handed her an oval of lavender-scented soap she'd bought in the market in Guluch. Temi flashed a timid smile, and Gilea waded to the rock, scanning the forest in all directions. There was no movement, no sound except for the burbling water, and she sensed no human presence anywhere nearby.

"It's safe," she said, laying Temi's bag on the edge of the rock. "I'll keep watch, but everything looks good. Take your time." She turned to face away from the pool, breathing in the pine-scented air as she steadied her nerves and struggled to sink into a watchful meditation. The sounds of Temi slipping out of her clothes and wading into the water pulled her thoughts away from her task, but she steeled her mind and settled her vision so she could see the forest in three directions. She pressed her hands together in front of her heart, concentrating all her muscles to focus on her posture, which helped anchor her mind against the images of Temi's pale body floating in the clear water of the stream.

Chapter Sixteen

Leo cooked the speckles over the fire, stuffed with herbs he had gathered near the clearwater stream. Sylvan's eyes rolled back and he let out a soft moan as he pushed the first bite into his mouth.

"Finally, something that doesn't taste like river mud."

Temi's laugh turned into a barking cough, and she wheezed a bit before flashing a weak smile and sliding a small piece of the fish into her mouth. Leo frowned as he watched Temi, and Gilea shot him a knowing look. It sounded a lot like Ulver's cough. It was rare for someone in good physical condition to contract it, and Temi seemed generally healthy, but the painted faces tended to be more susceptible to disease and infection than most people. Through the years, Leo had seen Gilea treat their charges for a number of minor infections and diseases, but Ulver's cough was notoriously difficult to control. The reports from the Great Library said the disease had gone dormant along the Agra, and the roughabout had been approved, but if Gilea was worried, Leo knew he should be too.

Early the next day, the white dome and flowing architecture of Endulai came into view in the distance, glowing in the bright sun. Gilea untied the canoe, knelt down, and paddled off, her face troubled beneath a mask of serenity. Leo watched her go with a heavy heart. He knew what the place meant to her, and how difficult it would be for her to get so close but be unable to enter. She had asked his leave to try to get some herbs for Temi, and though there seemed to be little danger, he felt exposed without her. He stayed closer than usual to Sylvan and Temi, and his stomach churned when he saw Temi wracked with coughing and wheezing while he and Sylvan pushed the sweeps.

"You need to keep at least arm's distance from her for a while," Leo said to Sylvan once Temi had returned to the cabin. "Just in case." Sylvan nodded, his serious face showing he had heard the subtext. There was no doubt about it. Temi had Ulver's cough, and while Leo and Gilea had had it as children, Sylvan would be vulnerable, though the fact that he hadn't started coughing yet might be a good sign.

Leo stood with Sylvan staring at the holy city as they floated past. The tall outer walls were white stone, and beyond them stood buildings with curvy, organic shapes and a large dome whose top was open to the sky. The city was surrounded by gardens so lush and colorful they were impressive even at this distance. The two long piers were decorated with flowerpots, and trellises covered in vines shaded the piers from the sun. A number of smaller craft were docked there, and people lined the piers, throwing something reddish into the water, which appeared disturbed somehow, though it was hard to see. Leo hauled himself up to the top of the raft and looked through his field scope. He saw the people on the piers pouring bottles and jars of red liquids and powders into the water, which roiled with scores of swirls. Leo turned his scope downstream and saw a line of swirls, reddish in color, streaming across the river and down along the right bank, in the direction of the wetlands he was convinced held The Living Waters, which he figured would be no more than two or three days downstream from Endulai. He scanned the pier for Gilea, but could not pick her out from the throngs. His eyes were drawn back to the swirls, which filled his troubled mind with a fleeting sensation approaching joy, though the mystery of their reddish tint nagged at him. First the inkworks, then the quicksilver, and now this. What were the red liquids and powder the Endulians were throwing into the water? Why were the swirls drawn to the color red? And where did the quicksilver fit in? His mind burned with urgency to get to the Living Waters in search of answers, but he worried Temi's illness would sidetrack them, and he might never find out.

Near dusk, they pulled the raft to an overgrown, muddy bank downriver from Endulai, on the opposite side, to wait for Gilea as arranged. The last of the red swirls were making their way along the slow current near the shore, moving in twos and threes, as he had seen them for the past several hours when the raft had crossed the line and pulled to shore, following the direction of the swirls. Leo's mind grew numb with the sheer numbers of swirls they had seen, hundreds or more likely thousands of them, slowly petering out until the last one, the largest of them all, pulled alongside the raft and paused, pulling bits of debris into its orbit. It was almost as wide as the raft itself, and several feet deep in the center, and it was river-brown, not red like the others. The large one they had seen near the alchemist's hut had been empty of the silvery flash of quicksilver. Leo wondered if it was the same one. He leaned over the edge of the raft so his head was over the swirling rim, and stared into the empty vortex, until at last, it spun off downstream, joining the others in their procession.

"Gilea!" Temi called out joyfully, followed by a barking cough and a long wheezing spell, during which she slumped against the cabin wall. Sylvan hovered nearby, his face pained, keeping his distance. Leo stooped by her, and she smiled through labored breathing. He put his hand on her sleeve, flashing her his best smile before turning his eyes up to meet Sylvan's, which were wide with pity and fear. Leo blinked at him, then turned to help Gilea tie the canoe to the back of the raft.

"How is she?" Gilea's face was drawn, the muscles along her strong cheekbones swollen with tension.

"Not great," Leo admitted. "She was glad to see you, though."

Gilea dropped her eyes, took Leo's hand, and hopped aboard the raft.

"Did you get what you need?" he asked in a low voice.

Gilea's eyes stayed down. "I got a few things, but..." When she raised her eyes to meet his, they were wet. "If it is Ulver's cough, there's only so much we can do out here. They won't take her at Endulai, and I can't say I blame them. Our only hope would be to somehow get back to Anari before..."

Temi pushed along the cabin wall as she made her way toward them, unsteady on her feet. She covered her mouth with her hands as she gave a silent cough, then stood wheezing, leaning against the cabin again. Her eyes were sunken into her face, and her lips were mottled, almost dirty looking, even through her paint. She smiled at Gilea and gave a faint wave, her hand glowing white against the growing dusk, except for the wet splotch of dark brown in her palm.

"You're back," Temi whispered, sounding feverish

and loopy. “It’s so beautiful, isn’t it?”

Leo stretched the tarp tight against the rear of the cabin, tying it off to the canoe cleat. Gilea had moved Temi’s mattress to the back of the raft, and Leo made it as weatherproof as he could. Temi did not protest, and Gilea held her hand as she made her way along the slippery side of the raft back to the little lean-to as Sylvan watched from the front deck.

As Leo tucked and tied the last corner of the tarp, Gilea knelt by the lean-to with a small steaming cup, which smelled like mint, honey, and alcohol. Temi took a sip, made a wretched face, then smiled and took a longer drink.

“Thank you. I feel better already.” Her gaunt face told Leo a different story.

“It will help you sleep,” Gilea said, sitting down on a stool, which she had brought to the small rear deck. “Don’t worry, I’ll be right here if you need anything. If the coughing starts up again, I have something to help with that.”

“So you’re just going to sit there and watch me sleep?”

Gilea looked out over the water, then along the bank, before turning back to Temi. “I’ll just be here, that’s all.”

Leo gave Gilea and Temi a nod and a curt smile and slipped away. He couldn’t stand to watch someone suffer when there was nothing he could do. He wished Gilea would send him off to find some rare herb or root to make a tea, or a poultice, anything to feel useful. He gazed out at the water, wishing he could leap out of his pants and swim out hard into the river, feel the current carry him, swim with it, then against it. But with Gilea occupied, he had to stay on the boat, with nothing to do. He pulled the throw net off its hook and started casting for minnows. Maybe with any luck, he could catch a decent whisker using them for bait. He pulled up a half-dozen small fish and dumped them into a bucket of water, then cast out several more times until he had close to twenty. He uncoiled the trotline and started baiting the hooks.

"Wait, is that a baby thinkfin?" Sylvan knelt next to him as he was about to thread one of the fish onto the hook.

"You might be right. It's so small I almost didn't notice." Leo dropped it in Sylvan's hand, where it flipped about, and he had to cup both hands to catch it.

"But look, it...it has eyes." Sylvan pointed with his pinky finger, and sure enough, the fish had wide yellow eyes, set in thick ridges of flesh along the side of its head, which would be replaced by hard protective scales when it grew to adult size.

"I guess they need them when they're small, but after that, they don't?"

"It's interesting," Sylvan said, dropping the fish back into the bucket and watching it swim around with the others. "They're said to be much more sensitive to vibration than other fish, and the plates on their head are thought to be some kind of sensory organ. I wonder if the optic nerve somehow connects to those plates as they grow over the eyes, so it can feed by feel alone."

Leo flashed a big smile and clapped Sylvan on the shoulder, almost knocking him down.

"It's not everyone who can show me something new in the water. I guess you really did learn something in all those books."

"I've learned twice as much just on the first part of our roughabout. I can only imagine what we'd learn if we..." He trailed off, his eyes darting toward the back of the raft. "I mean, we are going to get Temi back, aren't we? Surely she can't go much farther in her condition."

Leo shook his head, visions of the swirls dancing before his eyes.

"It's up to Gilea to make that call."

Gilea's face was sunken with fatigue when Sylvan spelled her and she joined Leo at the front end of the raft.

"She slept okay, but she's pretty weak," she said in a hoarse whisper. "I had to help her up so she could go to the bathroom."

"We could paddle her back up to Endulai and try to hire a boat to row her up to Guluch, or maybe Tralum. They should have doctors who'd know what to do."

Gilea shook her head. "They would, but she doesn't want to go. She keeps saying she'll be fine after a bit of rest."

Leo looked down at Gilea's hands, which were clenched tightly together. They both knew Temi was unlikely to recover on her own since the brown cough had started so fast.

"You think maybe she'd listen to Sylvan? They seem pretty close."

Gilea huffed out a little snort. "I told him to try. But he's half the reason she doesn't want to go back. She knows how excited he is about..." Leo swallowed, trying to hide his own desire to find the Living Waters, but there was no hiding anything from Gilea. She had always been able to read him like a book.

"What about the other half?" Leo squinted against the morning sun, and Gilea held his eyes for a long moment.

"I don't think she likes it much in Anari."

Leo picked up a leaf from the deck, spinning the stem in his fingers so the leaf whirled around and around. "So she'd rather die than go back?"

Gilea exhaled, long and slow. "Maybe. I don't know. But we can't take her back against her will, not if she's conscious. She did hire us, you know."

“Her mother hired us. If she...If something happens out here, something we could have prevented...” Leo spun the leaf into the water. He would probably still be able to work roughabouts if Temi died, though he might not get the highest paying jobs. But a minder who lost one of their charges would be put on permanent ban. It was a hard and fast rule, and Gilea knew that all too well.

“Well we’ll just have to make sure nothing happens, won’t we? I’ve got a few things I can try, and I got some medic’s balm at the market outside Endulai. I’m not sure if it will help, but it’s worth a shot.”

“Gil, how did you...” Even a small jar of medic’s balm would cost twice what she made on the roughabout. It was mostly used to heal cuts and infected wounds, but he’d never heard of it being used for anything internal. Then again, Gilea was a certified herbalist, so maybe she knew something he didn’t.

“Don’t you worry about me. Just make sure you get us down to whatever there is to see in one piece. Maybe a day trip in the canoe will be enough, then we can see about getting her back upstream.”

Chapter Seventeen

Temi lay in her lean-to, listening to the rain patter on the tarp Leo had stretched over the back of the raft, forming a little tent. It was pretty watertight, only leaking in one spot, in the corner of the mattress near her feet. Gilea had put a bowl there to catch the water, which she emptied more often than was necessary, her eyes clouded with worry. Temi always took as deep a breath as she could when Gilea checked in on her, just to show she was alive. She didn't want to feel like a burden to Gilea, or anyone else.

Temi propped herself up on one elbow and watched Gilea through the gauzy curtain they had fashioned out of her and Sylvan's veils to keep the suckflies out. Gilea sat motionless on her stool under the tattered tarp Leo had rigged for her, eyes half-open, and Temi could not tell if she was asleep or awake. More likely in some meditative state in between, since she seldom left her post, and no one could go without sleep for three full days.

Though she wished Gilea would go inside and get some proper sleep, Temi felt safe, secure, knowing Gilea was there.

"Gil, we need you on the sweeps," Leo called out with some urgency. Gilea opened her eyes but remained still for a moment, then turned to Temi, who gave her a little wave.

"Sorry," Temi croaked.

Gilea's smile only deepened the worry lines on her face.

Temi awoke to Sylvan's face hovering outside the veiled window.

"Tem!"

"Is it time for my medicine?"

"No. Can you get up?"

"Sylvan, I told you not to wake her." Gilea appeared next to Sylvan, her eyes hardening as she looked at him, then softening as they fell on Temi.

Temi took a slow breath in and pushed up to sit without coughing, but her head was too light to move any farther for a moment. When the faintness passed, she scooted her feet out of the opening as Sylvan took a step back, his eyes wild with excitement. Gilea knelt, and Temi took her hand and let Gilea pull her up to standing, holding onto her arm for a bit until she felt steady enough to support herself with one hand on the cabin. Sylvan pointed behind her, and she turned around to see a wide expanse of tall grass with wide, sharp-looking leaves. The river smelled different here, less rotten, and the air was thick with the chirping of frogs.

"We made it," Temi said, grabbing Gilea's arm and twisting back to smile at Sylvan.

"The Living Waters," he breathed.

Temi sat in the center of the canoe, leaning against Gilea, who stood and pointed this way and that, while Sylvan and Leo paddled. Leo steered the canoe, following Gilea's directions through a dense field of bladegrass. Temi ducked her face between her legs whenever the sharp leaves poked at her, especially when the canoe got stuck and they had to back up to seek a new path. At one point she looked up at Gilea, who had dozens of scrapes on her arms, bright red against the dark bronze of her skin. Dragonflies and half-moon butterflies danced above the grasses, tracing erratic patterns in the gray sky. Splashes, croaks, and the high-pitched humming of insects filled the air, occasionally pierced by brash calls like a child's shriek, but Temi could never see the source of the unnerving noises. Brown, green, and even blue stickbirds waded silently away as the canoe approached, their heads ducking as they moved on long crooked legs. Temi tried to fix the images of all these creatures in her mind so she could draw them once she got to a stable spot.

After an hour of slow travel, the bladegrass thinned, now growing in irregular clumps between open channels of clear water. A green snake, long and flat like a stalk of bladegrass, swam out from under the canoe and disappeared into the grasses. Schools of silvery minnows moved like flocks of blackbirds, billowing and narrowing in hypnotic patterns. Large specklefish cruised between the vegetation, watching the canoe with big, round eyes before disappearing in a flash of rainbow coloring. Sylvan gave a start, stopped paddling, and pointed far ahead.

"Look! Breathfins!" he whispered. Temi sat up to peer around him and was immediately seized with a cough that wouldn't come out. Her lungs pumped and pulsed, and for several long seconds she could pass no air, until at last her throat opened enough for her to bark out a spatter of brown, which she caught on her hand and quickly wiped on the bottom of her shoe as she wheezed herself slowly back to a slow, shallow breath pattern. Gilea's legs leaned into her, and she smiled up at Gilea, then turned to look ahead. The grass field had opened into a wide area like a lake, and as she watched, several tiny puffs shot out of the water, like steam expelled from a kettle.

"Well, I'll be," Leo murmured. "I've never seen one in freshwater, not this far away from the sea anyway."

"And they're so much smaller, look!" Sylvan pointed, then turned back, his eyes wider than his grin. "Did you see that? I saw one roll, and it was purplish-gray, just like Max said."

"It wasn't much bigger than a *chukin*," Leo said.

Temi raised up, still on her knees, and watched the water until two puffs of spray shot up one after the other, and two purplish-gray fins surfaced at the same time. Her breath caught as she watched the water roll away from where they had surfaced. Something about the way the little waves curled in the breathfins' wake stuck in her mind, and when she closed her eyes she could see the waves, the fins, and the spouts painted in delicate purple lines on a freshly glazed dinner plate. It was the kind of design that might freshen up the Yskan pottery line and maybe make it relevant again. She could just picture the half-smile that was the closest thing to approval her mother ever showed her. She shook off the thought, leaned back on her heels, and wrestled her drawing pad and pencil out of her bag.

She could feel Gilea's eyes staring down as she drew the outline of a plate, filling in the outer rim with little swirls. She made a squiggly line between the rim and the center and drew the rolling waves first, then the fins and rounded backs, adding the spouts after the rest of the scene was in place. It was a little rough, and one of the fins was crooked, but it was a start.

"What in the gods' shit is that?" Gilea's voice was

full of awe and fear. Temi looked up and saw her staring off into the distance. Temi started to rise up, but she was too weak. "Leo," Gilea said in a low voice.

"I see it, Gil."

"Leo, Sylvan, time to back the boat up." Gilea's voice was soft, but her urgency was terrifying. Sylvan sat down and splashed his paddle into the water, and Leo stroked hard from the back of the boat, and they began moving against the faint current.

"Steady, Sylvan," Gilea said in a voice that was anything but. Temi could hear Sylvan's breath coming in short huffs. Her own breath grew shallow, and her throat started sticking together. She tucked her head between her knees and coughed into her lap, wracked with silent wheezes, each of them siphoning a little more of her remaining breath, until her lungs felt flat, sticky, like they were filled with mud. Her body grew heavy, and her mind tried to control her limbs, but she flopped over sideways, and only Gilea's quick foot kept her head from banging into the gunwale. Gilea crouched down over her, making a shushing noise as she put her fingers on Temi's forehead and started massaging outward.

"Be here with me Temi. Be here with me now." Gilea took a slow, deep breath in, and Temi's lungs opened just a crack, and air came flooding in. "That's right, now out with me." Temi held the air for a moment, unsure if she would be able to get more, but Gilea's fingers sank into her hair, her thumbs tight against Temi's temples, and Temi breathed out with her, long and slow, then in again, a little longer than before. "That's my girl." Temi shook her head a little, propping her arm against the bottom of the canoe, with Gilea's strong hands supporting her back. The canoe was now back in the narrow grass channel they had come down, and Leo was holding it tight with a paddle in the grass.

"The tall men," Leo said. "The ones Max talked about."

“No man is that tall,” Gilea said, releasing her hands from Temi and rising to her knees to peer through the grass.

“But look at its face, isn’t it…long like Max described? I wonder…” Sylvan bit his knuckle, looking back at Temi, who gave him a nod, turning toward the grass, but she was still too weak to sit up for a proper look. She felt her breath growing shallow again at the tones of everyone’s voices.

“You think it saw us?” Gilea asked.

“It saw us,” Leo said. “You can bet on that. The real question is why it let us see it.”

“How tall?” Temi rasped, looking up at Gilea, who kept staring through the grass. “What did it look like?”

“I don’t…” Gilea shook her head and turned her eyes to Temi. They were wide with worry, but this time it wasn’t about Temi’s cough.

“Eight, nine feet, easy, if it stood up straight.” Leo sucked his teeth. “I don’t know what that makes it, but it’s not human. Look at the neck on that thing; it must be two feet long.”

Temi turned back to Leo, who wore a faint smile. She started to giggle, then swallowed it before the cough could bloom.

“I wonder…” Sylvan said again. Leo turned to him, and Temi and Gilea followed with their eyes. Sylvan turned halfway around. “I think it might be an *ipsis*.”

Temi gripped the gunwale with both hands and used all of her strength to pull up onto her knees, angling to see through a break in the grass. Across the calm water, past the swirls and spouts of the breathfins, a tall, thin creature stood, humanoid in shape, the upper half of its body rising out of the grass. Its long torso ended in wide shoulders, with a slender neck curving forward from its body. Its head was like a man’s, but narrower, elongated, and its arms held what looked like a spear poised above the water. Temi squeezed in a shallow breath as she watched the creature slowly raise the spear, which she could now see had several prongs at its tip. The spear flashed down into the water and brought out a large speckle, which splashed ferociously for a moment before the creature grabbed it, twisted it on the spear, and it went limp. The creature inserted its long fingers into the fish's gill slits, slid it off the spear, and dropped it into a bag at its side. Temi's cough rose up without warning, and she saw the creature's head swivel toward them as her hands gripped the gunwale, then she fell back into Gilea's legs.

"Shit," Leo whispered.

Gilea sat down in the bottom of the canoe, her legs around Temi, who sank into her as the wheezing started again, and a great silence enveloped her. Her body pulsed with each cough she was unable to expel, and the muscles in her back and abdomen screamed with the effort. Gilea was saying something to her, holding Temi's head in her hands, but her face faded into the gray light of the sky, which slowly faded to black.

Sylvan turned once the creature had vanished into the grass. Leo was hovering over Temi, who was curled up in Gilea's arms.

"She's hardly breathing," Leo murmured.

"She's breathing." Gilea held her hand in front of Temi's mouth. "But maybe not enough."

"Temi—" Gilea's eyes shut Sylvan's mouth, and he sank back in his seat.

"We've got this. You keep an eye out for that...what did you call it?"

"I think it's an *ipsis*. It's written in my book, in the margins, and I think it comes from an ancient Enduli word for thin."

Gilea propped Temi's head back and began unbuttoning Temi's dress. Sylvan reflexively looked away as Gilea peeled the dress apart to reveal her pale breasts.

"Leo, get the jar out of my bag." Leo handed her a

small ceramic jar with a copper lid. Gilea glanced up at Sylvan as she leaned down and put her ear on Temi's chest, squinting into space for a few moments. "So, you say you know ancient Enduli?" Sylvan blinked several times as Gilea's words filtered through his shock. How could she be asking about ancient languages at a time like this?

"A little. It's required study, as some of the scientific terms have their basis in it..." He trailed off as Gilea sat up, put two fingers in the jar, and spread a blue-tinted cream across Temi's lily-white chest, about where her lungs would be. A potent medicinal smell filled the air, and Sylvan shook his head to clear the tingling in his eyes and nose. Gilea held Temi's head on her knee and stared into her face, gripping Temi's hand tightly. After a few moments, Temi drew in a sharp breath, and her eyes opened, wild and erratic. Gilea smiled wide, showing all her teeth for a moment, before putting one hand over her face to hide what looked like the beginnings of a sob. Temi breathed again, and her eyes steadied.

"I'm here," she said in a small voice as she looked down at her bare chest and quickly pulled her dress back together as everyone looked away. "What's that smell?"

"It's medic's balm, isn't it?" Sylvan asked, staring at the jar as Leo screwed the cap on and put it back in Gilea's bag. Medic's balm was expensive even by his family's standards, though they always kept a jar in the kitchen cupboard, in case of emergencies.

"We take care of our charges," Gilea said, squeezing Temi's hand and helping her sit up.

"Will it cure her?" Sylvan asked. He'd never heard of it used for anything other than topical wounds and infections.

Gilea flashed him a quiet, piercing glance. "She's going to be fine. She just needs to get a little rest."

"I've had nothing but rest for the past three days."

Temi sat up, took a shaky breath, then covered her mouth with her hand as her body tensed like she was about to cough. She squinted and swallowed hard, then took in another breath.

"Tem," Sylvan said in a low voice, "we need to get you back, to Guluch at least, or Tralum. The hospital there is first-rate, and my father gave me a tunnel badge, just in case. We could go straight to the second circle, bypass all the—"

"I'm not going anywhere." Temi sat back on her heels, took a slow breath, then fixed Sylvan with a pleading look. "Not until I get another look at that thing we saw."

"We need to leave before it comes back with its friends," Gilea said. "Leo, turn this canoe around and let's make our way back out the way we came."

"I don't think they pose any threat." Leo avoided Gilea's eyes, looking up at Sylvan as he spoke. "Remember Max's story? How they took him in, helped him get back upriver?"

"Leo, don't be an idiot." Gilea's voice was harder than Sylvan had heard it before. "I'm ordering you to turn this boat around and get us out of here."

Leo winced, still avoiding Gilea's gaze. His eyes were bright with the same desire Sylvan felt: to explore the Living Waters, for there could be no doubt now as to where they were. But the fear that had seized Sylvan's heart at the sight of the *ipsis* was absent in Leo's expression.

"Gilea's right," Sylvan managed. "As much as I want to learn more, we don't know anything about them, and we're kind of sitting ducks in this grass." He turned to Temi, who shook her head at him.

"I thought you wanted this," she said. "Aren't you a scientist? What about those notes in your book? If we turn around now, do you think you'll ever—" She stopped for a second, her hand frozen in mid-air, then let out a hoarse cough, but she did not wheeze afterward.

Her words wrenched Sylvan's heart; he knew it was true. But she had almost died a few minutes before, and there was no question what the right thing to do was.

"Temi, the medic's balm won't cure you." Gilea looked Temi in the eyes. "It'll just keep the symptoms from getting worse for a little while until we run out." She hefted the jar in her hand. "If we don't get you out of here, and into a proper hospital, you might die."

"I'm...not...going...back," Temi growled through clenched teeth. She closed her eyes and breathed out unsteadily through her nose. "Not until we see it again."

Gilea put her hand over her face, nodding. "Okay," she said, moving her hand down to touch Temi's shoulder. "Okay."

"Uh, guys?" Sylvan said, pointing behind them, where three of the creatures had materialized and stood towering over the bladegrass, carrying stout spears with thick, wide blades almost like spades. Gilea eased away from the back of the boat, holding her arms around Temi protectively. Leo craned his neck around to look, gave a start, and tumbled back onto the bottom of the boat next to Temi. Sylvan's fingers gripped the paddle so hard it hurt, but he couldn't release his grip. Gilea pushed Temi gently toward Leo, then slowly stood up, her palms facing the creatures. She stood staring at them for a moment, then crossed her hands over her chest and bowed her head, and the *ipsis* lowered their long necks and clasped their spears to their chests with both hands. One of them raised its head, staring at Gilea with gentle brown eyes, then held out an impossibly long arm, with its index finger extended toward the right bank of the lake, where Sylvan could see an inlet or creek running off it.

The four of them sat silently in the canoe, hardly breathing, as the *ipsis* pulled them along the edge of the lake, one on the front end, one behind, and one wading ahead. Several swirls floated alongside them as they went, and as Sylvan stared into their empty centers, he noticed a strange shimmering underwater out of the corner of his eye, approaching from the center of the lake. It was hard to see because of the reflections on the water's surface, but it looked like a swarm of transparent snakes, or tentacles, pulsing in rhythm, moving toward the canoe. The swirls moved aside as the shimmering approached, hovering next to the boat, and the *ipsis* stopped pulling and turned to face it. The shimmering water formed into a kind of hump, which rose above the surface, thinning into a shape like a staff made entirely of water. Its top expanded into a wavy globe, which tightened until its edges were perfectly smooth, and the water within it stopped moving. Sylvan felt a strange warmth spreading down his legs, and it dawned on him that he'd wet himself, but he could not take his fingers from the paddle, or his eyes from the globe.

Leo stood up slowly, balancing on the gunwale, staring at the globe. Gilea whispered, "Leo," but his eyes were full of wonder as he leaned his face over the edge of the canoe until it was inches from the ball of water. A ripple flowed over the globe, and it hovered for a moment next to Leo's face before sinking back down and flowing along the water's surface like a fat snake toward the *ipsis* holding onto the front of the canoe. When it reached the creature's leg, it enveloped it, moving up like a watery sheath, then climbing its long torso, which glistened with the thin layer of water. The *ipsis* looked down with untroubled eyes as the wetness spread up its neck, covering its entire face and head, and it closed its eyes, its face tensing, as with concentration.

Sylvan's blood drummed in his ears as the moment stretched on for what seemed like an hour, though it couldn't have been more than a few seconds. When the *ipsis* opened its eyes, the water poured down from its body, collapsing into the snake-like shape once again, which Sylvan could see flashing as it sliced through the water to rejoin the shimmering mass next to the canoe. He watched as it sank and pulled away, trailing watery tentacles behind it like a squid from one of his books. Two dark shapes moved in and swam alongside it, then surfaced, blowing puffs of mist into the air. Sylvan followed the breathfins with his eyes as the shimmering mass was obscured by the water's reflection. The two swirls returned to the side of the boat, and the *ipsis* in front spoke to its companions in a language that sounded almost human, though it was unlike any language he'd ever heard. Its voice was two-toned, like a ship's whistle, one part higher than he expected, but with a bass undertone that vibrated his jaw. It nodded to Gilea, then turned and pulled the boat along the edge of the lake and into a narrow channel leading further away from the river.

Sylvan swallowed his fear and studied the *ipsis* pulling the boat. It was close to eight feet tall, though it walked with its neck stretched out in front of it, so it had to be at least nine feet when it stood to its full height. Its skin was mud-brown, with few hairs on its legs, though its torso and arms were as hairy as a man's, or perhaps more so. Its hands were little different than a person's, though the fingers were proportionally longer, and the fingertips flared out where they gripped the front of the canoe, like a lizard's toe pads on glass. Its feet were twice as wide as a person's, its toes splayed out with large gaps between them covered in flaps of skin, like a frog. Its privates were like a man's but tucked in tighter beneath its torso. Its head was like a person's head that had been pulled from both ends and stretched out, but its mouth jutted out beyond its small chin. The most unusual thing about it was its neck, which was about two feet long, covered in ropy muscle, with a wide range of movement. It occasionally craned its head around to blink at him and the others with deep brown eyes, which might have been reassuring in their gentleness had they not been fixed in such a bizarrely long face.

No one said a word as the *ipsis* pulled them through a maze of channels crisscrossing the bladegrass, following the lead *ipsis*, who studied the terrain ahead and pointed this way and that with impossibly long arms. Sylvan turned to look back at Temi, whose eyes were fixed on the creatures, widening, then narrowing, as if studying them. She flashed Sylvan a quavering smile, and tears welled up in his eyes, though he could not have said exactly why. Gilea crouched over Temi, scanning the area ahead with clenched jaw and hard eyes. Leo's face was fixed in the same wild smile he had shown when staring at the watery creature, like a child seeing a light show for the first time.

Clumps of trees began to break up the bladegrass as they moved farther away from the river, and before long they were in a shaded, swampy place, with moss hanging from the trees and frog songs filling the air with their solemn symphony. Several varieties of stickbirds stood poised in the shallows, black eyes staring down their long beaks at the water beneath them, paying the canoe, and the *ipsis*, little mind. Sylvan recognized one of them from his book, but there were several he had never seen pictures of before. He wished he could stop and open up the book and flip through the pages; there was so much to see, so many notes to scribble down, and he feared he would forget all the details, so he focused as best he could, hoping to commit everything to memory. Assuming the creatures did not kill them, it would take hours to write down just what he'd seen on this short tour, and he was sure he could spend a month studying the life forms here and barely scratch the surface.

After a time, the lead *ipsis* stopped and motioned them to get out of the boat as they approached a hill that rose out of the water, dotted with large stones. The *ipsis* that had been scouting ahead approached, looked to Gilea, and spoke. Gilea stood staring at the creature, her face narrowed with concentration, her eyes half-closed. When the creature stopped speaking, Gilea shook her head, crossed her arms, and closed her eyes completely. It was the second time she'd made the gesture, which Sylvan thought might be an Endulian greeting, though how she knew to use it with the *ipsis* was beyond him. The creature's neck curved down, bringing its head to her level, and as its forehead touched hers, she gave a little start, then stood perfectly still, not even seeming to breathe.

Chapter Nineteen

Gilea shuddered when the creature's forehead made contact with hers, then the shock of the strange touch melted and their connection was immediate, comfortable as an old blanket. It was deeper than the Endulian mindshares she had experienced, as if it bypassed the conscious mind entirely, and she struggled with the new sensations. She felt there was a more complex message, but she was too overwhelmed to make out the details. Welcome washed over her like the warm southern surf, and she returned it with thanks like a glistening starshell. Worry lapped around the edges of the creature's mind, and fear, but also warmth, the desire to protect. It meant to keep them safe.

The creature's forehead peeled away from hers and its head raised up as it arched its neck backward. It swept a long arm toward her and her group and gestured to the top of the rock-studded hill, which had a path zigzagging up the side. It eyed Temi, who stifled a cough as her gaze stayed locked on its face. When it turned its soft eyes down to Gilea, she felt its concern for Temi, as if the connection they had made was still faintly active. It blinked, and Gilea felt vaguely reassured. It walked up the hill, its long legs shooting forth and its body following, and Leo scrambled up after, taking two or three steps for each of its. Sylvan followed behind Leo, but at a more considered pace, his eyes darting from the *ipsis* back to Gilea and Temi, who walked arm in arm, Gilea gripping Temi's hand tight and holding her up by the elbow.

It was a short, steep climb up the hill, which rose no more than thirty feet above the swamp. As they neared the top, Gilea saw the hill was built around a lake, perhaps fifty yards in diameter. A rocky island sat in the center of the lake, roughly the size of a low house, partially obscured by a light mist in the air. Ripples in the water showed where a stream trickled down from the island into the lake. Everything was just like in Max's story. There were other ripples too, larger ones, between them and the island, but the light of a cloudy afternoon filtering through the trees did not allow Gilea to see what was causing them. They didn't look like swirls, but there was something unnerving about the way they moved, like the glimmering shape that had risen up to greet them before. The *ipsis* made a hollow whistling sound. After a moment of silence, another whistle came from the direction of the island, and shortly thereafter a huge dugout canoe emerged from behind the rocks of the island, powered by two *ipsis*. They paddled using shovel-spears, like the ones carried by the *ipsis* that had brought them here. The hulking canoe was made from the trunk of a thick tree, and it moved slowly under the considerable efforts of the *ipsis*, whose arms, she noticed, were thicker than their guide's.

Gilea turned back to glance at the other three *ipsis*, who stood at the base of the hill watching. They too had thick, strong arms and legs, in contrast to the guide, who was leaner, stood taller, and had ropy muscles.

"The heads of those paddles are way too small for that boat," Leo said, his face pulled wide in a smile that now seemed to be permanent.

"I think they're spears," Gilea whispered.

"More likely shovels," Sylvan's voice suggested his fear had mostly given way to wonder. "For digging up the roots of the bladegrass, I'd bet."

Gilea's eyes sharpened on Sylvan, and she found herself nodding. He could be so clueless sometimes, she tended to forget how smart he really was.

"Maybe a little of both," Leo said. "It's one tool, with many uses. I wonder what else they use those for?"

As the canoe plodded toward them, something in the water to one side of it moved, and a ripple formed above the spot, rising into a low hump, which shimmered and pulsed for a moment. Their guide stared at the hump, which quickly melted into the water, and the circle dissipated into the lake. The guide fixed Gilea with its eyes, telling her to stay, she thought, as it walked along the bank to the right. Its ability to project its thoughts, however vaguely, reminded her of Amini, with whom she'd apprenticed. She had sensed it from the first moment she'd seen them, and their response to her crossed arm greeting showed there was some connection between them and the Endulian practices, though how that could be was a mystery.

The low hump reappeared and began moving toward the *ipsis*, who stepped into the water about fifty feet away from the group. The hump reached the *ipsis*, and a wet glimmer spread up its body until it reached its head, which shone and shimmered in the shadowy half-light. The *ipsis* remained motionless for some time, then the shimmer drained from its body and it stepped back onto the bank and walked toward the group, arriving just before the slow-moving canoe.

The *ipsis* gestured at Temi, then toward the canoe,

and Gilea's stomach lurched as she considered what it might mean for Temi to step into this hollowed-out tree trunk with two creatures large and strong enough to twist her head off with their bare hands. She looked up again into the *ipsis'* eyes, which radiated calm and compassion.

"Are we really doing this?" Sylvan said in a shaky voice.

"Not we," Gilea said. "Just her and me."

"He only pointed to me," Temi said, clinging to Gilea's arm.

"I'm not sending you in there alone." She put one arm around Temi's shoulder and looked up into the *ipsis'* eyes, trying to project her determination to accompany Temi. The *ipsis* hesitated, then blinked what felt like assent. Gilea looked into the eyes of the two *ipsis* in the boat, who returned her gaze with curiosity, perhaps mixed with a little fear.

"Come on Temi. Let me help you in."

Temi gave a tight smile and nodded, and Gilea held her steady as she stepped into the boat, whose interior was lined with thick moss. Gilea looked up at Leo, whose smile had faded, his eyes grown serious.

"Trust this one," Gilea said, pointing to their guide. "And don't let Sylvan out of your sight."

Leo nodded and gave a little wave as Gilea stepped into the boat, pushing off with her foot as she did so.

Temi shivered in her arms, and Gilea pulled Temi's head tight to her chest, scanning the water for swirls, ripples, or humps, but the surface remained undisturbed, except for the faint half-circles where water trickled from the island into the water. She focused on the aura of the *ipsis* paddling the boat, but all she felt was duty, plus the whiffs of fear and curiosity from before. Despite their size, they didn't seem to pose any threat. She studied the lake as they paddled slowly toward the island. It was round, with a ten-foot-wide swath of earth surrounding it, a bowl of water set in a hill that was surely of *ipsis* construction. As they neared the island in the center of the lake, she could see enough through the mist to tell it was formed of large rocks, in an irregular but essentially circular pattern. The mist was warm on her face, and Temi's shivers subsided as they neared the island. The *ipsis* paddled around the back side and pulled the boat up next to an opening in the rock wall. They held the canoe tight to a stone dock with their paddles and eyed Gilea toward the opening.

Gilea lifted Temi under her arms, supporting her at first, until Temi took in a deep breath, stood up straight, and stepped off the boat under her own power. Gilea followed her through a dark passage, which opened into a kind of stone courtyard set around a pool of clear water with a strange fountain in the center, and benches scattered around the edges, with a seated statue on one of them. The fountain was about six feet tall, human-shaped, with water flowing over and around it, though Gilea could see no obvious places where the water was coming out. The fountain appeared to be made out of glass, as light shone through it, but it was so clear it almost seemed like there was no structure at all beneath the surface, as if it were made of nothing but water. Temi stepped to the edge of the pool, staring at the fountain, and Gilea moved behind her, one hand reaching out to grab her in case she started to fall into the water.

Gilea's gaze was pulled away from the fountain, and she froze when she saw the figure, which she had at first taken for a statue, sitting on a bench in a shaded corner of the courtyard. It was extremely rare for her to be in the same space as another living being and not notice. She had felt no drop-off in her overall awareness, even with the *ipsis*, but the figure barely registered as alive. It was an *ipsis*, or at least it had the size and head shape of one, and it wore a sheath of brown fabric over its body, but it had no visible arms; just legs, a torso, and a head. Its eyes were closed, and Gilea could only sense it weakly, but she did not think it was asleep. Its aura was muted, but what Gilea picked up from it was unsettling, a mind fragmented in ways she could not comprehend.

She pulled lightly on the back of Temi's dress, reaching one arm around her to point at the seated figure. Temi gasped as she turned her gaze to the figure, and took a step back into Gilea, who put a hand on her shoulder and tried to will calm into her.

"I'm sure it's fine. Let me..." Gilea trailed off as the figure opened its eyes and stood, summoning her with a firm blink. The other *ipsis* had seemed more attuned than most humans to the unspoken lines of communication, but Gilea could feel herself being almost physically pulled toward the figure. She could have resisted, but she was drawn to it, and she moved around Temi, letting go of her shoulder with a gentle pat. The *ipsis* turned toward Gilea as she rounded the edge of the pool to approach it, and the way it moved suggested it did not, in fact, have arms, though it was impossible to tell for sure beneath its brown tunic.

It bowed its head in the Endulian way, though it had no arms to cross over its chest, she could clearly see now. A wave of peace swept over her as if they had mindshared without even touching foreheads.

Gilea bowed her head and crossed her arms, pushing out a peaceful response.

The creature blinked at her, curving its neck to lower its head, inclining its forehead toward her. She took a deep breath, then let it out slowly as she stepped forward and touched her forehead to its.

Your friend is dying, said a voice in her mind. Hot tears rolled down Gilea's cheeks as the words sank in. She had known it on some level, had steeled her mind against the thought, but the intensity of the connection brought all her feelings to the surface.

We will take her to Tralum for treatment. Gilea's body

shivered as the words passed out of her mind. She had heard that Endulian masters could communicate telepathically, but she had never exchanged anything more than general emotions or desires.

There is no time. Gilea's legs trembled as the words reached her, and she almost reached out to the creature for support. *We can heal her here.*

Gilea's heart gave a painful flutter. *Please, do what you can.*

We will keep you safe until the Circle has decided.

Gilea tried to respond, to ask what the Circle was, but her thoughts stopped at the edge of her mind as if they'd hit a wall. The creature lifted its head on its curving neck, then looked to Temi and blinked. Temi stood staring, wide-eyed, and touched her chest. Gilea wiped away her tears and gestured her over.

"It's okay, they're going to help you. They said they can make you better." Her tears flowed afresh as she watched Temi walk unsteadily around the edge of the pool toward her.

Chapter Twenty

Leo hovered close to Sylvan, who sat clutching his ornate book box in one of the oversized carved wooden chairs, which the *ipsis* had piled with dried moss at their arrival in the little platform village. Leo couldn't help giggling at the sight of Sylvan's slight frame in the huge chair, the absurdity of his elaborate book box in such a place. Leo wriggled out of his chair and stood watching the *ipsis*, studying their hierarchy. The three stout ones with the spear-shovels deferred to the taller, thinner one, who carried a three-pronged fishing spear, which could easily double as a weapon. After a time, the taller one, who Leo had come to think of as Ranger, sent two of the three others back toward the river after some discussion. Leo had heard many dialects of Southish, as well as a bit of Islish, and a handful of maritime languages from the Southern Seas, but the *ipsis'* speech sounded absolutely foreign. Even Sylvan shook his head and shrugged as they talked.

Sylvan leaned forward and spoke in a loud whisper. "So, we just sit here, and hope they aren't preparing Gilea and Temi to be roasted for their feast?"

"No need to whisper," Leo said in a normal, conversational tone. He had determined to swallow his fear and accept these creatures as friends, despite their freakish appearance. "If they could understand us, don't you think they'd speak Southish to us?"

"Not necessarily," Sylvan hissed. "It's entirely possible to understand a language and not speak a single word." He turned to stare at Ranger, who made small but dramatic gestures with his hands as he spoke with the other *ipsis*. Several more emerged from one of the huts, and they listened to Ranger intently. "It's also possible they don't want us to know they understand us."

"Well, I don't know about that, but I think we're pretty safe here. If they meant us harm, we wouldn't be sitting here so comfortably now."

Sylvan sat back, shifting in his chair. "This moss is rather comfy, actually, now that you mention it. A bit scratchy, but all in all, not bad." He fiddled with the clasp on his box but did not open it. "Besides, I suspect they mostly eat fish."

Leo raised his eyebrows at Sylvan.

"Well we saw them fishing, and they live on the river, so of course, but look over there." Sylvan pointed to a pile of charred remains about thirty feet away from the edge of the village platform, which sat on a little rise ten feet above the spongy forest floor. Leo scanned the remains and saw nothing but fish bones. If there were mammal bones in there, they would have stood out. He clapped Sylvan on the knee.

"Good eye. See? Nothing to fear. Unless maybe they eat fish most of the time, but on special occasions when the river brings them something warm and tasty..."

Sylvan shook Leo's hand off his knee. "Glad someone's having fun."

"You aren't having fun? I bet you're studying these things like your life depends on it." The corners of Sylvan's mouth lifted ever so slightly. "So tell me, Doctor, what do you see?"

Sylvan shifted in his seat, leaning forward, looking down when Ranger glanced back in their direction.

"The neck, first of all, it almost suggests grazing tall branches? Or maybe ducking under them. Maybe a little of both. What else could a long flexible neck be good for?"

Leo scratched his beard. "Well some wading birds have them, stickbirds and the like, but I don't see the *ipsis* jabbing their heads underwater to catch a fish."

"Exactly. And did you notice their teeth? They're a bit like ours, but bigger, and they don't seem to have canines. They're definitely not designed for tearing flesh. So I figure they eat fish and plants. With their height, they could easily reach nuts and fruits higher up, but with a little more flexibility in the neck, they can move through tight spaces just about the same as us."

Leo nodded, impressed with Sylvan's analysis, and was about to answer when Ranger approached, stopping about ten feet away, bowing his head, and crossing his arms before continuing. He said something, then made a gesture, moving his fingers toward his mouth, and Leo's stomach growled. The creature smiled, at least Leo thought he did, and he called out to one of the others, who walked off to one of the pyramid-shaped huts and returned with a wooden bowl. It contained several chunks of dried fish and something gray and mashed, which looked a lot like cattail roots. Leo bowed his thanks, stuck two fingers in the mash, and slid a glop into his mouth. It was stringier and more bitter than cattail roots, but not dissimilar, though it had no salt whatsoever.

"I think it's bladegrass roots," he said, holding the bowl out to Sylvan, who shook his head with a grimace but picked up a piece of the fish, holding it gingerly between his thumb and forefinger. He tore a tiny piece off with his teeth and chewed, his face showing distaste, but not disgust.

"Smoked speckle," he said, pulling off a larger piece and sitting back in his chair as he chewed it. "Rather edible. Badly needs salt though." He leaned forward. "You didn't bring any of that everyspice, did you?"

Leo grinned and pulled the pouch out of his pack. "I made the mistake of forgetting it when we visited Max and Zander, but not this time."

Ranger watched, curious, as they sprinkled the powder on the fish, and Leo held out the bag. The creature's neck bent down to bring his nose close enough to smell, and his nostrils flared for a moment, then he smiled. Leo held out a piece of the fish they had sprinkled, and Ranger took it with surprisingly light fingers. He popped the fish into his mouth, making a strange face as he chewed, even by *ipsis* standards, then waved his hand and leaned his head back up.

"You get used to it," Leo said, looking right at Ranger, whose eyes showed intelligence, but not comprehension. Ranger turned as footsteps neared the settlement from the forest. Leo followed the sound and saw two more *ipsis* approaching through the trees, one of them hunched over a staff, the other seeming to glide on soft feet, touching each tree with her fingertips as she passed. Ranger stepped to the edge of the little plateau and bowed deeply with arms crossed, more deeply than he had for the other *ipsis*, Leo thought. Ranger spoke a few words, and the hunched *ipsis* inclined his head, his face grave. The other one bowed low toward Ranger, bending her torso neatly to the ground. Her neck and head stretched out in front of her, looking up at Ranger with big, sad eyes. She rolled back up when she saw Leo and Sylvan, and her eyes brightened a bit. She turned and put her hands on her companion's shoulders, and his neck craned up with evident difficulty. When his eyes fell on Leo and Sylvan, his mouth hung open, showing a mess of half-missing and broken teeth. Everyone fell silent for a moment until he emitted a deep, barking sound that might have been a laugh.

He muttered something to the willowy one, then accepted Ranger's hand and struggled up the stairs to the encampment. They exchanged words for a time, then he turned toward Leo and Sylvan and gave a crooked bow, but in the human style, with one arm at his side and the other leaning on his staff.

"Welcome to our village," he said with a thick accent, made all the more difficult to understand by his deep, marbly voice.

Leo stepped forward and held out his hand. His legs were shaking, and sweat beaded over his forehead, but he surged with energy from his toes to the tips of his fingers. It felt like he'd been waiting his whole life for a moment like this. The *ipsis* closed his mouth in a smile and wrapped his large hand around Leo's, swallowing it with gentle, soft skin.

"We are honored," Leo said, eyeing Sylvan, whose eyes were frozen wide. "I'm Leo, and this is my friend Sylvan." His breath failed him as the creature let go of his hand and smiled.

"You may call me Merk," he said. He gestured toward his companion, who moved closer but did not extend her hand, watching them with great curiosity. "This is my companion, whom you can call..." He stared at her for a moment, rubbing the thin whiskers under his chin. "Sadie. Our names would be unpronounceable to you, so I won't trouble you with them."

"Nice to meet you, Merk, Sadie." Leo bowed to them both, with arms crossed, and Sadie smiled a little. Her smile widened as she turned to Sylvan, who had slipped off his chair and approached on cautious feet. His eyes met hers, then fell to something dangling from Merk's shoulder, which Leo hadn't noticed before. It was a kind of tube, like an elaborate field scope, made of polished wood, perfectly round, with brass dials and end caps. Intricate coppery lettering, like fine wire pressed into precise grooves, ran across its surface, set inside thin copper rectangles. Merk whispered something to Sadie, whose neck flexed as her head bobbed in a kind of nod.

"I hear your friend has Ulver's cough," Merk said, closing his eyes for a moment. "We will care for her, but she must stay on the island until she is cured."

"And how long will that take?" Leo asked. Ulver's cough patients often convalesced for weeks or even months, depending on how advanced their symptoms were, and Temi already had the brown cough.

Merk spoke with Sadie for a few moments, and her head bobbled on her flexible neck as he turned to Leo and spoke.

"A week at most," Merk said, "if she is receptive to our treatments. Longer if not."

"What kind of treatments?" Sylvan's voice quavered, but he stood firm.

Merk looked Sylvan up and down, and his gaze fell onto Sylvan's book box. "Are you a scholar?"

"Of sorts," Sylvan said, clutching his book tightly. "A doctor of life sciences, to be precise."

"But not a real doctor?" Leo stifled a giggle; if Merk meant any malice by his statement, his face did not show it.

"Not a medical doctor, no. But I do have some understanding of medicine. What kind of treatments?" His voice was polite but firm, and he seemed to have lost any trace of fear. Leo was impressed.

Merk spoke a few words to Sadie, who eyed Sylvan's book, then turned to Merk and answered with a short phrase.

"A combination of chemistry and more...holistic methods, which only a few of us are privy to. I wish I could share, but...” He held out his hand with splayed fingers, then grasped it into a fist and let it fall.

“Can I assist? I spent a month shadowing a doctor of philosophical medicine in Anari.”

Merk raised his eyebrows, then shook his head. “I am sorry, but it is not allowed. We must go attend to your friend. You will be in good hands here.” He started to turn away, then paused, twisting his neck around to look at Sylvan. It seemed to Leo he was staring at Sylvan’s book, then he looked up into Sylvan’s eyes.

“When we return, I will give you a full report. And if you will let me examine your book, I will show you what this does.” He glanced down as his fingers grabbed the tube around his neck and shook it. “Deal?”

Sylvan’s head bobbed several times in rapid succession. “Keep her safe,” he said with a tinge of sadness in his voice.

Merk blinked and swung his head around, and his body followed. Sadie held his hand as they walked to the other edge of the platform, but her head swiveled on her flexible neck, her eyes lingering on Sylvan, then Leo, until they descended off the platform and began walking toward the hill. Leo watched as they plodded through the swampy forest, his heart feeling caged and squeezed at the thought of what might happen to Temi if they could not heal her. He wished there was something he could do other than stand there on the platform and hold his tears inside.

Chapter Twenty One

Temi watched as if through clouded glass as the hunched *ipsis* removed the brass lid from a strange wooden tube, and the willowy one poured a few drops of Temi's blood inside. The armless one stood staring at the strange fountain, their body motionless, like a pillar. Gilea tied a bandage around Temi's arm where the *ipsis* had drawn the blood, which she hadn't felt at all after the foul red concoction the *ipsis* had insisted she drink. Temi was comforted by the warmth of Gilea's gaze, and she watched with fascination as the willowy *ipsis* tapped the wooden spoon against the side of the tube, then closed her eyes and sniffed the spoon as the hunched one replaced the lid. Her head glided down over Temi on her gracefully curving neck, and she rolled out a long arm, moving Temi's dress aside and spreading her long, warm fingers over Temi's chest. The *ipsis* closed her eyes, and Temi felt her own lids grow heavy as the creature's fingers seemed to sink into her body, massaging her insides, palping her heart and organs. Temi's eyes flew open as the *ipsis* removed her fingers, and Temi sat up suddenly, sucking in a huge breath, then another.

Gilea held one hand behind Temi's back and the other clutched her forearm, and Temi fell back softly, with Gilea's help. She stared up at Gilea, whose outline was fuzzy against the gray clouds above, but the worry lines brought her face into sharp focus.

"I'm fine," Temi said as she ran her fingers over the smooth skin on Gilea's arms, then slid her fingers between Gilea's. "I feel like I'm floating."

"I've got you right here." Gilea's fingers squeezed hers so tightly Temi was sure she would get bruises, but she didn't care. The world where that mattered was so far away it must have been a dream, and the dream she was in felt so much more real.

"She touched me, inside," Temi said, glancing at the willowy one. "She touched my heart."

"She's just trying to help you get better."

"I'm not a child. I'm not your child. I'm not anyone's child!" Temi slipped her fingers out of Gilea's and propped herself up on her elbows. "I'm less than a child. I've not been born yet." The words flowed out of her like a poem recited in a dead language, devoid of meaning but oddly soothing in their foreignness. Gilea took a step back, casting her eyes down. Temi wanted to reach out to her, tell her she hadn't meant it. She didn't know what she meant, what she was saying, or what was happening to her.

The willowy one approached again, took Temi's hand, and held it, the soft length of her fingers wrapping around Temi's hand like a cocoon. The *ipsis* stared down with kind eyes, then turned and spoke words Temi could see traversing the air in liquid waves. The hunched one's head bobbed a few times, then he turned to Gilea and spoke.

"The next steps she must take without you." He spoke with a thick accent, but his words rang clear in Temi's ears. Gilea stepped to Temi, gripping Temi's hand in both of hers, and Temi let out a little giggle.

"I'm not leaving her alone, I—" Gilea stopped suddenly as a shadow fell over her face. Temi craned her head back to see the Pillar staring at Gilea with eyes both blank and piercing.

"You know you must leave her," the hunched *ipsis* said. "Go now. We will keep her safe."

Gilea let go of Temi's hand, ran her fingers over Temi's cheek, then turned away without a word.

Temi felt the gaze of the Pillar fall on her, and the mental haze suddenly lifted. She sat up, swung her legs off the moss-layered bench, and stood. Her legs were suddenly strong, and her breath came with little effort, though it still felt shallow and wet. She was aware of the hunched *ipsis* and the willowy one walking away, but the Pillar's gaze drew her toward them, and she stepped forward. The Pillar's head lowered to her level, and Temi found her hand reaching up to touch their face. The ridges of their skin were smooth and shiny, though their face was lumpy with wrinkles. As their foreheads touched, the world went silent, and the edges of her vision dimmed, until all she could see were two eyes, looking through her, and she through them, and the world went black.

Through the darkness, she saw a light, like a candle's unwavering flame, and it grew and grew until she could see nothing else. She sank into the light, which suffused her body with warmth until she had no body, only a mind, sinking into another mind, which was vast and unending like the ocean at sunrise. Thoughts came to her, formless, wordless, and they were not her thoughts, but soon she could not distinguish them from her own. She became aware of her body again, but not as a physical thing standing on stone. Her body was an ocean, contained in a shell of air, its tide ebbing and flowing more slowly with each second. She saw the bubbles created by the waves, and the tiny fish flashing silvery-gold in the sunlight. Her vision closed in on the fish, and she entered the space behind their eyes, then her perspective shifted as she was lost in the vastness of the water. She saw now as they saw, tiny creatures drifting among the waves, and there were smaller creatures still in a myriad of shapes, stars and snowflakes and spiky balls and fluttering discs. She moved toward those shapes, sucking them inside her, filtering them from the water and swallowing them down, bringing a sense of fullness, but a hunger remained to swallow more and more, and she moved through clouds of shapes, spinning with open mouth, heart, and mind.

Temi felt herself pulled out from behind the eyes, back into the waves. The tiny shapes became indistinguishable from the bubbles, and the fish grew smaller as she rose above the water, the brilliant orb of the sun growing and shrinking as it reflected off each wave. She rose higher and higher, and the waves grew smaller until they were mere wrinkles on the surface, fading into a blanket of sparkling majesty laid out below. As she ascended into the sky, the sea and the sun and the horizon merged into a field of brilliant blue-gray, and her consciousness flipped suddenly as she burst through a wall of wind and silence. She stared up into the sky, which flashed from deep blue to starry black, and as she flew outward, the stars streaked by her, forming a tunnel of twisting light. The streaks disappeared one by one until after a time, she was flying through utter darkness, and in the end it was impossible to tell if she was still moving or had come to stillness in the void.

The words reached her first, echoes in a cave, familiar but incomprehensible. Light filtered in, jagged, gauzy lines as her eyelashes parted and the gray illumination of the sky battered her like a sandstorm. The Pillar had moved away from her and stood ankle-deep in the edge of the pool, their body shimmering with the reflection of the breeze. The fountain was gone, but the water rose in a tall, thin hump whose profile was eerily reminiscent of the armless *ipsis* it stood next to. Temi steadied herself with one hand on the bench and stood catching her breath, which came shallow but relatively unimpeded. As she watched, the Pillar stepped out of the pool and bowed toward Temi as the liquid figure sank into the water. It emerged again a few seconds later in the center of the pool, as before, its surface flowing while maintaining its basic structure.

The Pillar's eyes fell on Temi for a moment, and she felt the urge to lay down on the moss-layered bench, which she did. It was comfortable, more comfortable than any bed she'd ever slept in, as though it had formed itself to her contours. She sank into the moss, which seemed to rise up and swallow her in its soft green embrace.

Temi awoke to low voices in the now-familiar sounds of the *ipsis*' language. Her eyes remained closed as her fingers caressed the moss, which was dry but still soft, with a pleasantly earthy smell. The bench was covered in several layers of the moss, lain across the bench in sheets. Temi wondered if they cultivated it or just harvested it from the forest. After a time, she opened her eyes, cautiously at first, but the light was lower now, late afternoon at least, though it was hard to be sure because of the cloud cover. She raised her head enough to see the hunched *ipsis* consulting with the willowy one, who was working what might have been a mortar and pestle. A shadow fell over Temi's face as the Pillar appeared above her, their deep brown eyes gazing down at her. She felt strangely comforted by their presence; though she could read nothing from their eyes, they seemed to radiate calm, and she knew she could trust them, and the other *ipsis*. The hunched one approached and stood at the foot of her bed.

"How is your breathing?" he asked in a low, hollow voice.

Temi took a shallow breath in and expelled it. "Better. I haven't been coughing, at least."

"But still shallow," he commented. "Sadie is preparing an ointment for you, which will help keep your lungs still. We have confirmed that you have Ulver's cough, and for that, we have a medicine, which will work, in conjunction with..." He moved to her side and lowered his head. "You have communed with the Pillar, who says you may be ready, or you may not." He paused, licking his lips with his fat purplish-brown tongue. "Are you familiar with Endulian meditation?"

Temi shook her head. "Gilea is. I've heard about it, but Endulian practice is frowned upon in Anari." Religion, Endulian or otherwise, was a taboo subject in her house. Her mother spoke with open disdain of anyone who followed what she called 'primitive belief systems.' A family friend had spent a year in Endulai after suffering multiple nervous breakdowns the doctors could do nothing about and had returned with remarkable self-possession and stability, but Temi's mother had scoffed at the suggestion that Endulian techniques had any role in her recovery.

"We will first treat you with the ointment, then we can discuss the next steps. I am called Merk, by the way. We never formally met, but Gilea says your name is Temi. It is a pleasure to meet you."

"Likewise. I'm so grateful." The willowy one, whom he had called Sadie, approached with a stone bowl. Temi felt suddenly alone and vulnerable as the three *ipsis* loomed above her. "Where are Gilea and the others?"

"They are safe in our village." He pointed, though Temi had no idea where she was or what direction he might be indicating.

"When can I see them?"

Merk blinked slowly. "The Pillar has decided Gilea will be allowed to return if she is willing to help. But it may be difficult, given her feelings for you. She will have to put them aside to do what must be done."

Temi's heart felt squishy as she heard Merk's words. The way Gilea looked at her, her attentiveness to Temi's every mood, her fierce protectiveness, left little doubt. It had occurred to her before, but she kept pushing the thought to the side, hoping it would just go away. She pictured Gilea, her strong face, her eyes deep with worry, and something stirred inside her. She'd never felt this way about a friend before, but she sensed it wasn't quite the same thing as Gilea felt. She gave a weak smile, blinking back tears, and nodded.

"I know."

"If you will allow it, Sadie will now rub the ointment on your chest. She says it will have a similar effect to the medic's balm, though its potency is less, and it will have to be applied more often."

Temi nodded, unbuttoning her dress and looking up at Sadie, who set the bowl down and scooped out a glob of an oily green paste, which smelled of mint and juniper. She closed her eyes as Sadie's warm fingers spread the mixture over her skin. A chill crept into her chest, and her lungs opened a little more with each breath. She kept her eyes closed, trying to chase away the images that crowded around her mind: three monstrous figures hovering over her bed; Gilea's penetrating eyes set in a face full of worry; the watery figure, whose eerie transparency refracted the green and gray world into an infinity of flowing stillness.

Chapter Twenty Two

Sylvan's fingers fiddled with the latch on his book box as Merk approached, one hand on his cane and the other clinging to Sadie's arm. Sadie's head swayed gracefully on her neck as she walked, her soft eyes staying with Sylvan's. They stopped ten feet away and bowed in sync, crossing their arms over their chests. Merk craned his neck up from his hunched position to smile at Sylvan.

"Temi is doing well," he said in a deep, hollow voice. "The Pillar thinks she may be receptive to treatment."

"Receptive? What kind of treatment is this?" *And what the hell is the Pillar?* he wanted to ask.

Merk's lips curled inside his mouth, then bloomed again, full and wet. He used his cane and Sadie's help to lower himself into the chair opposite Sylvan, then exhaled with a loud rasp.

"You said you have studied philosophical medicine?"

Sylvan nodded. The doctor of philosophical medicine

he had shadowed in Anari used traditional tinctures from the provinces, along with meditation techniques and talk therapy, mostly for those with mental health conditions. Though Sylvan tried to keep an open mind, it had seemed more like a placebo effect than anything.

"Then you know the body can heal itself if you can attune yourself to its rhythms and channel them. I expect you've only seen it used with psychological disorders if you learned in Anari."

"That's right," Sylvan said, wondering how Merk, who was so well versed in philosophical medicine and somehow spoke Southish, also knew of Anari medical practices.

Merk nodded. "Well as a doctor of life science, you must know that the brain controls most of the body's functions, yes? But sometimes the connection to the blood and the humors can be obscured by disease or imbalance. The brain cannot see the pathways, if you will, to make the necessary adjustments. Or it cannot direct the body to clear the obstructions. But there are methods that can be used to help the brain bypass these natural limitations."

"In theory, yes." Sylvan's professors had given little credence to philosophical medicine, but it was popular enough among the people that every student of life sciences had to take at least an introductory course.

"Mmm." Merk's eyes fell to Sylvan's book. "This book you carry, it is a book of science?"

"Yes, a foundational text of life science, called The Living Waters, by a late classical scholar named Servais. The first attempted encyclopedia of freshwater creatures. It's required study for everyone in my field."

Merk smiled. "Surely there have been more exhaustive and accurate books written since then?"

"Well, yes, but there's a kind of poetry to the language, and the illustrations are first-rate. It was a gift, from my mother. A collector's item."

"The book box alone is a great treasure. Do you mind if I take a look?" Merk unshouldered the strap holding his wood and brass tube and dangled it in front of Sylvan, who took the tube, hardly noticing as the book box was lifted from his lap.

The tube was about two inches in diameter and close to a foot long, made of dark, reddish wood, with brass dials, and brass caps fitted over both ends. The wood was inlaid with symbols made of copper wire, which had an ancient Islish look to them, though the symbols were not Islish letters or any other language Sylvan knew. A rectangle of the copper wire surrounded a cluster of tiny symbols arranged in groups of three to four, spaced out along lines running the length of the tube, almost like some kind of chart. Sylvan fiddled with one of the caps and found he could unscrew it. He glanced up at Merk, who had puzzled open the latch on the box and was staring at the book's mother-of-pearl inlaid cover with wide, smiling eyes.

"Unscrew both caps and hold it up to..." Merk glanced at the clouds between the treetops, which were looking heavier and darker than before. "You'd need a brighter sky or a flame." He whispered something to Sadie, who slipped away toward one of the thatched huts. "Go ahead, take a look," he said as he opened the book with delicate gestures. "See what you can see. Just try not to drop it." Merk's eyes widened as he gazed down at the pages, and his face glowed almost as if the book were emitting light. Sylvan wondered if the *ipsis* even had books, though Merk was clearly educated and literate, so who knew?

Sylvan unscrewed one cap, revealing a finely polished glass lens that rivaled any he had seen at study in Anari. Beneath the other cap was a crystal with an unusual pattern, two opposite spirals intertwining to form a dazzling array of tiny shapes. He marveled at the construction, which was too perfect to be natural, but he couldn't conceive how even the most skilled jeweler could craft this level of detail on the interior of the crystal. He held it up to a patch of sky that was lighter than the rest, but all he saw was a hazy dark blob surrounded by green leaves and gray sky in fractal patterns.

"The other end," Merk said, looking up from the book. "Look through the crystal to see inside the tube. The clear lens is for seeing far, but the tube has to be empty." He spoke a few soft words to Sadie, who had returned with a small reed taper, which burned with a low, steady flame. She nodded, then knelt before Sylvan, holding the taper low and fixing him with her kind, curious eyes.

Sylvan turned the tube around, put the crystal up to his eye, and pointed the tube toward the flame. At first, he saw nothing but the flame, cast in a thousand iterations by the crystal. He adjusted the dials, and the pattern dissolved, and he saw a shining sphere made up of tightly packed red globules, each with a brown dot on it. The sphere seemed to float in space, and it rotated slowly, in a slightly off-kilter pattern, so within the span of about ten seconds Sylvan saw it from every angle. He grew dizzy and lowered the tube, leaning back into the chair and closing his eyes until the spinning subsided.

Sadie reached out a tentative hand, laying it on Sylvan's shoulder when he made no move to deflect the gesture, though he did flinch a bit as her long, soft fingers draped over his neck. She spoke a stream of low, murmury words, then made a sound like a giant cat purring. He looked up into her eyes, and his mind grew clear and calm. She patted his shoulder, then removed her hand.

"It can be disorienting at first," Merk said, his finger pointed to something in the book. "This fish, what is it? It looks like a thinkfin, but the dorsal fin is much too short, and what are these teeth?"

Sylvan chuckled. "The illustrator seems to have taken some liberties. Some think Servais did the drawings himself, but I read a convincing paper by a calligraphy scholar who made a strong case that it had to be someone else."

"It's not easy to capture the essence of living things. If they are alive, they won't hold still, and if they are dead, you lose their true shape."

"Temi's the artist, not me. You should ask to see her drawings of the swirls and the breathfins. They're quite good, actually."

Merk fixed him with a curious eye. "What did you make of them?"

"I beg your pardon?"

"The swirls, as you call them. What does your scientific mind think about them?"

Sylvan screwed the caps back on the tube as he thought about the swirls, moving of their own volition, with no visible cause, and the watery beings they had encountered, which defied all laws of science he was aware of. He shook his head and leaned over toward the book.

"Servais doesn't mention them—he's the author—but there are notes in the margins, written in another hand, which speak of several unusual beings found in a place called the Living Waters, but the notes don't say what they are."

Merk raised his head from the book, his eyes fixed on Sylvan's. "What names does it give them?"

"Well, it mentions three: the *ipsis*, which I think means you—" He paused as Merk closed his eyes and nodded. "And it speaks of the *duni* and the *sitri*. I believe the *duni* refers to the swirls, and the *sitri* may be the... shape-shifting watery beings?" It sounded so absurd it was hard to say it out loud.

"Very good," Merk said. "You must have studied ancient Enduli."

"Of course, it's required study, though honestly, the course is a little rushed, as there aren't enough good teachers to go around."

"I expect not. Show me these passages."

Sylvan moved close enough that Merk's fish-and-stale-sweat body odor almost overpowered him, but he held his breath and flipped to the section about the myths and legends of the Living Waters.

"Here. It's written in Middle High Southish. Can you read it?"

Merk turned the book sideways and read aloud. "*How could Servais not have mentioned the ipsis? The duni? The sitri?*"

"Yes, exactly. How could he know of this place and make no mention of any of...this?" *And how can you read Middle High Southish?* he wanted to shout.

"Maybe it is as the curmudgeonly author of these marginalia suggests: he knew all about this place but chose to remain silent on the topic."

"Or maybe, as he says...over here." Sylvan turned the page and pointed to the marginalia. "Servais never came to the Living Waters, and his work is based on someone else's observations." Sylvan leaned back, studying the symbols on the tube.

"I'm not sure that it matters much. This book was written over five hundred years ago, was it not?"

"Six hundred, and yes, it matters. It matters even more since it lasted this long. There are so many things to learn from books like this, not all of them what the writer intended."

"You are a scholar's scholar," Merk said with a smile, closing the book and its box with care. "Tell me, what did you see in this tube?" He reached out one arm to put the box in Sylvan's lap as he gently took the tube from his hand.

Sylvan stared at the tube as Merk slung the strap over his neck. He shook his head and looked up into Merk's eyes.

"It looked like maybe...blood?" Merk nodded. "I've seen it under a magnifying lens at study, but never in anything like that kind of detail."

"Did you notice anything unusual about it?"

"Well, there were these little brown spots. I thought maybe...that is Ulver's cough?"

Merk closed his eyes for a moment. "It seems to attach itself to each globule of blood, and the body can't get rid of it. I theorize it is invisible to the body's healing systems."

"Then how do you make it visible?"

"Mmm." Merk shook his head. "We can't, as long as they're attached to the blood. But we can coax them out, using a special tincture, then the brain can sense them, and send its army after them and flush them out."

"Is that what the Pillar's treatment is all about?"

Merk gave a wry smile, wiping a spot of drool from the corner of his mouth. "Ulver's cough is smarter than you would think for such a tiny organism. It finds ways to hide, lurk, and bide its time until the tincture is spent, then it begins again. The medicine alone is not enough."

"Then what, some kind of meditation? Hypnosis?" Sylvan racked his brain, thinking of all the techniques the philosophical doctor he'd shadowed had used.

"Not precisely, but you're not far off. They can help Temi fight it off herself. I'd tell you more, but the Pillar never speaks, not in words anyway. And they're not very forthcoming with their secrets."

Sylvan opened his mouth to respond but wasn't sure what to say, or which question to ask. The world of science he had devoted his entire life to studying had suddenly been turned upside down, by a creature he could never have imagined in a place that was not supposed to exist. Sadie craned her head around, smiling as she murmured something to Merk. Out of the corner of his eye, Sylvan saw Leo walking on his hands between two of the huts, with several wide-eyed *ipsis* children following him, trying to push their gangly bodies into a handstand. They lacked the coordination or the strength to pull it off, so they tumbled to the ground, emitting deep, hollow giggles.

"I'm glad to see Leo has made a few friends," Merk said, watching the spectacle as he touched Sadie lightly on the shoulder. "And the children could certainly use a distraction after all that's been going on."

The tone of his voice suggested he was referring to more than the arrival of Sylvan's group. It also said he wasn't planning on saying anything more on the subject.

Chapter Twenty Three

Gilea sniffed the tincture Merk had prepared. It was not as red as what she was used to, and a little thicker, but when the boozy, metallic tang hit her nose, she knew it would work. She took a fingerful of honey from the bowl and rubbed it over her tongue, then sucked on her tongue to coat her throat. She gave Temi a weak smile and tipped the reed tube back carefully into her mouth. Her throat tweaked as the liquid slid down, but the honey had done its trick, and she sucked spit and swallowed several times until her throat stopped twitching.

Temi locked eyes with her, and Gilea tried to push out a calming vibe. Temi's eyes crinkled in response, and she dabbed her pale finger in the honey and stuck it in her mouth. The sun pushed from behind the clouds, and Temi squinted, then took the tube and poured it down. Gilea tensed her muscles to catch Temi if she fell, or to help her to the ground if she threw up, but Temi gave no more than a couple of twitches, then opened her eyes, holding a hand over them to block out the sun. The paint on her face and hands had been largely smeared away, and the unpainted patches of skin glowed pink beneath the bright sun.

"Can we move into the shadows for the treatment?" Gilea asked Merk. "Her skin...she's burning."

Merk blinked. "Of course. We can perform the treatment in the tunnel if you prefer."

"I'm fine right here," Temi said, turning her head halfway up toward the sky, her hand still shading her eyes. "It's late afternoon, and the clouds will return soon. And you have everything set up here." She gestured to the bowls, tubes, and assorted containers on the bench. Gilea gave her a hard stare, which Temi deflected with a smile. "Really. I'm ready." Her eyes shone from the soma she had been given, a small dose to lower her inhibitions but still keep her lucid. Gilea sighed and blinked her agreement. She needed Temi to be in an open mindset, and fighting her wasn't going to help. She pictured the tub of salve she would use to treat Temi's sunburn if they ever got back to the raft.

Merk nodded to Sadie, who stepped forward and lifted her hands to Temi's face, her long index fingers resting on Temi's temples. Sadie closed her eyes in concentration, and her lips moved, but she did not speak. Temi took a sharp breath in, then let it out slowly as her body relaxed, her shoulders slumped, and her expression faded to a serene blankness. Sadie lifted her fingers from Temi's temples, opened her eyes, and looked into Temi's, then leaned down and kissed Temi on the forehead. She muttered a few words to Merk, then wrapped one arm around him while she held his hand with her other.

"Now you must help her prepare," Merk said. "We will leave you to it." He nodded to Sadie, and they turned and walked over to a bench on the far side of the pool. The Pillar stood a few feet behind Temi, so still it was hard to remember they were not a statue.

Gilea gestured to Temi to move next to the pool. Temi blinked several times and smiled at her.

"Tell me what to do."

"Just relax," Gilea said, moving her hands slowly to the back of Temi's neck. "Close your eyes, and focus on the sound of my voice." Temi closed her eyes, and Gilea took a moment to steady her breath. She hadn't done a proper shared meditation in a long time, but the tincture had cleared her mind, and Temi's vibe was calm and open. Gilea put a hand on Temi's chest and moved Temi's hand to hers. "Breathe with me," she said, taking a slow breath in, not too deep, so Temi could match her, then pursed her lips to let it out with a steady hiss. "We're just going to breathe for a while until our breath moves as one."

Gilea closed her eyes and brought her focus to each breath, filling her lungs halfway, then letting them deflate at their own pace. She could feel Temi's breath, a little ragged but steady, and her heartbeat, which slowed to come in time with hers as they breathed together. The heat from Temi's body, the closeness, the touch, distracted her for a moment, but she willed these thoughts to the side and let the air flow in and out of her. Birds chirped, leaves rustled in the breeze, and water tinkled down the sluice leading out of the pool. Gilea used these sounds to anchor the edges of her consciousness, then pressed her hand harder into Temi's chest, where she felt Temi's heart beating, their breath rising and falling together, their bodies growing in tune with one another.

"I'm going to touch foreheads with you, and open my mind to yours," Gilea said. She pressed her forehead into Temi's, and she felt Temi's heart beat faster for a moment, then slow again, in sync with her own. As their breath mingled, Gilea allowed the boundaries of her mind to open, letting a little bit of herself flow out into the shared space between them. Temi's breath grew shallow, and Gilea gave her neck a gentle squeeze.

"What is inside me is open to you. Let go with the front of your mind, and move slowly outside yourself, one tiny thought at a time." Gilea knew that newcomers had a much easier time letting themselves out than letting someone in.

Temi took a deep breath, and when she let it out, Gilea felt her push out a tentative pulse, which Gilea touched with the tip of her mind, gently, then pulled back. A tendril of Temi's thoughts reached out into her consciousness, and Gilea relaxed her boundaries all the way, and let Temi in. It began as a warmth in her forehead, then spread throughout her head, down her neck, and into her heart. She fought for a moment to keep it from spreading further, but there was no point in fighting or hiding anything now. She let Temi's consciousness suffuse her body, accepting the desires it brought out in her without judgment. She struggled to hold her mind still as Temi explored what must have been a new sensation for her, swirling around Gilea's mind, finally coming to rest, like a cat settling into her lap.

"You have feelings for me," Temi whispered.

"I do," Gilea replied, with an odd sense of calm.

"I feel something for you too, but...I'm not sure what it means yet."

Temi's words wrung her heart like a sponge, but she retained a drop of hope at the word. *Yet.* "That's okay. We feel what we feel."

They stayed quiet for a time, locked together, body and mind, until Gilea felt Temi was fully acclimated.

"Now it's your turn to let me in," Gilea said, squeezing gently with her mind. Temi's breath faltered as she pulled back, opening her eyes, and Gilea felt hollow with Temi's absence.

"How do I..."

"Do you trust me?"

Temi gave a little nod as her eyes devoured Gilea's.

"It'll be just like before, but when you open your mind, you stay put and wait for me."

Temi closed her eyes again and leaned forward, putting her hand back on Gilea's chest and touching foreheads with her. The nape of Temi's neck was sweaty beneath Gilea's hand, and their foreheads stuck together in the muggy air.

"Breathe with me for a minute." Gilea closed her eyes, and the sounds of the world slowly gave way to the rush of blood in her ears, the soft thud of Temi's heart, the squishy sound of Temi's lungs laboring open and closed. After a time, those sounds too grew faint, and a space opened between their minds, wider and freer than before. Gilea imagined the front of her skull as a butterfly's wings, opening gently to soak up the sun, and she waited until she could sense Temi's mind opening, with more of a flutter. Gilea pushed herself out like a cloud of cheroot smoke, filling the space between them, until after a moment she was drawn in thin ribbons into Temi's mind. She let the ribbons float, limp and airy, then with a sudden gasp Temi pulled her all the way in. Temi clung to Gilea, pushing her hand into Gilea's chest as Gilea squeezed Temi's neck to keep their foreheads tight together.

Gilea saw flashes of movement, spinning wheels of clay, stained hands painting designs on bright white china, and a sea-green painted face, drawn with worry but stiff with pride, a face shaped by disappointment and dashed hopes. Temi's mother, studying her, taking her measure, and Temi always coming up just short. Gilea pulled back, not wanting to stir up difficult thoughts, and followed a brighter pathway, snaking down the glittering brown river to a city of billowing colors, of music, of great high-ceilinged studios where artists sat, each at their own huge table, hunched over half-copied manuscripts, maps, and works of art, while quiet boys brought steaming tea in little silver cups. Rontaia, or the version in Temi's mind, Gilea guessed. A good place.

A happy place. An anchor for the treatment to come.

Gilea summoned her own vision of Rontaia, the smell of beer and mussels, of salt air and smoke, of sweat and pitch and fried dough. She watered Temi's mind with them, adding the sounds of seagulls, crates thumping on docks, drunken laughter, languages and dialects swarming and mixing like competing birdsongs. The taste of tri-fries, the crunch when she bit off each corner, holding her mouth halfway open so the steam didn't scald her tongue. The colors of the market, the iridescent fish, the stands bursting with ripe fruit, the patterned fabrics she had to duck through, the freshly painted canvases for sale at Dock's End. She felt Temi squeeze these sensations, taking the time to examine each one until at last Gilea was sure the connection was stable.

She reached out with the back of her mind, and a thin column of water rose out of the pool like a snake, curling down to flow over her foot and ankle. It felt wet, but not in the usual way; it coated her skin with a thin, even layer, so it was more like being underwater than being caught in the rain. Gilea struggled to hold her mind still as the sheath of water flowed up her leg, enwrapped her torso, then crept up her neck and face. It paused for a moment, and she could feel a faint vibe of reassurance. She exhaled slowly, and the wetness flowed in through her mouth and nose and up over her forehead, pushing a thin layer between her and Temi that connected them even as it kept them separate. Gilea's mind bucked like one plunged underwater unexpectedly, but she held tight to Temi, with body and mind, and slowly brought herself under control. She relaxed and accepted the peace of another consciousness merging with hers, exploring her, massaging her temples from the inside.

Her mouth widened into a smile as she let the *sitri* take over, though she wasn't sure if she could have stopped it if she'd wanted to. It flowed through her into

Temi, following the bright copper path of the river to her vision of Rontaia, coiling around each of Temi's bright thoughts before moving to the next. Gilea experienced a sensation like hearing a faint echo around a corner; she could tell something was there, but she couldn't say quite what it was. She grew more and more distant from her own mind, but she could still feel her hands, one on Temi's neck and one on her chest, and Temi's on hers, warm, sweaty, and trembling.

"It's okay," Gilea whispered. "It's okay." She wanted to say something else, but she was drifting too far back, which was fine with her. It was all very, very fine.

Chapter Twenty Four

Leo struggled to follow Ranger through the soggy moss. His feet kept getting stuck in the mud beneath, which came up to his knees in spots, though it didn't seem to slow Ranger down much with his freakishly long legs. Leo felt a sudden pang as he pictured Sea Wolf trotting on light feet through the marsh. He would have absolutely loved this forest, with its little streams, its population of tree rats, and its myriad smells of life and decay. Ranger would have liked Sea Wolf too, Leo was sure of it. He wondered how his dog was getting along by himself on the raft. Water would be no problem, but besides the two small whiskers Leo had left him, he would have nothing to eat. Would he stay there guarding the raft like a good boy until Leo came back, or would he get too anxious all alone and paddle down toward the Living Waters to try to find him?

Being in the claustrophobic platform of the *ipsis* village was a bit like being trapped on the raft, and Leo had jumped at the chance to get his feet wet. Sylvan was busy poring over his book, and Gilea was with Temi at the little lake, so there was nothing for Leo to do to burn off his insatiable need to move. He'd spent several hours doing gymnastics with the kids, walking on his hands and doing tricks, but they'd been called off to what looked like a class. They'd sat on their knees with their gangly legs tucked under themselves and listened to a lively *ipsis* who spoke with great animation and many sweeping gestures. As Leo walked behind Ranger through the dim forest, he wondered what the *ipsis* children were learning in those classes. He bet it was more practical than what was generally taught in human schools.

After a time, they reached drier land, and Ranger began examining the north side of some tree trunks, especially the parts seven or eight feet off the ground. Leo quickly realized Ranger was focusing on one type of conifer, whose name Leo could not recall. Ranger stopped to study a faint purple patch on one of the trees, some kind of lichen from the look of it. Ranger used the tip of his spear to scrape off a bit of it, taste it, then spit it back out, frowning and nodding. He pointed to the lichen, holding his fingertips almost touching, and shook his head. He spread his fingers a little wider, then nodded.

"We need to find where it grows a little thicker. Got it," Leo said. Ranger gave a slow blink, then turned and continued through the dim, swampy forest.

Two hours and a dozen false starts later, Leo hit the jackpot. He spotted a patch as wide and thick as the *ipsis*' hand, just out of easy reach.

"Over here."

Ranger reached him in several long strides, craning his head forward on his slender neck to study the lichen closely. He flashed Leo a smile, then deftly pried off the lichen-encrusted bark with a bone knife and tucked it into a pouch tied around his waist. He touched his pouch, then held up two fingers, eyeing the forest ahead.

"We need two more like this. Sure thing."

It got easier now that Leo knew exactly where to look, and before long they had collected three more patches, and Ranger's pouch was bulging. Rain had begun to filter through the irregular tree canopy, and the sky was darkening. Leo followed Ranger back to the village in a drizzle that turned into a steady rain until at last the sky opened up all the way, soaking Leo to the marrow. Fortunately, it was still warm out, and he was getting a workout pulling his feet from the greedy mud. When they reached the platform, at last, Ranger stepped into a round pool lined with stones and swished his feet around for a while, then emerged, clearing the stairs two steps at a time. Leo rinsed his feet in the pool, then joined Ranger, who was taking shelter with the children and their teacher under a circular pavilion.

The teacher finished what she was saying, then added a short phrase, and the children relaxed. Ranger stepped toward her and showed her the pouch. She smiled, glancing back toward Leo, who gave a little wave. Her smile grew a little wider before she turned back toward Ranger. Her face turned serious, and she said some forceful words, adding gestures Leo could not puzzle out, but he gathered she was talking about the lichens. It made sense that a teacher might know about medicine, which he became more and more convinced was what the errand had been all about. Merk or Sadie must have asked Ranger to harvest ingredients for some kind of tincture to help with Temi's healing. Leo hoped they knew what they were doing. He didn't usually make room in his heart for guilt, but he was starting to worry that his decision to push into the Living Waters instead of heading straight back to get Temi to a hospital was a mistake that might wreck all of their lives.

The teacher touched Ranger on the arm and took a step toward Leo, stopping and crossing her arms at the ten feet distance that seemed customary to them. Leo crossed his arms back, and she smiled again.

"Hello. How are you?" she said with a garbled, almost incomprehensible accent.

"I'm fine, thank you. How are you?"

"Fine, thank you," she managed, then shrugged and held her palms to the side.

"Don't speak much Southish I take it?"

She shook her head and spoke a few hopeful-sounding words in her language.

It was Leo's turn to shake his head. "Sorry, I don't speak *ipsis.*" She nodded at the word.

Sylvan walked out from behind a partition, his book clutched to his chest.

"Leo," Sylvan said, pointing at him, then added a couple of syllables of what must have been *ipsis*, then pointed to the teacher and said something like "Peree," though he clearly struggled to pronounce it.

"You speak their language?" Leo asked, moving to clap Sylvan on the shoulder.

"Just a couple of words I picked up from the children, with Peree's help. But I can see there's some connection with Enduli, so with time, I'm sure I can learn it. So can you, or anyone else, though there are some sounds I don't think we have the hardware to make."

"I guess all that book learning comes in handy after all," Leo said.

"How'd you make out in the forest? I gather Ranger brought a pouch of something back; was it moss?"

"Lichens. For medicine, I think."

Sylvan nodded. "For Temi. After the...treatment."

"Did you ever figure out what that was about?" Leo was intensely curious, but Merk had played coy about the whole thing.

"Not as such," Sylvan said, tucking the book under one arm so he could gesture with the other hand.

"But you saw Gilea touch foreheads with Ranger before, right? That's an Endulian thing, a way they have to communicate without words. And I might be stretching, but I think the treatment might involve some kind of..." his hand flapped about a bit as he paused. "They say the most highly trained practitioners can heal with their minds. I know it sounds preposterous—"

"It doesn't sound preposterous to me," Leo said, scratching his beard. He'd always believed in the power of traditional medicine. "The mind is part of the body, right? And the body can heal itself."

"Yes but not from Ulver's cough, not at this stage." Sylvan's frustration was palpable, but was it because he thought the treatment was a waste of time, or because he was starting to think it might not be?

"Well, we don't exactly have a lot of options. And Gilea's a certified herbalist. If she says it's the right thing to do, we can trust her."

Sylvan studied Leo for a long moment, then raised his eyebrows.

"I suppose. I'm not sure what evidence there is for this kind of treatment, but it can hardly make things worse."

Leo opened his mouth, then shut it again. He wanted to ask Sylvan what evidence could account for the swirls, and the water rising of its own accord and flowing up the body of a creature that surely wasn't in any of Sylvan's textbooks. He wanted to ask what proof could be shown that a sunset was beautiful, that living creatures were miraculous, that the pleasures of the flesh could rival those of the mind.

"Find anything else in that book of yours?"

Sylvan sighed noisily through pursed lips. "Not really. Servais makes no reference to any of these creatures, or phenomena, whatever you want to call them. And the marginalia don't have much more to say than what we know already. The only thing..." he paused, sitting on a stump and flipping delicately through the pages, stopping near the back of the book. Leo leaned in, but all he could make out were strangely shaped letters, upside down, in a language he couldn't quite read.

"Ah, yes. Here." Sylvan sat up straight and took on a distinctly professorial expression. "It reads, *The natives living near the Living Waters are said to be among the tallest on the continent, and local legend attributes their height to the salutary properties of the Living Waters themselves."* He sighed and closed the book. "That's all there is. And believe me, I've read every page at least twice."

"Well, there's clearly a lot that got left out of the textbooks. What do you know about lichens?"

Sylvan sat up straight again, raising his eyebrows. "Lichens are believed to be a form of fungus, perhaps ones that have been colonized by other organisms, or infected with some sort of disease, with which they form a kind of symbiosis." He looked off into the rain, squinting, then shook his head. "Not really my area of specialty. They are used in some traditional medicines, which a few scientists have tried to study, but..." He held his palms up. "There were too many unknown variables for consistent lab results, as I recall."

"Well there's a lot out here that hasn't been studied in a lab, but that doesn't make it less real." Leo's mind returned to the water, rising up like a staff, and the globe that formed on top of it. Watching him, he was sure of it. He could have stared into its shimmering clarity all day, but it had drained away too quickly, and now his mind struggled to hold onto it, the way it caught the light, the tension of its surface. He would have given anything to return to that moment, to stare into the sphere's liquid infinity.

Sylvan was clutching the book to his chest, staring out at the rain, in the direction of the lake in the hill. Leo stared with him, though there was nothing to see but driving rain obscuring ghostly trees. After a time, Sylvan rose and walked over to observe the *ipsis* children in their lesson, and Leo turned and walked to where Ranger squatted, scraping the lichen from the bark with a bone knife and tossing it into a wooden bowl. Ranger nodded toward a rack on the wall, which held several more knives, and Leo pulled one off and squatted by Ranger, watching as the *ipsis* peeled and pried the lichen away with gentle movements. Leo got the hang of it pretty quickly, and they finished as the rain subsided. The lesson must have ended, since the children stood up, rushed over to the edge of the stairs, and went streaking across the forest, laughing and shoving each other.

Sylvan and Peree approached, Sylvan gesticulating as he stammered to spit out a few words of *ipsis*. Peree's long neck arched back in laughter, and she spoke a few words, slowly and clearly. Sylvan repeated them, and she closed her eyes and smiled. She said something to Ranger, then stepped out of the pavilion and entered one of the huts. When she returned, she carried a reed bag that must have been heavy, since she leaned to the other side as she walked. She set the bag down and pulled out a large stone mortar and pestle, several bundles of dried herbs, and two stoppered gourds. She put half the lichens in the mortar, splashed some brownish liquid from one of the gourds over it, and began grinding, releasing a penetrating odor like rotten mint mixed with pine needles.

She stopped after a moment, leaning the pestle toward Leo. "You...?" she managed.

"Sure!" said Leo. His fingers brushed against her soft, warm hand as he took the pestle, which was a little big for him. He smiled at her and leaned into the task, crushing the lichen into the viscous brown liquid, which splashed up on his face, its vapor stinging his eyes though it had not touched them. He wiped his face on his sleeve, smiling at Peree with one eye shut against the pain. She blinked at him, then pulled off half of one of the bundles of herbs and tossed it into the mortar, brushing his hand with hers again as she did so. Leo smiled up at her, unsure of what the gesture meant, but it was nice to touch someone for a change, even if that someone was an *ipsis*.

Chapter Twenty Five

Temi lay on the moss bed, eyes closed, listening to the songs of the frogs and crickets. Her chest felt light as it rose and fell, with very little of the gurgling and wheezing of the previous days. Her mind felt even lighter, open somehow, the boundaries between herself and the world thin and iridescent like a soap bubble, and it was difficult to tell which side of the membrane she was on. She could still feel a part of Gilea inside her, along the bright lines of Temi's own thoughts that led always to Rontaia, or how she imagined it to be. Her childhood visit, which her memory had embellished to the point she could not trust any single detail, remained etched in her mind as the last perfect moment with her parents, before her father's downfall. Before the collapse of the Yskan pottery empire. Before her mother's slow fade into bitterness. She knew intellectually that the real Rontaia would be nothing like her vision, but that vision had helped her bear many nights of wistful silence in her mother's house.

She could feel Gilea's smile at the simplicity of her vision, but also the joy as Gilea thought of her own Rontaia, the version she had reconstructed from her childhood. She felt how Gilea tended her memories like a garden, pulling unwanted thoughts and pruning excess growth. Her Rontaia was dirtier and messier than Temi's vision, but it was also warm, alive with rich tastes and smells, and their visions merged in Temi's mind into a city that glowed more fiercely than anything she could have imagined on her own. Temi pictured herself walking along the docks with Gilea, hands brushing together, then intertwining, and her heart swelled with the thought, which stole the breath from her chest.

She heard Sylvan talking from far away, and though she couldn't hear well enough to figure out just what he was saying, she could tell he was pleading, trying to convince someone, and having little success. She heard Leo's voice too, filled with enthusiasm, then Gilea's, low and protective, and the other voices dropped to a murmur. Temi opened her eyes a crack, saw the dusky sky fading to black, and propped herself up on her elbows. She started to turn over sideways to push herself to standing, and Gilea appeared, crouched beside her.

"You're awake." Gilea's voice was soft with concern, but also hope.

"I feel...better." Temi rose to her knees, wobbling a bit, then steadied herself on Gilea's outstretched arm. "A little."

"Easy does it," Gilea said as Temi leaned on her arm and stood up slowly. She turned to see Leo and Sylvan next to Merk and Sadie, who were holding large smoky tapers. She pulled Gilea along with her for a few steps as she passed by the Pillar, who stood impassive, staring at the fountain, which Temi believed was the *sitri* that had joined with her through Gilea. Sage, Merk had called it, speaking in reverent tones. Temi released

Gilea's arm, flashing her a gentle smile as she breathed deeply and found balance on her own. She stepped toward Sylvan, who eyed her, wincing, his arms held out awkwardly as if he weren't sure if he should hug her or keep her at bay.

"Merk says you shouldn't be contagious, but I'm not supposed to touch you for another day or two just in case. I guess Leo and Gilea have already had it, so they're more or less immune."

Temi smiled at him and glanced at Gilea, who flashed a quiet smile, then looked down at the ground. "Thank you. Thank all of you." She turned to Merk and Sadie, who blinked and smiled, and Leo, who stood watching with his usual joyful smile. She looked over her shoulder at the Pillar and at Sage, who remained locked in their eternal staring contest.

"We brought you some tea," Sylvan said, holding out a steaming clay pot. "Merk says it will help build you back up."

Temi clenched her jaw, suddenly dizzy, her legs wobbling beneath her. Gilea helped her sit on a bench, keeping one gentle hand on her back. Temi steadied herself with her arms and took in a deep breath, deeper than she had taken in quite a while.

"It's made from some kind of lichen Leo helped Ranger harvest from the forest, along with some herbs." Sylvan poured her a cup. "I hope it tastes better than it smells."

"It can't be any worse than that tincture they fed me before." Temi's hand trembled as she raised the cup, inhaling an earthy, rotten perfume tinged with something minty, which did little to blunt the smell. Temi tried not to breathe through her nose as she took a sip, but she still almost gagged. She looked up at the expectant faces around her, steeled herself, and drank a large gulp. The tea burned its way down into her stomach, and she feared for a moment she would throw up. She covered her mouth and let out a foul belch, which would have horrified her in any other circumstance, but she could not bring herself to care.

"I take it back. It definitely is worse."

Sadie reached out her long arm and held out a pale green disc, murmuring something in her language.

"You need to eat something to help absorb it," Merk said. Temi examined the disk, which had char marks on one side, and looked a bit like a pancake with leafy greens cooked into it. "Bladegrass patty," Merk said. "Very nutritious."

The patty had an almost meaty texture, and though it was bland for lack of salt, it was not altogether unpleasant. She took a few bites, chewing thoughtfully before swallowing. It was a bit like the perflower pancakes Dina, the family cook, used to make, before they'd had to let her go.

"Thank you," Temi said, taking another gulp of the tea, then chasing it down with a bite of the patty. Everyone watched in silence as she finished her little meal. When she had down the last sip and the last bite of the patty, she shook her head to clear the taste, and Sadie handed her a cup of water, which she drank greedily.

She pushed up to stand, blinking away Gilea's extended arm. The weight of everyone's expectant eyes was too much to bear, so she turned toward the fountain, which rippled in stillness, glinting in the faint light from the *ipsis'* tapers. "Thank you," she whispered, and for a moment it seemed the surface of the fountain flickered in response. She moved to the edge of the pool, feeling Gilea's silent presence behind her; their connection was near-constant now, and Temi took comfort from the unspoken support. She could also feel Sage's influence inside her, lodged deep in her mind, a gentle pressure extending from her head into her heart and lungs, a cleansing energy flowing through her. And beneath it all she sensed the nebulous force of the Pillar, filling all the empty nooks and crannies. She wondered if this made her any less Temi, now that her mind held elements of three distinct consciousnesses besides her own.

The Pillar's head swiveled suddenly, and the two *ipsis* guards disappeared into the tunnel leading out to the dock. She heard their paddles splash, and the sound of the giant canoe being powered through the water. She looked in the direction the Pillar's head was facing but saw nothing other than the stone walls of the island's enclosure. Gilea's hand touched her shoulder, and Temi turned to see Gilea gesturing her back toward Leo and Sylvan.

"I think we're about to get visitors."

Temi followed Gilea, her legs shaking a little, and sat down on the bench.

"It will be a message from the council," Merk said. "We will be summoned to Circle at sunrise."

"Circle?" Sylvan asked.

"A meeting of *sitri* and *ipsis*, in a circle, as the name suggests."

"What kind of meeting?" Gilea asked, her voice hard.

"We must decide what to do with you. Humans are not as a rule allowed into the Living Waters, and they are very rarely allowed to leave."

"Are we prisoners?" Temi asked.

Merk shook his head. "No. Not yet." He paused, staring down at his long fingers. "But not all on the council feel as we do. There are factions. It is...complicated."

Everyone stared at Merk, who continued examining his fingers as the splash of the paddles approached. Merk stood, with Sadie's help, and used his cane to walk toward the tunnel, where the Pillar stood already, though Temi had not noticed them moving. The fountain in the center of the pool had vanished, and a low hump formed in the water just outside the channel where the overflow from the pool ran down into the lake. Gilea stood between Temi and the tunnel, and Temi had to lean sideways to see the entrance. The paddling stopped, and two figures emerged from the darkness, carrying a large earthenware jug between them, which they set down with care.

Out of the jug rose a rounded cylinder of water, forming a humanoid shape, whose surface was dotted with small circles. The hump at the edge of the pool, Sage, rose up again in their fountain shape, and the two stood still for a moment as if staring at each other. The *sitri* in the jug bowed toward the channel and poured itself into it, moving to the edge of the pool as a rounded lump, then stretched upward into its dotted shape, moving next to Sage. Fat tendrils emerged from what would have been the center of the two creatures' chests if they were human, linking together, with a faint blue luminescence at the point of contact.

The newcomer's surface rippled and pulsed, forming dots, circles, and other geometric shapes, which moved and rearranged themselves into patterns so fast it was hard for Temi to follow, but she sensed there was a logic to them if she could slow them down and study them. The newcomer's surface went smooth, and Temi could see Sage forming similar patterns, though they were distorted, as she saw them through Sage's watery body. The two *sitri* went back and forth several times, then remained still for a moment, their surfaces glassy smooth. The newcomer glided toward one of the *ipsis* it had come with, a female, who moved to the edge of the pool and closed her eyes. The *sitri* melted down around her feet and flowed up her body and face, which shimmered with its wetness. The *ipsis* opened her eyes and spoke. Temi turned to Merk and Sadie, who listened with hands clutched together. Though Temi had no idea what the *ipsis* was saying, she spoke slowly and distinctly, going on at some length with what somehow felt like eloquence. Merk responded with a few short sentences, and the *ipsis* blinked as the water drained from her face and body, and the *sitri* re-formed. It flashed another series of patterns on its surface, then it sank down into the water. It rose again as a hump, then formed into an arc and poured itself back into the vessel. The two *ipsis* bowed, picked up the vessel, and turned back toward the tunnel.

No one spoke as the *ipsis* guards followed the others into the tunnel and paddled them back to shore. The Pillar walked over to Merk, whose head rose from its hunched position to look up into the Pillar's eyes. Merks' face froze as they touched foreheads, and they remained connected for a long moment. Merk's head sagged, and he turned slowly back to the group as the Pillar stood, impassive, staring at the stone wall.

"It is as we thought," Merk said in a tired voice. "We will join the Circle tomorrow at sunrise." He paused, giving Sadie an inscrutable look. Sadie's head lowered slightly, and she turned to look at Sylvan, then Temi and the others. She said something to Merk, who blinked slowly.

"What happens at the Circle?" Leo asked, his eyes brighter than Temi felt they had a right to be.

"The Circle will decide what is to be done with you. You will join us, though you will be unable to participate." He hobbled over to Sadie, leaning on her arm for support. "You should go back to the village and get some rest. I have research to do."

Temi looked up at Gilea, who stood staring at Merk. Gilea turned to Temi, and for the first time, Temi saw something like fear in her eyes.

Chapter Twenty Six

Sylvan sloshed through the swampy forest in the gray half-light of dawn behind the Pillar, Ranger, Sadie, and Merk, who was the only one who seemed impeded by the mucky terrain. Temi, Gilea, and Leo followed, and no one spoke, either due to the uncertain outcome of the Circle meeting or because the Pillar's silence was contagious. They walked parallel to the channels, and whenever they had to cross one, Ranger stopped and studied the water for some time before waving the rest of them forward. It was hard to tell, but from the light filtering through the trees, Sylvan thought they were not heading toward the river but alongside it. The maze of channels and pools seemed to stretch on endlessly, and Sylvan could hardly take in the menagerie of creatures he saw: stickbirds and ducks of various colors and shapes, frogs that plopped into the water at their approach, snakes twisting up mossy trees, fish flashing silvery rainbows in the water, groups of *chukin* and *dimura* congregating in the pools. He recognized many of the creatures, but there were more that he did not, and he longed for his book, to stop and study each creature, its appendages and patterns, how it moved, how it grouped with its fellows or acted alone.

They passed by a wide round pool that was separated by lines of rocks into dozens of smaller circles, each of them with a small *duni* swirling around in the center. An *ipsis* circled the edge of the pool, tossing bits of what looked like moss into the circles as she passed.

"Is this some kind of nursery?" Sylvan asked Merk, marveling at the setup.

"Yes. This is where the *duni* are protected until they grow of a size to go out with the others," Merk said. "It takes several years."

A hundred questions swirled inside Sylvan's head. Were the *duni* merely baby *sitri?* Was there an in-between stage? Were they conscious? Merk did not seem inclined to discuss further, and Sylvan took a last look over his shoulder before they continued out of sight of the nursery.

After a time, the ground became sandy, the vegetation a bit sparser, with various conifers dominating the canopy. Ranger held up his hand for them to stop, and he and the Pillar continued across the sandy ground. They stopped atop a mound, where Sylvan could see several other *ipsis* standing, spaced in a wide circle. Ranger seemed to speak with the other *ipsis* for a moment, then he turned and gestured with a long arm.

"By tradition," Merk said, "the *ipsis* gather first, while the *sitri* wait in the channel nearby. The others are from the downstream village, and they live in closer contact with the *sitri* than we. It looks like we are the last to arrive. You will stand behind us on the circle of sand, well clear of the water. You may observe, but not speak, not that anyone but me would understand you anyway. Come." He gestured by curving his head toward the mound and leaned heavily on Sadie. Sadie craned her head around to blink at Sylvan, then turned back around and helped Merk make his way over the unsteady sand, which seemed to give him more trouble than the swampy forest.

As they made their way up onto the small sandy hill, Sylvan could see it was a circle, broken only by a channel on one side. The hill rose ten feet above a round, clear pool of water about thirty feet in diameter. In addition to Ranger and the Pillar, three unknown *ipsis* stood spaced around the edge, casting unfriendly glances at Sylvan and his friends. They crossed their arms over their chests in greeting, showing bluish lines tattooed across their forearms. Merk and Sadie repeated the gesture, and Sylvan followed suit.

"Stay here with me," Merk said. Sadie left him and moved to stand about ten feet farther along the circle, so there were now seven *ipsis* in total surrounding the pool. Merk gestured with his chin toward the Pillar, who stood with eyes closed, their neck curved in the direction of the channel. A few moments later, six humps of water moved into the pool, then rose up to form the now familiar humanoid shape the *sitri* took when dealing with the *ipsis*. Sylvan thought of the other shapes he had seen them in: humps above the water, squidlike shapes beneath the surface, and the staff of water that had arisen next to their canoe, forming a globe as if to study them. They could clearly take any shape they chose, but they could not exist outside of the water, as evidenced by the fact their ambassador, or whatever it was, had been transported in a large jug.

One of the *sitri* moved to the center of the pool, and the others lowered down to humps. The center *sitri*'s surface went smooth, then formed a pattern of dots and circles, as the one back at the island had done. Sylvan glanced at his companions and noticed Temi staring at the *sitri*, her face scrunched in concentration, with Gilea hovering just over her shoulder, eyes closed, one hand on the back of Temi's neck. Leo stood gaping at the *sitri* like a child at carnival. The *ipsis* all stood watching the *sitri* with attentive faces, some showing comprehension, others confusion. If Sylvan interpreted correctly, those who understood were not happy about whatever the *sitri* was communicating with its flashing patterns. After a time, the *sitri* went smooth again, and the other *sitri* rose back to their humanoid shapes.

One of the unknown *ipsis* spoke, her voice low and careful, looking at each of the others as she talked. By now the patterns of the language were quite familiar, but Sylvan still couldn't make out what she was saying, except perhaps a greeting at the beginning, and possibly the word *please* near the end. He was far from sure, but he had heard a similar word from Peree and the *ipsis* children several times, and it was not far off from the Enduli word. Ranger responded, his voice rising with animation as he spoke, making wide, sweeping gestures with his long arms. Sadie said something, and Ranger waved her off, but then Merk interrupted him with a raised finger, and Sadie continued, speaking at some length in what sounded like a patient explanation, though her face looked tense. One of the other *ipsis* started speaking but stopped in mid utterance as the Pillar descended from the sand rim in two long steps and stood with both feet in the water.

The *sitri* in the center drifted over to the Pillar, who lowered their head, leaning their forehead down toward the *sitri* as it stretched toward them. A faint blue light glowed at the point of touch, and the group's silence deepened. Sylvan turned to Temi, who looked confused and a little annoyed, and to Gilea, who had released Temi's neck but kept her eyes closed. Leo flashed Sylvan a grin, then turned to watch again, the wonder in his face tinged with a note of worry. Sylvan watched as the two figures stood touching, but the *sitri* did not seem to be flowing over the Pillar's body as they did when communicating with the other *ipsis*. This was similar to what had happened between the two *sitri* back on the island, and what the Pillar had done with Merk. Clearly, the Pillar had some special skill or ability the other *ipsis* lacked. They stood still for some time, then the Pillar's head swung back up, and they moved up the sand hill in several long strides to stand next to Merk. Sylvan took an involuntary step back, as did Gilea and Leo, but Temi did not flinch. She stood gazing up at the Pillar and Merk as their necks leaned forward, touching again. After a few moments, the Pillar returned to their place on the rim.

Merk spoke for some time, slow and serious, ending on what sounded like a resigned tone. The other *ipsis* crossed their arms and bowed their heads, and the *sitri* leaned outward for a moment in what looked like a similar gesture, then sank down to their hump forms and filed out of the pool into the channel, where they disappeared. Sylvan watched as the water in the channel roiled, and the swirling mass of water moved swiftly away and vanished around the bend.

The *ipsis'* bodies relaxed, but their faces remained tense. The Pillar turned, long-stepped down the mound, and strode off through the forest without so much as a glance. The others stood together in a sandy patch below the mound, talking in low but earnest tones.

"What the hell just happened?" Sylvan said to his friends.

"The *sitri* said we should not be allowed to leave," Temi said, staring at the channel where they had disappeared. Gilea touched her lightly on the arm, and Temi looked up at her, then back at Sylvan. "At least that's what I think they said."

"How on earth do you know that?" Sylvan asked. Endulian mindshares were hard enough to swallow, but this was beyond any science Sylvan could even imagine.

Temi shook her head. "The patterns they make... are starting to make sense. Ever since...ever since my treatment, there's a part of Sage that's still in me, and if I let it, it helps me see how they see." She blinked up at Gilea. "You feel it too, don't you?"

Gilea nodded, her face curling into a frown. "I only feel an echo, the traces Sage left as they passed through me. I can't see what you see. I can't read the patterns." Sylvan wanted to stop her and ask a hundred questions, but he kept his mouth closed and listened as Temi spoke.

"Well I don't know if I can read them, but I can get the gist. With a little help." She touched Gilea gently with her elbow.

"That is so cool," Leo said, his head bobbing in appreciation. "I wonder if you're the only person in the world who can understand the *sitri*."

"Not the only one," Merk said as he stepped close, lowering his head. "But one of the very few."

"Who else can read them?" Sylvan asked. "Do you have to be...treated, or whatever happened to Temi, or can you learn the patterns, like a language?"

"It takes a lot longer if you have to learn on your own," Merk said. "Years, in fact. But it is possible."

Sadie slid her arm into his, and their fingers intertwined as she whispered into his ear. Merk nodded.

"We should return to the Island. There is much to discuss." He looked each of them in the eye. "From now on, you should all be extra careful whenever you are within reach of water, any water. We have been given three days to prepare our appeal, but there may be some *sitri* whose minds are made up, and they might not follow the agreement."

"And after three days, once you make your appeal, what if it's denied?" Gilea's face was a mask of calm, but her voice did not hide her concern, which Sylvan shared. The *sitri* could hide in water, and there was no way to escape without crossing through large swaths of wetlands, not to mention the river.

Merk sucked his lips inside his mouth, then popped them back out and licked them with his fat purple tongue. "In theory, we could agree to keep you in the village indefinitely, and swear an oath not to allow you to leave."

"In theory?" Sylvan asked, his heart sinking at Merk's tone.

Merk blinked as his head dipped. "If tradition were followed, yes. But in light of recent events, protocols that have been broken..."

"They'll kill us," Temi said in a small voice. "Won't they, Merk?"

Merk sighed. "It's not beyond the realm of possibility. Which is why we need to get you back as quickly as possible."

Sadie spoke to him with a serious, warning tone, looking at Sylvan and the others, but mostly at Sylvan. Merk patted her hand and nodded.

"We will carry you across the channels on the way back. Just to be safe."

Chapter Twenty Seven

Gilea sat next to Temi on the bench, nibbling the bladegrass patties Sadie had given them, which seemed to have a few mushrooms mixed in. Temi stared off at the fountain, at Sage, Gilea reminded herself. She could see why Merk had picked that nickname. Though Sage had only used her as a vessel to enter and heal Temi, Gilea could still feel little echoes of their ineffable knowledge, vibrating her mind at odd moments like sail ropes when the wind turned just so. In those instants, she saw the world as if through a fine crystal lens that rendered everything a little bit crisper, making the smallest details obvious in their relevance to the whole. The tone of the moss under the slanted rays of sunlight could predict the weather, or lead her to the nearest source of sweetwater. In such a moment she saw the peeling skin on Temi's nose, curling away from the tender, shiny skin beneath, which would harden, crack, and dry the next day, revealing an even softer, more fragile layer, one that had never dreamt of being kissed by the sun.

"I want to take a walk," Temi said, popping the last piece of green patty into her mouth and chewing with her mouth twisted sideways. "Just around the pool," she added, touching Gilea on the forearm in a way that said, *Stay*.

Gilea watched Temi move with soft steps toward the wall, running her fingers along it as she walked. Gilea turned her focus to the Pillar, who sat on a bench opposite her, staring at Sage, whose surface flowed in stillness. Gilea wondered if the state were akin to sleep, which she herself desperately needed. She closed her eyes halfway and grounded into her seat to dim the edges of her consciousness so all she saw was Sage. She imagined her mind opening with the grace and precision of a lotus flower, ready to receive the sun's blessing, the bee's kiss. Her thoughts flowed out across the surface of the water toward the soft, vibrant energy surrounding Sage, but just as she was about to connect, she felt hers slowing, stretching to its limits, then being pulled back just as the static crackle had begun to form between them. Sage's surface stopped flowing for a moment, shining clear and still, then collapsed into a hump, moving across the pool toward the Pillar, who stood from their bench and moved to the edge of the pool.

Temi sat down just as Gilea was standing up to get a closer look, and Leo and Sylvan sidled up behind her.

"What are they doing?" Sylvan whispered.

Gilea waved him off, pushing out again with her mind as Sage rose up in humanoid shape, the orb that passed for their head stretching forward on a fluid column like the *ipsis'* necks. The Pillar leaned their head in, and Sage's orb flowed over the Pillar's head, forming a thick, oblong mass that shimmered in the light reflected from the breeze rippling the pool's surface. They stayed motionless for a time, and Gilea tried but could not reach them, as if they were surrounded by an invisible shield that kept all other minds out. But though she could not feel them directly, she could sense trouble beneath the surface. A disturbance radiated out from them, and even when Sage pulled away, the Pillar's head remained englobed by a watery sheen. They stepped back from the pool, turning toward the tunnel leading out to the lake. Gilea heard Merk shout, and the two *ipsis* guards by the pool swiveled their heads toward him, then looked down at the channel.

Forms like glass tentacles snaked out of the water, wrapping themselves around the guards' legs and rushing up their bodies. One gave a shout and leaped back, and the water splashed onto the stone, then slithered back into the channel. The other *ipsis* froze, his body enveloped in a thin sheen, and Gilea clenched with her mind to slow the scene unfolding before her so she could see every detail as it was happening. Sadie lunged toward the standing guard, who hoisted his spear and reared back to throw it. Sadie's body slunk low as her long legs flowed forward and she reached out her arms toward the guard, hooking him around the neck just as he released his spear. The projectile streaked through the air, its large blade spinning as it flew, and the Pillar's body curved away from the point, which would have struck them right in the chest. Sadie pulled on the guard's neck and he lost balance, his feet slipping on the wet stone, and he fell backward, water splashing from his body as he struck the stone. Sadie dragged him away from the tendrils of water swarming around his feet, and the tendrils melted and rushed back into the channel, joining a large hump that had formed there.

The hump sank into the channel, and a watery V sped forward into the pool, like the wake of a charging fish. Gilea straddled the bench, hooked one arm under Temi's knees and the other under her arms, and hauled her back against the wall as Leo and Sylvan scrambled out of the way. Temi gave a startled cry as Gilea pushed her into Sylvan's arms, then moved to stand between them and the pool.

The water churned and bubbled in zigzags and circles, which moved toward the center of the pool, then around the edges, splashing waves up onto the stone, which slithered back into the roiling mass. The water rose up in an unruly column, which flailed and morphed into a furious array of wild shapes, growing taller and thinner, the top billowing like an uncontrolled chemical flame. The sides of the column grew straight and smooth, the tongues of water at the top grew smaller and less frantic, and the column froze in place, more than ten feet tall, glistening in the sunlight filtering in through the clouds.

The Pillar stepped to the edge of the pool in two long strides, their head still enveloped in a liquid globe, which leaned toward the watery column. The column began to tremble, its surface jiggling ever faster, then started melting and shrinking, coalescing in a perfect shimmering sphere. Gilea felt the sphere's tension in the air, the tight surface strained against a force on the inside struggling to escape. The sphere exploded with an almost inaudible pop, spraying water over the courtyard and soaking Gilea to the skin, though the surface of the pool showed not a single drop had fallen on it.

Sadie shouted at Merk, eyeing Gilea's group as she stood and waved them over with an impossibly long arm.

"You must go with Sadie at once," Merk said to Gilea, his voice shaky. "Take them back to the village, where you will be safe. She will—" He stopped, turning toward the Pillar, who stood staring at him, their head still encased in water. Merk nodded as the Pillar turned their head down to scan the pool for a moment, walking around its edge and down to the channel, their eyes on the water.

"They are going to make sure there are no other *sitri*

in the lake before the guards paddle you across." Merk shook his head, chewing on his lips as he watched the Pillar disappear into the tunnel.

"Is it dead?" Gilea asked. Merk nodded, his eyes closed. "And Sage?"

Merk shook his head. "The Pillar holds their essence."

"How did it get here?" Leo asked. Gilea turned to see his face, earnest behind a hint of a smile. "They can only travel in water, right? So how did it get to the lake?"

Merk observed Leo with what looked like respect in his eyes. "It can only have been brought by the *ipsis* allied with the Spreaders." Leo shook his head a little, looking to Gilea, then Temi, then toward Sylvan, who was crouched near the edge of the pool, studying something on the ground.

"The Spreaders?" Leo asked.

Merk gave a great sigh. "We don't have much time, but there are those among the *sitri* who wish to extend their domain beyond the Living Waters."

"And how would they do that, exactly?" Gilea asked. Merk had referenced political divisions among the *sitri*, but this was a new detail.

"By extending the Living Waters themselves, as you do with cities, growing ever outward, up and down the shore, transforming the land to suit their needs. But come, we can talk more later." Merk's face went slack as he stared at the Pillar, who had returned and stood across the channel facing him, their head englobed in a watery sheen. Neither moved for a long moment, then Merk swallowed, licked his lips, and gestured with his cane. Gilea marveled at this ability to communicate without even touching foreheads. It must have been Sage's ability, shared through the Pillar, that allowed it.

"The Pillar says whoever brought them has gone, so it is safe to cross, for now. But you must hurry."

Gilea watched the Pillar as she followed Temi and

the others into the tunnel. The Pillar knelt by the pool, lowering their head until the liquid surrounding it slipped off and into the water, which began turning like a small whirlpool at the water's edge. Like the swirls they had seen in the river. She gave a start as she felt a tug on her mind, and she turned to see Merk looking at her with kind eyes.

"Sage is re-forming. The Pillar dispersed both Sage and the interloper, but the part of Sage that remained with the Pillar can return to their normal state in a day or so. Now come, Sadie can tell you all about it in the village." He touched Gilea on the shoulder as she passed, and she felt a calming warmth flow from his long fingers. She blinked at him and walked into the tunnel.

The mood in the village was tense. The children huddled around Peree, who spoke with calming tones, eyeing Sadie and the group from time to time. Sadie said something that sounded final to Ranger and a few other adults, then gestured for Gilea to follow her into a large hut.

Inside the hut, a low fire burned, and long log benches framed the fire in a square. Sadie sat down on the end of one of the benches, eyeing the end of the adjacent bench. Gilea sat, and Sadie lowered her head to Gilea's level, her eyes soft and deep, then leaned her forehead toward Gilea, just as Ranger had done before. Gilea closed her eyes, took a deep breath in, and touched foreheads with Sadie.

The connection with the *ipsis* had a different feel than what Gilea had experienced with Endulian mind-shares; it was somehow more direct, as if they had less filter than humans. As if this were natural to them. Gilea relaxed her mind as Sadie's thoughts flowed in gently, gracefully.

The Spreaders have clearly decided to take matters into their own hands. They will be coming for you.

Are we safe here in the village? Gilea asked.

They control some of our number through fear, even when not connected. They may come for you here as well. Sadie's thoughts had a defeated tone, but a spark of optimism surfaced. *Merk and I have been working on a tincture to prevent us from being controlled. If we can make enough of it, it will help. But the ingredients are rare and difficult to find. It will take time. The joyful one, whom you call Leo, I think? May be able to help.*

I'm sure he will. What can I do?

Stay watchful and protect the others. Especially the wise one. Sylvan. Gilea felt a warmth in Sadie's mind at Sylvan's name, something she had never felt before, an emotion between familial protectiveness and romantic love. She had noticed Sadie looking at Sylvan differently than the others, but she had not been able to determine what was behind it. Gilea gasped as Sadie's forehead pulled away, and it took her a moment to center her consciousness. She blinked at Sadie in thanks, and Sadie blinked back.

When she emerged from the hut, Sylvan was talking excitedly to Merk, holding something carefully in his hands. Merk's eyebrows raised, and he moved to sit next to the table where they had mixed and ground the ingredients for the poultice they had used on Temi. Gilea stepped closer and saw Sylvan cupping a leaf in his hands as Merk unshouldered his Seeing Tube and unscrewed the lid. He nodded to Sylvan, who moved the leaf over and poured several drops of water inside.

Chapter Twenty Eight

Leo watched as Sylvan and Merk conferred over the Seeing Tube, holding it up to the light as they looked into it, moving the brass dials this way and that. Leo wasn't sure exactly how it worked, but they were studying the water Sylvan had brought cupped in a leaf. It made sense; the water would have landed on the leaf when the Pillar had scattered the fighting *sitri*, so maybe it was like *sitri* blood. Ranger consulted with Merk, who listened, nodding, then summoned Leo with his eyes.

"Ranger has asked that you join him. He needs to hunt for a...creature, like a very large salamander, whose secretions we will use to make a tincture that will prevent us from being controlled by the Spreaders. If he can catch one. They are very reclusive, and it is forbidden to kill them, but it is also forbidden to try to assassinate *sitri* and *ipsis*, which the Spreaders have done, so we may need to make an exception."

"How large?" Leo asked.

"Smaller than an *ipsis.*" Merk gave a small chuckle. "But not by much. They tunnel under large fallen trees, especially darkwoods. Ranger will show you where to look."

Leo's stomach fluttered at the thought of coming face to face with a salamander as big as he was, or bigger. But that flutter warmed as it entered his heart and mind, becoming the pure joy he used to feel as a child lifting up creek stones in hopes of finding something wriggly beneath. Ranger handed him a long pole with a length of fiber rope on one end and three prongs of bone on the other. Leo hefted it and smiled. No explanation was required. He just hoped he didn't have to use the pointy end.

Ranger packed a small bag with some leaf-wrapped bladegrass patties, nuts, dried fish, and several skins of water. Leo found his own bag and held it open, and Ranger put half the supplies into it without a word, then nodded and turned toward the stairs. Leo followed him down onto the spongy path that wandered through the bog, away from the river, the village, and the lake. They walked without slowing through the area they'd combed previously looking for lichens, and Leo even spotted a few patches he had missed before as they passed. Leo's feet seemed to find the stable spots more easily this time, and he was able to keep up with Ranger's long strides without getting too out of breath. As afternoon faded into evening, Ranger slowed, made a 'wait' gesture with one hand, then stopped in a crouch, staring at a large moss-covered fallen tree ahead. Leo wasn't sure, but the veiny shape of the tree carcass resembled a darkwood.

Ranger curved his neck around, squinting at Leo, then gestured slowly with one arm, drawing a wide oval in the direction of the other end of the tree. Leo nodded. Ranger wanted him to creep around the other side, in case one of these giant salamanders had made this tree its home. Leo pointed to the trident end of his stick, then the loop end, and Ranger blinked when he indicated the loop. They were to try to trap the creature, not kill it, though Leo was mentally preparing himself for either possibility. It may have been forbidden to kill these creatures, but he didn't intend to get killed by one just to keep the *ipsis* tradition.

Leo gave the tree a wide berth, picking his way gently through the puddles and mushy spots until he saw Ranger signal for him to stop, at the point where the trunk began to narrow and separate into two smaller branches. Leo studied the tree, looking for obvious holes where its trunk met the ground, but he saw nothing. Ranger pointed two fingers toward his eyes, then back at Leo, and crept around the other side of the tree, moving in complete silence. He walked sideways, his long legs pulling him along like a crab, low to the ground, his eyes fixed on the tree trunk. When he reached the spot where the trunk split, just opposite Leo, he crouched, staring at the ground, and crept forward, poking his stick around the base of the trunk. He raised his head on his long neck and waved Leo over.

Leo circled around where the long branches melted into the ground, enveloped in thick moss and lichens, then crept in behind Ranger. Ranger's head curved around to blink at him, and he pointed to a wide hole beneath the tree, which was half-covered by leaves and branches. He shook his head, and Leo nodded. This had once been the lair of one of the creatures they sought, but it was no longer here. Ranger leaned against the tree, closing his eyes, his face drawn with fatigue. Leo moved to lean next to him, feeling Ranger's heat radiating off him. The *ipsis* seemed to run a little warmer than humans, Leo had noticed, though in most other ways they were the same—they ate and drank as humans did, slept, talked, even fornicated, much the same way, though from what Leo heard of their nightly couplings, they showed less privacy and more abandon in their sexual activity.

Ranger stood up with a grunt and hunted around until he found a conifer branch, which he used to sweep the ground in a semicircle near the fallen tree. Leo found another branch and pitched in, noting that the spot was a little higher and drier than the surrounding forest, and had cover on one side, so it would make a suitable place to camp. They sat in silence, eating a meager dinner in the darkening woods. Leo appreciated the companionable silence between them, but he longed for conversation or some form of interaction. It was always like this; either he wanted to be alone with his thoughts, or surrounded by good people, but as soon as he had one, he wished for the other. Being with Ranger was a lot like being alone, which he enjoyed, but it made him long for some other kind of company. He had seen Gilea touch foreheads with Ranger and seem to communicate, and though Leo had no Endulian training, he had always been curious, and he hoped he could convince Ranger to give it a try.

He touched Ranger on the shoulder, pointing toward Ranger's forehead, then touching his own. Ranger stared at him with what might have been amusement, though it was difficult to tell in the growing darkness. At last, Ranger sighed through his nose, blinked, and lowered his head to Leo's level. Leo closed his eyes and leaned forward, leading with his forehead. He could smell Ranger's breath, feel the heat from his face, the softness of his fingers on Leo's shoulder. When their foreheads touched, Leo felt a surge of heat, and a film of sweat broke out on his face. His head felt light, a little dizzy, and he held onto Ranger's muscular arm for support as he struggled to steady his breathing as he did in meditation with Gilea. After a while, his breath settled, and his mind followed.

A strange sensation crept over him, a seriousness of purpose, an urgency, pushed on by an existential dread, the fear of losing control. This fear did not rise from Leo himself; rather, it flowed from Ranger into him. Leo relaxed his mind further, giving in to the warmth flowing between them, wrapping himself in Ranger's emotions like a blanket. Other fears and concerns mixed in, with points of anger and consternation and hope, swirling together faster and faster, and Leo felt his balance failing, the strength of his grip weakening. As Ranger pulled his forehead away, Leo slumped backward, and the only thing stopping him from flopping onto the mossy earth was Ranger's long arm wrapped around his shoulders. Ranger lowered him to the ground, his dark eyes hovering like moonlit ponds. Leo's breath returned suddenly, and he smiled as Ranger lowered himself to the ground and nestled in beside him, easing his arm over Leo's chest. Leo turned away and snuggled into Ranger's body heat, his head spinning, but in a pleasant way, as if he'd had just the right amount to drink and everything was fine, just fine. He smiled and sank into the echoes of their connection, like distant music, lulling him to sleep.

They trekked for several hours the next morning, examining two fallen darkwoods before they approached a third, where Ranger stopped, crouching low and motioning Leo down with his hand. The tree lay across a narrow, winding stream, and moss trailed down from the trunk into the water. Ranger kept his hand close to his body as he pointed with a long finger, and Leo could see a hole where the bank sloped down beneath the tree, a muddy strip between moss, like the chutes *chukin* used between their burrows and the water. Unlike the other burrow they had found, this one was active. As Leo studied the stream, he noticed a half-submerged log with an unusual sheen, and he touched Ranger on the shoulder as he pointed. The upstream end of the log was oddly rounded, and Leo's heart pounded as he realized it was the head of a salamander over seven feet long. Ranger pointed to Leo and indicated the hole beneath the tree, then touched his own chest, eyeing the creature. Leo blinked his acknowledgment, hoping he'd understood correctly that he was to block the hole while Ranger tried to wrangle the beast. Ranger took a deep breath, held up five fingers, folding them down one at a time: four, three, two, one, at which point one of his long legs reached forward, pulling his body down toward the stream.

Leo crept toward the fallen tree, moving with practiced silence, studying the bank beneath the hole, which was muddy and likely too slippery for easy purchase. He would have to hope the moss on either side would hold enough for him to use the loop to catch the creature's head. He timed his approach so he would arrive at the hole just as Ranger reached the stream. Ranger moved with slow fluidity along the streambank, and when he got within ten feet of the creature, it turned its head toward Ranger, and the water thrashed with its sudden movement as it turned and scrambled up the bank. The loop on Leo's stick snagged in the underbrush as he tried to swing it forward, and he dropped it and made a desperate dive for the creature's neck.

A birdlike shriek erupted as the creature's mouth opened wide enough to swallow Leo's head, flashing rows of small, sharp teeth. Leo grabbed hold of a stubby branch protruding from the tree and swung his legs toward the creature, kicked the top of its head, and sent it sliding down the bank. Ranger was on it in an instant, straddling its body as he whipped the loop end of his stick around. He slid the rope over the creature's neck and pulled back as it thrashed beneath him. Ranger lost his balance and fell back into the stream, and the beast flopped over, twisting and whipping its tail as its mouth opened, straining for Ranger's foot. Ranger kept it at pole's length, but the loop appeared to be slipping. Leo retrieved his pole, leaped across the stream to get behind the creature, and looped the rope around the creature's neck, his feet slipping on the mud as he strained to pull it away from Ranger. Ranger scrambled to his knees, twisting his pole, tightening the noose, and the creature flopped wildly for a few moments, then went still.

Its mouth opened and closed rapidly, and Leo released some of the pressure in his noose as Ranger straddled the creature again, coming to sit on its back, pinning it to the ground. He gestured for Leo's pole, and Leo handed it over. Ranger held both poles in one hand, twisting them slightly until the rope was snug, but the creature was still breathing. He gestured for Leo to take the poles, which he did, holding them in the same orientation. Ranger reached for his bag, which was wet from having fallen into the creek, and retrieved a wide-mouthed skin, which he propped on his knees. He unsheathed his knife and ran the dull side along the top of the creature's head, then scraped a dollop of slime into the skin. His neck curved around, and his wide smile filled Leo with joy.

Chapter Twenty Nine

Sylvan's arms were tired and his eyes bleary from holding the Seeing Tube toward the sun. He handed the tube to Merk, rubbing his eyes until they stung.

"You need to go lie down," Merk said. "This thing takes it out of you."

"You're not wrong about that."

Merk blinked and smiled. "Go to my hut. Your lean-to lets in too much light, and you need darkness. Sadie is there already, and she can help you rest."

Sylvan cocked his head at Merk. Sadie's role in the village seemed to be of a spiritual nature, but he was a little unsure exactly how she would help him rest.

Merk breathed out a long sigh, leaning in close to Sylvan with deep, gentle eyes. "You must have noticed Sadie treats you differently than the others."

"She's very kind to me." Sylvan had noticed, but he hadn't been sure what to make of it.

"We have a tradition, a special kind of...relationship, what you might call support. Sadie would lend you some of her strength, her calm, if you will. It will help you be refreshed."

"Well, if you think..."

"Do not worry. It is nothing sexual. Think of her as a chosen aunt, who will help nurture and support you. If you accept, of course." Merk's voice remained neutral, but Sylvan saw a spark of hope in his eye.

"I accept, with many thanks," Sylvan said, picturing Sadie's gentle smile, her gentleness toward him. He could see how much Merk wanted this for him, and his lids grew heavy, his mind eager for the darkness of sleep. "Come get me when Leo gets back, or whenever you need me."

He turned and crossed the platform, past the students, who were on a break playing some kind of game with pebbles of various colors arranged along the planks. The smell hit him even before he entered the hut: Merk's lingering body odor intermixed with stale smoke, dried herbs, and various chemical smells to form a dizzying perfume. He steeled himself with a deep breath of fresh air and walked through the reed curtain into the cool shadows of the hut. He squeezed between tables laden with various crocks and implements, most of which were of natural materials, standard *ipsis* make, but a number of glass and metal objects were mixed among them, not to mention the dozens of books stacked in odd corners. Sadie stirred from the shadows of the bed, and she rolled halfway over, her eyes still closed, emitting a rumbly sigh. Sylvan sat on a bench and quietly unlaced his sandals, wincing at the faint burn marks around the straps. He'd worn sandals instead of shoes on this outing because he expected to get his feet wet, but he was going to pay for that decision. Despite how careful he had tried to be about keeping his paint coverage intact, his time among the *ipsis* had made personal care a challenge. He was pretty sure the family skin doctor could help the burns fully heal, but he would have to wear shoes at social events back in Anari to hide his feet for a while, so everyone would know something was up.

He eased himself onto the bed, letting the breath flow out of him as he sank into the moss-covered straw, inches from Sadie, whose body heat radiated across the bed. She smiled at him through sleepy eyes, and he took a deep breath, laughing a little as he let it out.

"*You okay?*" she asked in *ipsis*.

"*I'm fine,*" he answered, glad she had asked one of the few questions he could respond to. "*You...*" He closed his eyes for a moment and put his hands under his cheek like a pillow.

"*Yes,*" she said, closing her eyes and reaching out her long arm, which she lay over his chest. Sylvan tensed for a moment, but her touch was so gentle, so comforting, and it felt nice to touch someone, to be touched. He'd hardly touched anyone on the trip except in work or by accident, and the warmth in his heart showed how much he missed it. He ran his fingers over Sadie's arm, which was strong and a little hairy, and she emitted a sound, not unlike a purr. Sadie pulled him toward her, and Sylvan turned his back to her and settled in against her large frame, feeling oddly comforted by her presence, the shelter of her body. A cocoon of security and calm seemed to emanate from her, and he grew drowsy as he sank into her warmth, letting her breath flow across his cheek as her long fingers tucked in under his ribcage.

"They're back."

Sylvan opened his eyes a crack, squinting at Merk, who stood in a triangle of blinding light from the half-open curtain. Sylvan wriggled out of Sadie's grasp, and she ran her hand over his shoulders as he sat on the edge of the bed and retied his sandals. His tin of paint was in his lean-to, but he found it hard to care at the moment. A smile bloomed on his lips. Though he was a little groggy, something of Sadie's warmth stayed with him even as her fingers withdrew, and he hadn't slept that well since leaving Anari. He looked up at Merk, whose kind eyes regarded him and Sadie with something at once paternal and a little wistful. He had noticed this look before, whenever Sadie showed Sylvan her little signs of affection, which were different from the way she touched Merk. It seemed like Merk needed him to accept Sadie's support as much as Sadie needed to offer it, and though the dynamic was unfamiliar, Sylvan felt comforted by the growing closeness between the three of them. He blinked shyly at Merk as he ducked out of the hut, and Merk handed him the Seeing Tube.

"I will have work to do to prepare the tincture, but let me know if you need anything."

"Right, well, of course." Sylvan looked down at the tube, his mind spinning as he thought of the shapes he had seen in the water. He had studied animal and plant tissue under fine lenses at the Great University, but the level of detail the Seeing Tube provided was many times greater than even the best lenses there, which had been touted as the finest in existence. There were always rumors of magical devices allowing one to see the prime elements that made up all matter, but he had never believed such a thing possible. Some people believed in magic, and those thought to be "gifted" often trained with the Endulians, who were said to be capable of impossible feats, but no one could put their finger on exactly what. Besides the light shows, he had never seen magic at work, and even then, he was convinced it was some form of northern alchemy rather than anything truly beyond the realm of science.

Leo and Ranger sat on a bench, their legs still wet from rinsing in the footbath. They both looked exhausted, but Leo's smile nearly erased the fatigue lines on his face.

"Did you find the creature?" Sylvan asked, eyeing a wide-mouthed skin in Ranger's lap.

"We did." Leo's grin almost reached his ears. "Sylvan, you wouldn't believe it. It was bigger than me! And its head..." Leo held his hands a pumpkin's width apart.

Sylvan shook his head in amazement. He had never heard of salamanders bigger than a person's arm, but since his arrival in the Living Waters, he had come to realize there was much more in the world than was written in his textbooks. He wondered, as the author of the marginalia had suggested, if Servais had really been here, since there was nothing of the sort in his book.

"Did you have to..."

Leo shook his head. "We wrangled it, and Ranger scraped some of its slime off with the dull edge of his knife. Enough to fill half this skin." He pointed with his thumb at the skin on Ranger's lap, the size of a tube squash. Leo's smile faltered for a moment. "I hope that doesn't kill it."

Sylvan flashed a grim smile. Losing its slime coating would make the creature susceptible to infection. "If it was healthy, it should be able to rebuild its coating and recover."

Merk motioned to Ranger from the door of his hut, and Leo followed Ranger, poking his head around Ranger's wide frame to look inside. Sylvan walked on soft feet past the class that was in session and found one of the big chairs with a slightly filtered view of the sun through the canopy. He scooched to the back of the chair, propped an elbow on one of the arms, and held the tube up to the light.

At first, he saw only large, blurry blobs, but after adjusting the brass dials this way and that, he was able to get the water back into focus. Not the water per se, which appeared as a liquid sparkling with fractals, but the kernels at the heart of the fractals, linking together the interlocking shapes in an infinitely repeating pattern. The shapes looked different than before, less crisp, less perfectly interwoven, as if whatever held them in that pattern was breaking down. He twisted one of the knobs further until the fractals became blurry but the kernels came into sharp focus, and he zeroed in on one of them. It was shaped like a short, fat tube with rounded ends, and dozens of filaments streaking out from its center. He tilted the tube and followed several of the filaments, which touched other filaments connected to other kernels, each at the center of a hazy fractal array. Some of the filaments moved, which he had noticed before, but others remained still, limp, falling away from the point of contact. Sylvan's breath caught as he realized what it meant.

Before, they were all moving, but now some of them had stopped, and those that still moved did so in slow pulses, like fish gasping on a dock. These were the prime elements of the *sitri's* bodies, and they were dying, one by one, now that they were separated from the whole, or from the water. He lowered the tube into his lap, covering his eyes against the sun glaring down through the trees. These tiny creatures, if that was the correct word, could be a form of the *parthi*, theoretical organisms too small to be seen with any lens. Some scientists even attributed sickness to invasions of malicious *parthi* in the body, though most of his professors spoke of the theory, if at all, with the same derision they leveled at philosophical medicine. Sylvan had studied a book of such theories, and though the author's intent was to prove how impossible the idea was, his arguments had seemed no stronger than those he sought to contradict.

A distant roar pierced the forest, and Sylvan sat forward, cocking his ear to figure out where it had come from. Another roar sounded, more high-pitched, and the clatter of wood, and a full-throated scream. This time he was sure: the sounds were coming from the direction of the lake. Ranger appeared, Leo hot on his tail, and a group of adult *ipsis* gathered around him as he spoke in a burst of rapid speech, which Sylvan could not make out, except for the last word, *Now*. Merk and Sadie helped Peree herd the children into the largest hut, and two stout *ipsis* moved to block the entrance with their shovel-spears once the children were inside.

Sylvan slipped off the chair in a daze as shouts rang out all around him. Gilea grabbed his elbow and dragged him toward the large hut, where Sadie gestured from the doorway with her long arms, her eyes wide with concern. Sylvan saw movement from the forest to his right, and four *ipsis* leaped up onto the platform. Two of them rushed the large hut and the others advanced on him and Gilea, spears jutting forward, blocking their path to the hut. Gilea shoved Sylvan backward, crouching with her hands in claw shape, facing the *ipsis*. Their faces were wet and shiny, their pupils wide and black, swallowing their irises. One of them lunged at Gilea with his spear, and she slipped aside as the spear thrust forward. She spun her leg around and kicked the spear sideways, and it flew from the surprised *ipsis'* grasp and clattered on the deck. She rolled underneath the *ipsis* as he reached out to grab her, kicking him in the crotch, then sweeping his legs out from under him as he doubled over in pain.

The other *ipsis* jabbed at her with his spear, and her body bent backward beneath the bladed point, which jabbed again, and she fell, scrambling back to stay out of its reach. The *ipsis* charged her, then fell suddenly on his face as Leo stood behind him, holding a stick with a loop wrapped around the *ipsis'* ankle. Water splashed onto the wood, and the *ipsis* appeared dazed for a moment, then the water flowed back over his head and he scrambled to his feet, whirling around to face Leo, who had dropped his stick. Sylvan noticed a wide skin slung over the *ipsis'* shoulder, with water snaking up to cover his head. He must have been controlled by a *sitri* contained in that skin. The *ipsis* that Gilea had kicked was on his feet again, moving with shuffle-steps toward her, feinting and jabbing with his spear as she backed up near the edge of the platform.

Leo gave a cry as the *ipsis* lunged for him with his spear, and Leo tumbled out of the way. He ducked behind a bench, which the *ipsis* threw out of the way as if it weighed nothing and jabbed down with his spear, which struck the deck next to Leo's head. Sylvan dashed toward the *ipsis*, half-dizzy with fear, but he knew what he had to do. The *ipsis* yanked the spear from the wood and advanced on Leo, who was backed into a corner. Sylvan took two quiet steps as he drew his knife, pulled on the strap holding the skin to the *ipsis'* back, and slashed the strap with his blade, cutting it clean through and digging into the *ipsis'* shoulder. The *ipsis* whirled around, his eyes wide with confusion and rage, then faltered for a moment as Leo pulled on the strap from behind. The wetness drained from his face as Leo yanked the skin off his back and tossed it off the platform into the forest.

A shriek erupted from in front of the hut, where two *ipsis* lay on the ground bleeding, and one slumped against a pillar, doubled over in pain. The fourth swung the curtain wide and put one foot in the doorway, then a long arm shot out of the hut's dark interior, plastering the *ipsis'* face with yellow powder, which billowed into the air around his head. He fell to his knees, water sloshing onto the deck, then flowing up his body into the skin hanging from his shoulder. Sylvan eyed Leo, who rushed forward, knife in hand. Leo severed the strap and tossed the skin into the forest, and the *ipsis* hunched over, holding his head in his hands.

"Leo!" Sylvan cried as water arced out of the pack of one of the prone *ipsis* and flowed up Leo's torso. Leo took two quick steps backward and did a backflip, scattering the water across the deck. Sadie bolted out of the hut with a reed broom, sending showers of water this way and that as she swept the broom hard across the deck. She jammed the broom into the skin attached to the prone *ipsis'* back, flinging splashes of water into the air, then swept the deck with vigorous strokes as the water landed. Her right hand was coated with yellow powder, and the *ipsis* she had smacked with the powder sat with his head between his knees, rubbing his eyes and moaning.

Sylvan heard scuffling behind him and whirled around to see Gilea sprawled out against a bench, her chest heaving, and an *ipsis* churning through the boggy forest in the direction of the lake.

Chapter Thirty

Temi pressed the tips of her tented fingers together, and they turned as if of their own accord in the direction of the lake. The sounds of battle had died down, and the forest was quiet again. Something tugged at her mind, and she crawled out from under the chair where she had hidden when the controlled *ipsis* stormed the village. She had sensed that they were different, even before she saw their wet faces, as if she were faintly connected to them. She stood up, dusting off her tattered dress out of habit as Gilea pounded up, out of breath, and took her by the arms.

"Thank gods, we thought you'd been taken."

Temi put her hands on Gilea's forearms, pushing them down gently. "We have to go." She pointed with her head toward the lake.

"You think it's safe there, after what happened before?" Gilea's plaintive tone belied her otherwise calm demeanor.

“You think it’s safer here? Sage and the Pillar will protect us. And Ranger and the others.”

A group of six *ipsis* came running through the forest, bowing quickly to the group before rushing over to where Sadie was tending the *ipsis* wounded in the fight, including those who had been controlled. They spoke with Ranger, who pointed this way and that, then took off sprinting through the forest toward the lake.

“There are ten of them now, plus Sadie, Merk, and Peree.” Gilea’s voice pleaded. “It’s safer here.”

Temi took a step back, lowering her eyes for a moment. Gilea would understand. She was the only one who could. “Sage is calling me, or maybe the Pillar, I’m not sure. But they need me there. I can’t explain it but I can feel them.”

Gilea put her hands together and pressed them to her nose, breathing in deeply.

“Okay,” she said after a pause. “Let me get Leo and Sylvan.”

“I’m staying,” Sylvan said from behind Gilea. He stepped forward and flashed Temi a warm smile, lifting the Seeing Tube in one hand. “Merk and I may have found out something important about the *sitri*. We need a little more time.”

Gilea closed her eyes and nodded. “Leo will stay with you. Tell Merk and the others.”

Sylvan blinked at her, then at Temi. “Be safe.”

A female *ipsis* Temi didn’t recognize stepped from behind a tree as they approached the lake, waving them forward with her non-spear hand. She stuck two fingers in her mouth and gave a piercing whistle, which was returned from above. When they reached the top of the embankment, they saw Ranger and two muscular *ipsis* standing on the opposite end of the lake, in the direction of the river. One of the *ipsis* trotted over and escorted them to where Ranger was standing as the big canoe churned across the lake. One of the *ipsis* paddling had a square of green leaves strapped over his shoulder, and he winced with every stroke. Temi watched as Ranger touched foreheads with Gilea, wondering if she could communicate with any *ipsis* in the same way, now that she had communed with Sage and the Pillar.

Gilea shook her head as if to clear her thoughts as she pulled away from Ranger and turned toward Temi.

"They're expecting us." Gilea locked eyes with Temi. "Expecting you."

The canoe reached the shore, and Temi ignored Gilea's outstretched hand, hopping into the heavy craft and settling down onto the moss coating the bottom. Gilea stepped in after, then Ranger pushed the front end of the boat away from shore, and the *ipsis* steered the craft toward the island. Temi scanned the water for any unusual movement but saw none. When they reached the dock, Temi stepped out, holding out her hand to Gilea, who flashed a warm smile as she took it and let Temi help her up.

The Pillar stood staring at Sage, who was at their usual place in the center of the pool. Sage flashed a pattern of dots at Temi, who approached the water's edge in response without thinking. Sage glided across the pool, stopping a few feet from her. More dots bloomed on their surface, an invitation. Temi blinked, and Sage moved closer, the orb atop their body stretching out into a long liquid arc, which stopped inches from Temi's face. Temi closed her eyes and leaned forward, and her legs trembled as she felt Sage's cool, wet touch on her forehead. Her body felt light, like the slightest breeze would knock her over, and she wished Gilea were there to support her, to keep her from falling out of herself. Warm hands touched the sides of her neck, and she felt Gilea's presence, the heat of her body, the calm control of her mind, grounding Temi in place. She wondered briefly if she had called to Gilea, or if Gilea had just known what she needed. She kept her eyes closed but opened her mind.

Before her was a vast expanse of liquid blue, with ripples around the edges, which slowly grew into wavelike humps, rolling with infinite slowness toward the center. A face appeared amid the watery folds, like Temi's own face seen through a dreamlike mirror. Dots and circles appeared around the face, blooming, shifting, and fading. There were no words, but Temi felt the message, understood on some level deeper than language, beyond thought or emotion. She saw a great shallow pool, divided by rocks into hundreds of squares, and in each square a swirl, slowly growing as they spun, wavering but turning ever faster. The edges of her vision blurred, and the swirls rose up into humps, watery tentacles slithering over the rocks and pulling them into the next square. They moved in chaotic unison, racing to a corner of the pool, toward a channel running around the edges, which swarmed and roiled with hundreds of *sitri.* A lone *ipsis* dug into the bank, with *sitri* swarming all around it. Behind the *ipsis,* separated by a narrow strip of earth, Temi could see a creek snaking its way through the forest toward the river, which glittered in the distance.

Temi slipped half out of the vision as a sad pause sank over her, over the space she shared with Sage. No shapes or patterns disturbed her thoughts as they wandered in and out of her mind. There was a reason Sage had called to her, why they needed her. There was a reason they were talking to her and not the *ipsis.* And Sage could not, or would not, tell her exactly what it was.

Be prepared to do what must be done, the ripples in her mind whispered, then Sage went blank and faded from Temi's consciousness. Temi opened her eyes and saw the tubular arch re-forming into a sphere atop Sage's humanoid form, which flashed three times in rapid succession, then went blank again and glided back to the center of the pool. Gilea let go of her neck and took a step back, and Temi felt the intensity of her gaze as she turned around, but Gilea said nothing.

"They showed me something, but I'm not quite sure what it was." She flashed Gilea a hard look, not sure how much she should say in front of the Pillar, if they even understood, if they even needed speech to understand.

"We should talk to Merk," Gilea said, seeming to return Temi's stare in kind, then faltering, cocking her head to the side. She turned to face the tunnel, putting a protective arm behind her back. Temi heard crashing in the forest, followed by shouts, then a single blood-chilling scream, deep and powerful, a sound only an *ipsis* could make. Temi moved close behind Gilea, who stood stone still, muscles tensed. Footsteps pounding across earth, more shouts, grunts, then another scream. The sounds of fighting and exertion echoed from several directions, but Temi could see nothing beyond the walls of the island's enclosure.

"It must be more of the controlled *ipsis* like the ones who attacked the village," Gilea said. "They'll have a hard time getting across the water though."

A large splash sounded from the lake, followed by a lot of grunting, then another big splash.

"Stay right here," Gilea said, then sprinted into the tunnel and out of sight. Temi looked over at the Pillar, who had moved near where the channel entered the pool and stood staring into the tunnel. Sage remained in humanoid form, water flowing evenly over their surface as if nothing in the world were wrong. Gilea burst back out of the tunnel, holding a long wooden gaffe with a bone hook on one end.

"Two groups of *ipsis* are rowing across on logs, eight of them in total, all controlled." She made a circular gesture around her face. "I don't know how long those two guards will be able to hold them off."

A splash sounded from the lake, followed by shouts and cries, and more splashing. The sounds grew closer, echoing through the tunnel. Gilea stepped forward, holding the gaffe out sideways. Temi moved along the pool's edge to the far end, putting as much distance between herself and the tunnel as possible, while remaining close to Sage, who she felt instinctively would protect her.

An *ipsis* burst out of the tunnel, barked something over his shoulder, and four more emerged. Two of them charged the Pillar, and two lumbered across the courtyard toward Gilea, while one stayed behind, guarding the tunnel. Everything happened so fast Temi could hardly keep track of it. The two *ipsis* charging the Pillar stopped suddenly, dropping their spears and falling to their knees, their hands gripping their heads. The other two advanced toward Gilea, who braced the gaffe against her arm and deflected one spear, swinging the gaffe up to whack the *ipsis* in the face. He shook his head and shouted, and the other *ipsis* darted around Gilea, running along the edge of the pool. She swung the gaffe around, hooking his foot, and he tumbled halfway into the water as the gaffe slipped out of Gilea's grasp. She spun around, ducking under the other *ipsis'* spear and tumbling past him, reaching up toward his pack but falling back as he swung his spear around. The *ipsis* in the water muscled out with a roar, picked up his floating spear, and charged toward Temi.

Temi froze, watching helplessly as the creature bounded toward her. A glittering tentacle shot out from Sage, and the *ipsis'* spear clattered to the ground as his arm was enwrapped in a watery sheen. The *ipsis* tipped over and fell into the water, which erupted in frenzied thrashing as Sage dragged the *ipsis* under. Temi heard Gilea cry out, and turned to see her pinned to the ground, with the other *ipsis'* spear jutting from her chest.

Temi's body moved of its own accord, sprinting

toward the *ipsis,* who braced against the spear as Gilea's legs flailed and kicked at him. The edges of Temi's vision went dark as she leaped up onto the *ipsis'* back, pressing her forehead into the back of his head. Power surged through her, and she felt the surprise of the *sitri* controlling the *ipsis* quickly turning to fear as she squeezed with her mind, like wringing a towel dry, and the water flew off the *ipsis'* head and boiled out of the skin slung over his shoulders, splashing into a wide puddle on the ground around Gilea. The *ipsis* staggered back, letting go of his spear, and Temi slipped off his back, whirling to Gilea, who grasped the spear weakly, her chest heaving as clouds of red bloomed in the puddle surrounding her.

Temi turned toward the *ipsis*, consumed with rage. The creature's eyes grew wide with fear, and he dropped to his knees, saying something in his language as he held up his palms. The Pillar appeared, and the *ipsis* scuttled back, then moved to sit against the wall, burying his head in his hands. The water in the pool went still, and Temi knelt over Gilea's face, which had taken on a waxy look, her eyes wide and distant.

"Temi," Gilea whispered. "Temi."

Temi took Gilea's face in her hands, hot tears streaming and dripping down onto Gilea. Temi looked up as the Pillar knelt beside her, their body glistening and wet, and their eyes flashed with calm and compassion. Water flowed down in a column from the Pillar's chest, surrounding the spear wound, and flashed a pattern of dots and circles. Temi stood up without a thought, braced her foot on Gilea's shoulder, and yanked out the spear, then fell backward with horror as blood spurted out from the wound.

Chapter Thirty One

Gilea's body arched, then collapsed with the pain, which morphed into an icy numbness spreading from her chest up the back of her neck, a cold so intense it was hot again. The only part of her that was genuinely warm was the skin of her torso, where blood pumped and flowed from the hole in her chest. Then another wave washed over her, a literal one this time, as the water surrounding the Pillar's head slipped off as a single mass, splashing over the wound. But rather than flowing off onto the ground, the mass began swirling, grinding against Gilea's chest, boring into the hole. Gilea's thoughts floated upward, away from the tumult around her heart, to the Pillar, whose intense gaze was fixed on the action of the *sitri,* of Sage. Gilea felt her mouth widen as comfort flowed over her mind like the smell of pitch and saltwater, of tri-fries, of her mother's musk-wood incense. Her memory slipped as a sudden heat built in her chest, combined with a pulsing sensation, but she pushed through the sensation and returned to Rontaia. Only now she was walking on the docks, arm in arm with Temi, who pulled her from one sight to the next with contagious joy. A seagull swooped down for Temi's tri-fry, and she whirled away from it and fell into Gilea's arms. She looked up at Gilea, crumbs stuck to her laughing lips, her eyes wide with delight.

Temi's eyes froze in that instant, and Gilea was pulled away like a child sucked into an undertow. She crashed back into her body, took in a huge gasp of air, then let it out with a moan.

"Oh, gods Gilea are you—what—" Temi's hands hovered over Gilea's chest and her fingers pulled at a torn hole in the fabric, then retreated to cover her mouth. Temi's wide eyes overflowed, looking from Gilea's face to where the hole in her body used to be. Gilea's fingers found the spot, which was like scar tissue, but hot to the touch. Feeling returned to her entire body in a flash, and she clutched her elbows, forming a bowl with her shoulders and arms as if that could somehow soothe the burning inside her chest.

Temi crouched on the ground next to Gilea, putting one arm around her shoulder. She lay down on her side facing Gilea, leaning in so their foreheads touched.

"I've got you, I've got you," Temi whispered, and other words too, but Gilea had partially withdrawn from her physical body to dull the pain, and she heard Temi as if through a heavy door. She managed to roll toward Temi slightly, and Temi's body heat radiated into her, pulling her back to the moment, to the pain, which still burned, but with less intensity. Gilea took in a shallow breath, and she felt Temi breathe in with her, then out. With each deeper breath, the pain lessened, until after a time sound returned, first birds, then Temi's soft breathing, the sound of water trickling into the channel. Voices, *ipsis*, discussing, concerned, but not angry voices. She let go of Temi's shoulder and rolled flat on her back, wondering if she had the strength to sit up, or if she even wanted to.

Temi's warm hand touched her cheek, then Temi stood and walked away, Gilea's hand reaching in vain for her as she disappeared. Gilea rolled her eyes up, as she could not easily move her head, and saw the Pillar lower their head toward Temi, and their foreheads pressed together. Gilea closed her eyes, focusing her energy on the pulsing within her chest, around her heart, which beat slowly, as if being squeezed by a gentle, invisible hand. In time the pressure diminished, and her heart felt free, but weak, fluttering every third or fourth beat as it struggled to maintain cadence on its own. Warm hands slid under her neck and knees, and she was lifted up and carried to a bench covered with soft moss. She opened her eyes halfway and Ranger's big eyes stared into hers as he laid her down, easing his fingers out from beneath her. Temi's face appeared, then her hand, warm on Gilea's cheek, and she spoke, but Gilea could not hear the words. She felt Temi's gaze, the soft touch of her hand, the pleading look in her eyes. Gilea smiled, wrapping her fingers loosely around Temi's wrist as the blue-gray sky faded to smoky blackness, and she released into it.

Gilea awoke to Leo's face, which burst into a smile as she opened her eyes.

"Gil," he said, his eyes lighting up as worry washed from them. "You're back." He gripped her hand in his, and she squeezed, then released, pushing up gently onto her elbows. Her chest twinged at the effort, but the pain subsided as she held her position, and she sat up, with the support of Leo's other hand on her back.

"Water," she croaked.

Leo held up one finger, then rushed away and returned with a cup brimming with water, splashing a bit on her leg as he handed it to her. She took a small sip, let it unseal her sticky mouth, then drank, each sip larger, until she had drained the cup, which she set down with shaky hands. Temi appeared next to Leo, her eyes oddly calm, and flashed a gentle smile. Gilea smiled back, then suddenly noticed the absence of her other charge, and panic stung her heart.

"Where's Sylvan?" Gilea fixed Leo with a stare.

"He's with Merk and Sadie in the village. He's fine. More than fine, actually. They're working on a tincture to..." He looked around and his voice turned lower. "To protect them against being controlled by the *sitri*. But they took a break so Sadie could make this for you."

He held up a little reed vial with a stopper but kept it just out of her reach.

"Sadie said you need to study this before you drink." He pulled a wooden disk from his pocket and handed it to Gilea. It was smooth, as if it had been polished, and the center bore a design, engraved into the wood. She recognized it instantly: the eye within the eye, an Endulian symbol for self-awareness. Gilea studied the symbol, which looked to have been burned into the disc, with more delicacy than she might have expected from the *ipsis*. There were even eyelashes and dozens of thin lines in the iris of the outer eye. Gilea closed her eyes to slits, focusing on the outer eye, as she had done in meditation many times before, circling the iris five times with her mind before sliding through the pupil into the inner eye. She let the smaller iris frame her vision, and as she stared into the inner pupil it seemed to expand, drawing her deeper, until the rest of the design disappeared, and she was staring into pure blackness. A point appeared in the darkness, sending ripples to the edges then ricocheting back toward the center, which grew calm, shiny, and her face appeared reflected as in a still lake. She closed her eyes, unstoppered the reed tube, and downed the bitter liquid.

Gilea lay back down, glancing up at Leo and Temi and giving them a soft blink.

“I have some work to do.” She could feel the tincture taking effect, her awareness drawing inward, toward her heart. Leo squeezed her shoulder, then drifted away, but Temi’s face still hovered above her, hazy, as if seen through a dirty window.

“I’ll be right here,” Temi said, curling her fingers around Gilea’s. Gilea blinked at her, then let her hand relax into Temi’s, and her mind drifted away, deep down inside herself.

Gilea awoke to Temi’s sleeping face resting against the moss next to hers, her body slumped over at an awkward angle. Gilea slid her hand out of Temi’s, then lowered her legs as she pushed up on her elbows, as quietly as she could. She felt almost whole, despite what she had gone through, and echoes of Sage floated in the corners of her mind. She had heard of Endulian masters who possessed great healing powers, but what Sage had done was beyond anything she had imagined possible. It made her wonder if the Endulian practice didn’t come from the *sitri* and the *ipsis*, rather than the other way around, as she had assumed.

It would go a long way to explaining the Pillar, who stood at their usual post, staring at Sage’s humanoid fountain shape. Gilea had seen Endulian masters at the temple in Rontaia stare at a blank wall for hours at a time, in a state of waking meditation, but her own practice, which she had learned at smaller temples outside the city and further developed on her own, involved more movement.

“You’re up,” came Temi’s sleepy voice from behind her. “Like, up, up.”

“I feel...alive.” Gilea turned to Temi, smiling as she saw the pattern from the moss imprinted on her right cheek. “Hungry, though. You think they got any of those bladegrass patties around?”

Temi shook her head. "I already asked. I think the Pillar only eats once a day, in the evening."

"Well, it shouldn't be too long then." Gilea looked at the weakening sunlight, then her head swiveled back to Temi. "Wait, you asked how?"

Temi looked down as if embarrassed, then looked back up shyly, tapping her forehead.

"I guess I can do that telepathy thing now, with the Pillar at least. Ever since—"

"I know. That's amazing." Gilea closed her eyes for a moment, remembering the long years she had spent training just to learn how to share emotions; sharing thoughts was another level entirely, one only the masters were capable of. "What else did they tell you?"

Temi glanced over at the Pillar, screwing her mouth up, then nodded. Gilea could feel her hesitancy without even trying, as if they now had a running emotional link. She had only ever felt that with Amini, one of the masters she'd studied with.

"They have a plan to strike at the...I think you would call them Spreaders? The *sitri* that want to expand the Living Waters. The ones that want us dead."

Gilea took a step toward her. She could tell the plan was troubling Temi. "What is it?"

Temi shook her head. "They didn't say exactly, but I don't think it involves us. I think we're meant to stay here." *But not Leo.* Gilea heard the words as a whisper in her mind.

"What about Leo?" Gilea asked, her heart suddenly feeling constricted.

Temi's eyes widened, and she touched her head absently. "Sorry, I...I didn't realize I had..."

"It's okay. What about Leo?"

"They're going to send him on some kind of mission."

"A dangerous one?"

Temi nodded weakly. "I think it's...something they

can't do themselves, not the *sitri* or the *ipsis*. Something... forbidden, for them."

Gilea's fingers twisted together as tears threatened to form in her eyes.

"Sounds right up his alley."

Temi blinked, stepping toward Gilea. "The Pillar is very sad about all of it, and Sage too. It makes me sad to think about it, and I'm not even sure what it is." She reached out and touched Gilea's arm. "But if the plan is successful, I think we'll be able to leave."

Gilea nodded, gripping Temi's forearm. "No matter what happens, I'll make sure we all get back." She paused, watching Temi's eyes drop, as a wave of melancholy flowed from her like spreading fog. "If that's what you want." *Rontaia*, she thought, pushing the word through the air toward Temi, whose brows knit together.

"I don't know what I want anymore. I want..." Temi sighed, letting go of Gilea and turning away. She stood still for a moment, and when she turned back around, her eyes had grown wider, more peaceful. "I want to see Rontaia, I do, but..."

Gilea smiled. Their connection had grown deep indeed if Temi had heard the city's name. "I will take you."

"But I need to go home first. I can't just leave my mother alone, and I have an idea how I think I can help."

Gilea gripped Temi's elbows and leaned her face close. Wanting to kiss her. Knowing she could not.

"Whenever you're ready. I'll wait for you."

Chapter Thirty Two

Sylvan held the reed vials while Sadie carefully poured three thick drops of the almost sparkly tincture into each of them. Merk and Sadie had made it from the salamander slime Leo and Ranger had retrieved, mixed with some other ingredients. When they had exhausted their supply and filled and stoppered twenty-two of the vials, Sadie left to get Merk, and Sylvan sniffed the mortar Sadie had been pouring out of. The mortar smelled of pepper, citrus, and something musky he couldn't quite guess. A silvery sheen coated the bottom, which Sylvan was fairly sure was from quicksilver. He knew alchemical processes often used it, but it was considered too toxic for human consumption. Maybe the *ipsis* were more tolerant of it than humans, or perhaps their situation was so dire it was worth the risk. He wondered what else was in it, and he'd tried to get a closer look as Merk and Sadie mixed the concoction, but they had performed most of the work inside their hut as he sat outside holding the Seeing Tube up to the sun to study the tiny creatures inside the *sitri* sample. All but a few of the creatures had stopped moving, and those remaining showed only the faintest pulses.

Merk appeared at his elbow, reaching for the tube with his long, soft fingers.

"They're almost all dead," Merk said as he held it up to the sun.

"Which got me thinking," Sylvan said, his mind spinning. "What would happen if..."

Merk lowered the tube and his head craned down to Sylvan's level, his eyes serious. "If?"

"Well, if you could spare just the tiniest drop of quicksilver, I'd like to see what happens if we add it to the water in the tube."

Merk's eyes narrowed, then widened again. "I haven't much left since we made the tincture, and I'm not sure when I'll be able to get more. Maybe you could use the film stuck to the bottom of the mortar?"

"Well I would, but I'm not sure what the other ingredients would do. I'm not even sure what the other ingredients are, which, I know, you probably can't tell me."

Merk grunted a laugh. "The quicksilver helps the slime to bond with the mucous membranes. The rest is essences of bark and a flower, to thin it out, and ease its passage through the body. What is your theory?"

"Quicksilver is toxic to humans, and many other organisms. Is it not to the *ipsis* as well?"

"It is, in sufficient doses, and it accumulates in the body over time, but at the level of the tincture, it's reasonably safe."

"Well, I thought it might kill the...tiny organisms, or whatever they are, that make up the *sitri*."

Merk held the tube up to the sun again, then handed it to Sylvan, an odd smile on his huge lips. "I don't think the other ingredients will interfere with your experiment."

Sylvan sat on the bench, secured the Seeing Tube in the little wooden rack that seemed designed for this exact purpose, and unscrewed the cap. He used a tiny silver spoon from Merk's odd collection of tools and scraped a minuscule amount from the bottom of the mortar, then held it over the tube for a long time as it slowly formed a small drop, which fell into the tube. He reclosed the tube, shook it, and held it up to the sun.

At first, Sylvan thought he was looking through the wrong end, or that he'd turned the dials out of whack. The water inside the tube seemed to shimmer and shake like the leaves of the forest beyond fluttering in the breeze. Except there was no breeze, and there were no leaves between the tube and the sun. The water in the tube was pulsing, the fractal patterns swelling, multiplying, and recombining in a frenzied dance. He lowered the tube and held it out to Merk.

"Merk, look here, it's..." Sylvan trailed off as he saw the knowing look in Merk's eyes. "You knew?"

Merk blinked, taking the tube and unscrewing the cap. "Quicksilver speeds their growth, beyond measure." He dumped the drop of water onto the floor, and it splashed, then re-formed into a drop half the size of a pinky nail. The drop quivered, then began spinning in a slow circle. Filaments rose up out of the center of the swirling drop, which flattened and expanded to a thin disk the size of a two-lep coin. Merk stepped away, and Sylvan bent over for a closer look. The disk began to move along the grooves in the wood, spinning and oozing forward, its filaments bending on all sides to touch the surface as it moved. Sylvan stood up as Merk returned, holding a reed broom in his hands. Sylvan gasped as Merk lowered the broom and erased the drop with several hard sweeps in different directions until nothing remained but a damp spot on the boards.

"We need to move my lab," Merk said. "They will come for it, for me."

"The...Spreaders?"

Merk nodded. "I have only a small amount of quicksilver, but they do not need much. Once they realize I have some, they will not stop until they get it. And once they have it, there may not be much we can do."

"Because they would use it to grow?"

Merk blinked. "The *sitri* grow slowly from *duni*, over a long period of time, usually at least ten years, less if they are tended with great care. They stay in the nursery for two or three years until they reach a certain stage of development. Some substances can speed their growth somewhat, but with pure quicksilver, they can grow a thousand times as fast."

Sylvan snapped his fingers. "That explains...we saw a group of swirls near Guluch. They swamped an alchemist's lab and made away with all her quicksilver."

Merk's face hardened into a frown. "How long ago was this?"

"Just before we came here. I've kind of lost track of time, but maybe a week?"

Merk closed his eyes, letting out a deep, rumbly sigh. "This explains a lot. Come, we have little time. We must get to the Pillar right away." He called out in his language, a long, twisted sound that Sylvan had figured out was Sadie's real name, though he could not pronounce it. Sadie emerged from the hut, reaching them in several long, graceful strides, her face twisted with worry. Merk and Sadie exchanged a few words, and Sadie flashed Sylvan a hopeful smile.

"We will need to bring as much of my lab as we can to the lake." Merk touched Sadie on the shoulder as she turned back toward the hut. "Can you help us carry a few things?"

Sylvan followed Sadie, who laid out a strange basket

on the bed, made of two wide boards attached to webs of mesh looped around long poles. She started placing objects on the boards: covered ceramic pots, books, skins, unusual brass instruments, and an elaborate glass alembic, which she wrapped in several layers of moss and laid carefully on top. Merk stood in the doorway, barking out a few words, and Sadie added several more things to the basket, then picked up one end of the poles and motioned Sylvan with her eyes to the other end. He hefted his end, which was much heavier than expected, and shuffled out the door, feeling Sadie lower her arms to take most of the weight.

"Want a hand with that?" Leo appeared out of nowhere, his mouth spread in a wide grin, and took the poles from Sylvan's hands one at a time. "I figure we need your brain more than your arms right now."

"Your friend is not wrong," Merk said, craning his neck around to look at Sylvan. "Walk with me."

They followed behind Leo and Sadie, who were accompanied by two of the stout *ipsis* Sylvan had come to think of as diggers. He had not yet figured out if they were a subspecies or some other variation, or if their muscles were just bulky from doing physical labor, compared to Ranger and the others, who were leaner and, he thought, more flexible. The diggers certainly walked differently, with their weight more centered, as opposed to the others, who tended to lead with their long legs.

"What kind of plan do you think the Pillar will come up with?" asked Sylvan as he walked alongside Merk.

Merk sucked in his lips, shaking his head. "I cannot see any way to counteract what is happening, but if there is a way, between the Pillar and Sage, they will know."

"What exactly *is* happening? Our lives are at stake here, and yours too. If you tell me a little more, maybe I can help."

Merk's head turned and his eyes probed Sylvan's for

a long moment, then blinked softly.

"There is a faction among the leadership of the *sitri* that seeks to expand the Living Waters, partly in response to the increase in human activity and pollution upriver. For this, they would need to vastly grow their numbers. They would also need the cooperation of the *ipsis*, for they rely on us to tend the bladegrass that filters the water and creates the conditions for them to thrive. They have made a separate nursery near the other *ipsis* village, where they have obviously taken to controlling some of the *ipsis*, as we have seen. They are adding quicksilver to the water in the nursery to stimulate the *duni's* growth. They started with the red dyes and powders from Endulai, which contain some mercury in the form of cinnabar, but it was not enough, so they looked for other sources. They sank a ship carrying a load of ink, which sped up their process considerably, but pure quicksilver would speed things up exponentially. We may already be too late."

Sylvan stroked his beard, which had started the trip as a neat goatee but now spread unevenly across his face like mussels on a dock. "If quicksilver makes them grow, I wonder what makes them stop?" He racked his brain to recall basic chemistry lessons he'd had years before, but it had never been his strong suit.

"They cannot live in saltwater, or water that is too fouled with human sewage and pollution," Merk said, his arm straining on his cane as he made his way through the mucky forest. "Though I don't see how that helps us."

Sylvan could almost feel dormant nerves in his brain re-activating as he recalled an offhand comment made by one of his professors about quicksilver.

"Are there any natural sources of sulfur around here that you know of?" His professor had mentioned cleaning up a quicksilver spill by throwing powdered sulfur on it, which bonded to form a relatively inert compound.

Merk squinted, licked his lips, then turned his head toward Sylvan. "There is a hot spring not far off in the swamp. We go there for certain...rituals."

"How concentrated is it?" It would take a lot of sulfur to do any good, and he wondered if the water would suffice.

"The spring itself is moderately concentrated, but the rock around it is crusted yellow with sulfur." He turned his head to the ground, his face tense and pensive.

"What's wrong?"

Merk let out a sigh. "What you are suggesting may do more than slow their growth. It may kill them."

"Correct me if I'm wrong, but didn't they try to kill Sage, and my friends and me, and a number of the *ipsis* as well?"

"The Spreaders may have to be rooted out, but to stop this thing, we would need to eliminate more than just the *sitri*."

"The *duni*?" Sylvan said in a low voice.

Merk's head dipped slowly. "Such a thing cannot be done. It would be like killing their children. Even those inclined toward our side would have trouble accepting this."

They walked in silence the rest of the way to the lake. Sylvan tried to puzzle out the relationship between the *ipsis* and the *sitri*. Clearly, not all *sitri* were Spreaders, but he wondered if even the *ipsis* could tell the difference. And Merk had mentioned another *ipsis* village, near where the Spreaders had their nursery. Some of the *ipsis* might have been sympathetic to the Spreaders' cause, or perhaps the *sitri* merely controlled them. If the Spreaders were using quicksilver to speed the growth of the *duni,* they would quickly grow into *sitri,* though how that worked was beyond Sylvan's imagining.

A half-dozen *ipsis,* including Ranger, guarded the perimeter of the mound leading up to the lake, looking equal parts tense and fatigued. Sylvan and Leo sat in the front end of the huge canoe, while Sadie and Merk leaned against each other in the back. Two burly *ipsis* paddled them across the lake, where two more *ipsis* waved them through the tunnel.

Temi lay on a moss-covered bench, her arm draped over her eyes, while Gilea sat in what looked like wakeful meditation, staring blankly at the *sitri* in the center of the pool, whose surface flowed and swirled in gentle patterns. The Pillar reached them in a few long strides, then leaned in to touch foreheads with Merk. Merk's cane wobbled, and his face contorted in what looked like pain. Sadie glided up and supported his cane arm, and her head sagged low as she stood holding him. Her eyes found Sylvan's, and his heart clenched to see the deep sorrow etched into her features.

Chapter Thirty Three

Leo watched as Merk pulled away from the Pillar, leaning heavily on Sadie, and turned to face him, shuffling on the stone like a lame horse. His face was grim, and his eyes fell heavily on Leo.

"I cannot give voice to what you must do. It is forbidden." Merk's head fell, then rose again, slowly. "I can tell you the way, but these words cannot be uttered by any *ipsis*."

"I will say the words." Temi stood up from the bench, her eyes deep and distant. "If the Pillar will consent to touch minds with me again." She held out her palm to Gilea, who looked ready to leap in front of Temi and press her forehead into the Pillar's. Leo had never seen Gilea like this, out of control, and it was more than a little disconcerting.

"Temi, are you sure—" Gilea began, but Temi's gaze stopped her in mid-sentence.

“I am sure.” Temi stepped to the Pillar, closed her eyes, and leaned up with her forehead. The Pillar’s armless body angled awkwardly as their head lowered on their long neck to Temi’s level, and their foreheads pressed together. Leo watched Temi’s face, which relaxed after the first moment of contact, then grew tenser as they remained connected, until at last, she broke away, gasping and leaning on her knees. She looked for all the world like she was going to throw up, but her breath steadied after a while, and she stood up and beckoned Leo toward the far end of the pool with a tilt of her head. Leo followed her with a growing sense of dread as she walked with light steps, almost seeming to glide across the stones. When they got to where the fountain that was Sage blocked their view of Merk, she fixed her piercing eyes on him. Leo did not recognize the woman who stood before him, so different from the painted princess who had come aboard the raft only two weeks before. It was as if she had aged ten years, and her eyes thirty.

“They want you to poison the nursery with sulfur, to kill the growing *duni* before they can metamorphose into *sitri*.”

Leo swallowed. “Kill them all?”

Temi closed her eyes. “The Spreaders have a special nursery where they’ve been using quicksilver to heighten their growth. Sage showed me before, but I didn’t understand what it was. Within days, hundreds of *duni* will transform into *sitri*, and the Spreaders will overrun the Living Waters, and beyond. They could even threaten Endulai before long.”

Leo’s mouth twisted, and he shook his head to clear the sour taste. This takeover, if it happened, might be a natural evolution in the *sitri* and *ipsis* societies, and in the environment. Perhaps it was just the inevitable result of the human activity along the river, the ecosystem’s attempt to restore balance. He wasn’t sure if it was right to intervene; in fact, he was pretty sure it wasn't.

"That would explain them attacking that alchemist's shop," he said, stalling.

Temi nodded. "Yes, and the inkworks too, come to think of it. They use cinnabar to make the red ink, and it's full of mercury." She stared at Sage for a moment, then snapped her eyes back to Leo's.

"They'll kill us, Leo. You, me, Sylvan, Gilea, not to mention Sage, the Pillar, Merk, Sadie. All of us."

Leo looked down at his hands. "So we kill their babies to save our skins?" Tears formed in his eyes as he thought of the swirls, whose mystery had drawn him here in the first place. He had only ever killed to eat or to defend himself, and he was not sure if he could do it.

"Not all of them. Just the ones in the secret nursery. The ones they've been feeding quicksilver."

"Why me?"

Temi leaned around Sage to glance at the group. "The *ipsis* can't do it. It's forbidden. You heard Merk; he can't even talk about it or hear it. And I don't see me or Sylvan having what it takes, so that leaves you or Gilea."

Leo took a half-step back so he could see Gilea, whose eyes were focused on Sage, or on Temi behind Sage. If Leo said no, Temi would ask Gilea, who would agree without a second thought, and Leo could never live with himself if something happened to her. After everything he'd put her through on the past few trips, it wasn't fair to put her life in danger just because he had a moral qualm. And in truth, he did not like the idea of the Spreaders overtaking the Living Waters, and he liked the idea of him and his charges being killed by them even less.

He stepped back out of sight of Gilea and turned to Temi. "What's this about a secret nursery?"

Leo peered up out of the bag as Ranger lowered a clump of wet bladegrass roots on top of him, flashing an amused smile as he covered Leo's face. The *ipsis* carrying the bag exchanged a few words with Ranger, then joined her companions plodding through the marshy forest, spear-shovels in hand. The ride was bumpy, and Leo's hands and feet started to tingle after a while from being scrunched up into a ball. After a while, sunlight filtered through the mesh of the bag, and the *ipsis* began splashing through water, which soaked Leo's backside as they walked along what he believed to be the edge of the lake where they'd entered. The *ipsis* stopped and dug for a while, piling more roots on top of Leo. Water dripped from the hairy roots down into his mouth, which helped quench his growing thirst. After a time, they continued walking, then stopped again, and Leo heard the other two *ipsis* digging. The one carrying him continued, passing into the shadow of the bladegrass fields beyond the lake.

The *ipsis* slipped the bag off her shoulder, setting it down in the water, which soaked Leo to the stomach. The bag opened and the roots were pulled from atop his head, and he saw the *ipsis'* face peering down on him, her mouth twisted in a funny little smile. Leo took her long outstretched fingers and pulled himself slowly up to standing, moving only as much as his screaming muscles and joints would allow. He held onto the *ipsis* for support for a moment until feeling returned in his limbs, then dug the oval-shaped *ipsis*-made wooden box out of the bottom of the bag. He checked the strings, which were triple-wrapped and just as tight as when he had tied them, and tucked the awkwardly large box under his arm. The *ipsis* crossed her arms over her chest and bowed, and Leo repeated the gesture, as best he could with the box under his arm.

He waded through the bladegrass slowly enough that he wouldn't make waves or get scratched up too badly, and after a time the ground rose beneath his feet, and he walked onto a muddy sandbar covered in thorny bushes. He picked his way through the thorns, which were hard and sharp enough to draw blood, until at last, he could see the river stretching out ahead of him, muddy brown with an aroma of rotted moss and mussels. He felt a smile grow on his face as he soaked up the hazy summer sun. He had missed this, the open air, the hot sun, even the muddy river. There was something oddly wholesome about its odor of growth and decay, the plants and animals that thrived in it, despite the best efforts of the human cities to foul it.

He opened the box, which was thankfully still dry inside, and recoiled at the rotten-egg stench as he retrieved one of the bladegrass patties. It smelled and tasted of sulfur, but he knew he needed energy for the endeavor that lay ahead of him. He stared out into the river as he chewed, watching for any signs of the *duni*, but all he saw were the swirls of a few big whiskers and the occasional stick turning slowly in the current. He retied the box, stretching and checking the strings several times, then laid it on the water's surface, where it floated with several inches to spare between the water and the box's seam. He listened for any *ipsis* activity, but the only thing he heard was some digging far away behind him. He saw no tracks or any other indication the *ipsis* ever came here; this stretch of bladegrass and thorns served as a buffer between the river and the Living Waters, as the *ipsis* surely did not want to be seen by passing boats.

Leo pushed the box with his foot as he crept through the shallow water at the river's edge. The mud sucked his feet down to his calves, and he was glad when it got deep enough that he could swim without moving too much water. The late afternoon sun was on the wane, and he wanted to make sure he had enough daylight to cross the river and double back below the nursery. Merk had explained that there was a clearwater creek about a mile downstream, which the *ipsis* had blocked with rocks to discourage entry. Few *ipsis* were even allowed there, except for one Merk referred to as Trover, who tended the nursery. Leo knew there would probably also be *sitri* there, so he had a dose of the salamander slime tincture in a reed vial tied around his neck. In theory, it would protect him from being controlled, though the *sitri* could probably find a way to kill him using their ability to change the shape of water. He would have to be stealthy and decisive and hope for the best.

He tied the box to a string around his waist and set out across the river at a steady breaststroke, careful not to kick his feet above water or splash with his hands, so as not to draw attention. It felt good to stretch his muscles after more than a week pent up on the confines of the *ipsis'* limited domain. The river was about a mile and a half wide at this point, and when he reached the other side he sat on a rock and had a drink from his waterskin and a short breather, scanning the horizon for any sign that he was being watched. When he saw nothing, he returned to the water, trying to swim straight, despite the slow, steady current. He pushed himself, though the rope chafed at his waist as he swam and would surely leave a blister. He stopped about halfway across, treading water and scanning the shoreline. He saw a pile of boulders a little way downstream, which must have been where the creek let out. He scanned the shoreline for any sign of *ipsis*, but he saw none. He swam to shore about a mile below the dam and slow-crawled through the bladegrass at the water's edge until he reached a forest of spindly pine trees soaring toward the sky, now streaked with the pink and purple of the setting sun. He brushed aside the sticks and pine cones in a narrow space between the trees and lay down on his back, watching the sky's colors intensify, then darken. Frog and insect songs grew with the dwindling light, and when he could no longer see the tops of the trees, Leo sat up and looked around at the ghostly streaks of the tree trunks.

He checked the powder, which was still dry, and stuffed the remaining bladegrass patty in his mouth, wincing at the sulfury taste, but he was just able to keep it down. He noticed some of the sulfur was stuck together in hard chunks, which he set about crumbling in his hands until the box was full of fine powder. He held his nose to avoid the rotten-egg stench, but it penetrated deep into his mouth, his nose, and his stomach, which balanced on the edge of nausea. He drank some water and stood up, breathing in the wafts from the muddy river that mixed with the piney scent of the forest. He could see well enough to walk, but not fast, especially barefoot as he was. He leaned his back against a nearby tree and did some of Gilea's breathing exercises, inhaling slowly for a five-count, then exhaling for a seven-count. In time his body and mind relaxed, and he could see the task ahead with clarity and calm. There were several ways it could go wrong, and several solutions to each of them, which he allowed to swirl around in his mind, releasing control as they sorted themselves out and locked into place. Once he reached the nursery, there would be no time for reflection or weighing options. He needed to move like a creature of the land, in tune with his environment, certain of his quarry. And when the time came to act, he would do so without moral or strategic reflection.

Leo lifted the corners of the rough cloth that lined the box, jets of powder leaking out of the corners as he lifted them toward the center and tied them together, checking to make sure he had left room to reach his hand in and grab the powder. He slung the makeshift bag over his left shoulder and made his way slowly through the dark forest. Despite the occasional sharp stick or pine cone, it felt good to feel the moss and pine needles beneath his feet, and he padded along in near silence until he could see the silvery glints of stars on the creek ahead. Merk had said the nursery was about a half-mile up the creek, and Leo followed parallel to it, far enough into the woods that he would not be seen. After a few minutes of slow creeping, he saw where the creek gushed out from an embankment, above which lay a wide, square pond, divided into many smaller squares, with only a few trees spaced out among them.

He stopped and studied the pond, which shone more clearly than the creek, as the sparse tree cover above it allowed more starlight to shine through. The pond was square, with a strip of rock lining the edges. On the far side, he could see where the stream flowed calmly from the wetlands into the nursery, and in the opposite corner, the creek gushed out below a thicker barrier of rock, leading to the stream he'd followed on the way in. There were twelve rows of twelve squares, a hundred forty-four in total, each of them about five feet across, separated by thin rows of rocks. In each square, the water moved in a slow swirl, all in the same direction. He pictured them as a hundred forty-four *sitri*, rising up together into their humanoid form, racing en masse toward the Living Waters. While the *ipsis* would be safe in their protected village, there would be no way they could access the water with so many *sitri* around, and they would have to move elsewhere or quickly be overrun and controlled by the *sitri*.

He stood still, studying the dark edges of the pond, and noticed a mounded shape near where the still creek entered the nursery, which resembled one of the huts in the *ipsis* village. As he stared at the mound, he could see a thin stream of smoke rising from a slightly lighter shape against the darkness of the hut. The shape shifted slightly, and Leo could make out the contours of an *ipsis*, seated, and the smoke seemed to be rising from its head as if it were smoking a pipe. It could only be Trover, watching over his flock under the starlight.

Leo watched for what seemed like an eternity, fighting back the urge to pee, to take a drink of water, to do anything except stand perfectly still in the dark forest. Trover sat smoking for a long time, then stood and walked slowly around the edge of the pond, dipping his toes into the squares here and there. The swirls moved over to lap at his foot as he did so, then returned to the center of their square after he passed. It was as if he were petting them, and they moved to feel his touch. Trover's movements were slow and careful, and he walked with a slight limp. Leo surmised from his gait that he might be older, though not as old as Merk. This might bode well for Leo's chance to escape afterward, but even a slow *ipsis* might be able to catch him with such long legs.

After a long, slow round, Trover disappeared into the hut, and all was still except the slow spinning of a hundred forty-four *duni* under the stars. Leo wished he knew how deep the water in the cubicles was. He had studied the grid of stones separating the cells, and he worried about losing his footing if he moved too fast, but there would be no time to waste with so much ground to cover. He moved out of sight behind a larger tree and practiced thrusting his hand into the bag and pulling out a fistful of the powdered sulfur until he could do it in one smooth motion. He stood watching and listening for a long time, but detected no activity from the hut, or anywhere else. He unstoppered the tube around his neck and downed the bitter tincture, bracing his hand against a tree to keep it down. Once his stomach had settled, he walked forward with calm and purpose, careful to avoid stepping on anything that might make a sound, until he got to the edge of the forest, where a strip had been cleared between the pond and the surrounding trees. He paused to look at the hut one last time and listened for any sound, but he heard nothing. He took three deep, steady breaths, matching his exhale to his inhale, then crossed the buffer at a fast walk.

He walked left along the edge of the pond, tossing a handful of the powder into the closest three squares, and continued as fast as he could, fanning his fingers as he released for maximum spread. As he rounded the first corner, the water in the first squares began to bubble and splash, and Leo moved at a slow jog, tossing fistful after fistful. A large hump rose from the center of the grid and sped toward him, growing tentacles as it approached. Leo dug both hands into the bag and hurled as much of the powder as he could toward the *sitri*, which collapsed with a splat into the roiling water.

As he rounded the second corner, nearest the hut, he heard sounds from within, and he pumped his legs down the barrier, tossing sulfur haphazardly as he ran. He rounded the third corner and looked back to see a large figure burst out of the hut and run down the edge of the pool, obviously limping but moving much faster than expected. Leo turned toward the center of the pond and splashed along a line of stones halfway down, slowing to toss sulfur in both directions, then hurrying along the next couple of squares, his feet slipping for a moment as he stopped and threw powder to both sides. The *ipsis* stood at the edge of the pond, reared back, and hurled his spear through the dark air. Leo ducked and fell back into one of the squares, nearly hitting his head on the rocks on the other side, but the pool was only a couple of feet deep, and he managed to hold the bag high and dry as the spear clattered against the stones and into the pond.

Leo scrambled up as he felt a swirling suction around his legs, and got up onto the next line of rocks and started hopping and walking along the line, tossing sulfur as he went. The *ipsis* turned and ran back down in the direction it had come, then turned left and picked its way along a line of stones across the pond toward Leo, who by now had turned away and was covering the last third of the squares. Leo reached the end of his bag and the edge of the pond a few seconds before the *ipsis* chasing him, and he bolted into the forest, heedless of sticks and pinecones and rocks, hoping to the gods no stump or deadfall would bring him down. He ran straight for a minute, then headed left, back toward the place he had landed, slowing a bit to listen for footsteps behind him. Leo skidded to a stop as he heard the sound from far away, perhaps as far as the pond, a deep, mournful wail, like a great beast felled by a hunter's spear, raging with its very last breath.

Chapter Thirty Four

Temi watched Gilea walk in a slow circle around the edge of the courtyard, her hand touching the walls, just as Temi had done while she recovered. It was difficult to watch Gilea, who she'd come to see as strong, steady, and invincible, moving with such stiffness. Thinking how close she came to losing her. Imagining how it was affecting her. Gilea's shoulders cocked straight as she approached the bench with bold strides, then sat down with a pained wince. Temi took Gilea's hand and gave it a squeeze, thinking, *You don't have to pretend with me.* She could feel Gilea's spirits lighten, and it brought warmth to her heart. Not, perhaps, the same heat Gilea felt in her own, tempered though it was by her chitinous mental discipline. But they were connected somehow, and as she felt Gilea's pride battling her weakness, Temi's heart lurched, and she longed to lend her strength, to support Gilea as she had helped her.

Temi's ears perked at the measured splashing of the

tree-trunk canoe being paddled across the lake. Four *ipsis* soon appeared, carrying two earthenware jugs between them, which they set down next to the drainage channel. From the way Merk and the Pillar reacted, Temi could sense they trusted the newcomers. Sage sped over as twin columns of water rose from the two jugs, spreading wide like mirrors and flashing symbols back and forth with dizzying speed. Temi couldn't catch all of it, but there was something about the Circle, and digging, and it all seemed rather urgent. The Pillar pressed foreheads with Merk, who then spoke to Ranger and the half-dozen other *ipsis* they had gathered together, and they all nodded, gripping their shovel-spears tight.

Merk swung toward Temi's group, who stood clustered awkwardly around the bench. Gilea stood behind Temi and touched her lightly on the shoulder as Merk spoke.

"Sage and the Pillar have decided we must take you to the Spreaders, at the Circle. It is the only way."

"Take us to them?" Gilea's voice was incredulous, her hand grasping Temi's shoulder.

Merk closed his eyes and held out his hand in a calming gesture. "This is what they will think we are doing. The reality will be otherwise. Come. We must make haste. The morning is half over."

"What about Leo?" Temi asked softly.

"Leo accomplished his task." Merk's face drooped for a moment, then he lifted his head, though his eyes were heavy. "I believe he is safe for now, but they are out for blood, and if we do not go to them, they will come to us in full force. Their numbers are too great; there will be no more subterfuge, no more sneak attacks. It will be war, or more properly speaking slaughter, unless..." He clenched his long fingers into a fist. "Leo will find his way back. We can't worry about him. We must go. Now."

They tramped through the marshy forest, with the Pillar leading the way along with four other *ipsis*, including Ranger. The four in front carried two of the jugs, and two more *ipsis* behind Merk and Sadie carried the jug with Sage inside. Temi walked with Gilea and Sylvan behind the front group and would have struggled to keep up had Merk's slow pace not defined the group's speed. Gilea's jaw was clenched and sweat beaded on her forehead, but she marched steadily onward, flashing a tight smile when Temi gave her a worried look.

"I'm fine."

"I didn't say anything."

"I know, it's...it hurts, but I can manage the pain. I'm thinking of Leo, what he had to do..." Gilea closed her eyes for a moment. "He's going to have a hard time carrying that."

"He's not the only one." Temi had spent enough time around Sage, had enough of Sage still in her, that she knew the *sitri*, even the Spreaders, had a moral code, deep intelligence, and a sense of social bonds that was very much akin to emotion. They would see what Leo had done, what they all had done, as mass murder at least, if not genocide. And Temi wasn't quite sure they'd be wrong. Were the *duni* essentially baby *sitri*, or were they something else? Were they conscious? Could they make decisions? It was impossible to know, but there was no question how the Spreaders saw it, the revenge they would seek. Sage's plan was risky, but far less so than waiting to be overrun. They had no choice but to trust Sage.

They traveled much the same path as the last time, stopping to check for *sitri* before crossing each stream or channel through the marsh. They passed a group of six musclebound *ipsis* digging rather halfheartedly at a patch of bladegrass, and Ranger flashed them a hand signal, which they returned. Temi didn't know what the signal meant but assumed they were somehow part of Sage's plan. They continued for a time until at last the forest floor grew sandy, meaning they were close. Ranger bade the group stop, and he crept out into the forest, sweeping wide to check for any *ipsis* aligned with the Spreaders who might be lurking about. He returned and gestured for them to follow, but Merk stopped them, holding out a box with a dozen stoppered reed tubes. Ranger and Sadie each took one, and Temi, Gilea, and Sylvan followed suit, along with the rest of the *ipsis*, except the Pillar, who did not partake. Merk uncorked his tube, held it up with a smile, and poured its contents onto his huge brown tongue, wincing as he swallowed. Temi touched tubes with Gilea and Sylvan and they drank together. It was not as bitter as the healing tinctures, and though it was rather slimy, a pleasant numbness quickly spread from her mouth throughout her head and chest.

Ranger shook his head as if to clear it, handed the empty tube back to Merk, then gestured them to follow him. He led them a short distance toward the Circle, where four *ipsis* with the blue lines on their forearms stood on the sandy rim, spears in hand, faces stern. They exchanged a few curt words with Ranger, then all eyes turned toward the channel, where four *sitri* in hump shape moved toward the pool. As they entered, they rose up in humanoid form, and Sage and the other two *sitri* rose from their jugs. One of the *sitri* in the pool stretched their body wide, and a single dot appeared in the center, then flowed in ripples out toward the edges. Sage spread wide and flashed a similar pattern, but starting from the outside in. Bird calls and the sound of shovels in the distance were the only things that broke the silence.

Temi watched as Sage's form shimmered and undulated, their surface forming dense mazes of intricate lines and shapes she could not read. The *sitri* in the pool responded by forming an array of tightly packed circles of various sizes, which looked like one of the pattern practices Temi used to have to do in art school. Some of the circles grew and connected, and Temi noticed something familiar about the shapes they made. Though she couldn't work it out exactly, it seemed like they were showing agreement with whatever Sage had communicated.

Step toward the water now, came a thought in Temi's mind, like a voice echoing through a labyrinth. It was Sage. Temi nodded to Gilea and Sylvan, and together they took a careful step down the sandy bank toward the pool below. Three of the *sitri* moved to the edge of the pool, their bodies becoming taller, longer, thinner, splitting into multiple strands as if to enwrap them. *One more step,* came Sage's thought. Temi took Gilea's and Sylvan's hands, flashing them each a grim smile, and took another step with them, still at least five feet away from the watery tentacles hovering in the air. Sylvan's hand was clammy and his breath came short, but Gilea radiated calm, and something like acceptance. Temi wasn't sure, but it seemed like the tincture was making her more aware of others' feelings, particularly Gilea, almost as if their minds were touching at the edges.

Be ready.

Temi tensed as the *ipsis* who had carried the jugs burst into action, two of them rushing toward the point where the channel entered the pool, the others leaping toward the four *ipsis* standing on the rim opposite the group, forming a wall with their spears spread wide. The two by the channel tossed fistfuls of yellow powder into the water as they rushed past, then flung huge amounts into the portion of the channel nearest the pool, so a twenty-foot swath of it was stained mustard yellow.

The watery tendrils stretched out low and swept Temi's feet out from under her, and Sylvan and Gilea too. They all fell and slid down toward the pool, and the tentacles wrapped around Temi's legs and swarmed over her neck and face, tendrils like tiny fingers prying at the corners of her mouth, her nose, her eyes, her ears, then sliding back down her body as quickly as they had arisen. They rose again in humanoid form, then fell upon Temi and the others again as they tried to scramble to their feet. Water blanketed Temi's entire body, balling up around her face and head so she could hardly see, hear, or breathe. The tincture had prevented them from entering her body, but it would not stop them from suffocating her. She heard muffled shouts and saw flashes of movement through the cushion of water surrounding her head. Her breath was coming to an end, and she could not pull herself out from beneath the weight of the water, nor wipe it away with her hands, as it had formed a strangely hard, rubbery surface.

You have my strength, came a thought from Sage. Temi's hands stopped struggling, and she stopped fighting for breath. She lay still, her mind suffused with a clarity that lifted her out of herself, into a space filled with infinite light. She looked down on her face, pale and serene beneath the blueish tint of the water. The eyes on the face that was hers opened, and the water peeled itself off her head, rolling down her body and collapsing into the water. Her body sat up, holding one hand toward Sylvan and the other toward Gilea, and the water surrounding their heads slipped away, sliding down the sand to re-form into humanoid shapes in the edge of the pool. But the shapes were different now, less defined, and they sank down to humps with a great splash and rushed toward the channel. They stopped when they reached the cloud of yellow billowing into the pool, then roiled furiously away toward where the four *ipsis* from the other group faced off against the *ipsis* Ranger had brought. Those four began moving down the bank, but stopped suddenly, frozen in place, as a low sound emanated from the Pillar, a hollow, humming vibrato that hit an impossibly low note combined with an almost inaudibly high one, at the same exact pitch.

The *sitri* in the pool stretched and slithered up the bank, but the *ipsis* above were frozen just out of their reach. The *sitri* swirled and splashed around for a moment, then moved at lightning speed toward the yellow cloud, bursting out of the water like breathfins. They landed halfway through the yellow patch, where they splashed and thrashed along the surface, propelling themselves into the clear channel beyond. They formed into their jellyfish shape and sped off down the channel.

Temi floated back down into her body with the softness of a tiny feather, her hands clutching the warm sand beneath her. She heard shouting and pounding footfalls as Ranger led the *ipsis* from their group along the channel, spears in hand, moving with incredible speed through the forest. In the distance, she heard more shouting and splashing, but the chaos dissolved as Gilea's hand found hers. She looked up into Gilea's eyes and slid her hands up Gilea's arms, over her strong shoulders, and clasped them around the back of her neck. Gilea's eyes fluttered as Temi leaned in, drawn by a blind urgency, and kissed her soft, hot lips. Temi's heart pounded and her head grew light, and she pulled back, staring into Gilea's eyes. Gilea blinked away tears, wrapped her arms around Temi, and pulled her into a fierce hug. Temi clung to Gilea like a starfish to a rock, impervious to the waves crashing around her.

Temi heard Merk and Sadie's quiet voices, and she released her hold on Gilea and helped her to her feet. They walked back up to the top of the sandy hill, joining Sylvan, Merk, and Sadie. Sage and the other two *sitri* faced each other, their flat surfaces forming into moving shapes and patterns, like the story lamp she'd had as a child. They didn't seem to be communicating in their normal way; it appeared to be some kind of visual narrative. As she watched, she felt drawn into the performance, guided with gentleness from within, by Sage. They were sharing memories of the *sitri* they had just had executed, the Spreaders, but in these stories they swam joyously through the clear waters of the lake, flowing in and around and through each other. They had grown from *duni* side by side, had worked together with the *ipsis* to maintain the Living Waters, to tend to their *duni*, to keep themselves hidden from the world. The other two went blank as Sage flashed patterns Temi could see as buildings, riverside docks, ships, and at last a detailed image of Endulai that was so clear Temi heard Gilea gasp beside her.

No more. Sage went blank, then flashed the pattern again. *No more*.

Chapter Thirty Five

Sylvan sat turning the Seeing Tube over and over in his fingers, studying the symbols on the side and struggling to decipher any of them. He did make out what he thought were several numbers, three and nine, though he was less sure about the nine. He had at first surmised they might be a form of Islish or perhaps one of the alchemical scripts, but the longer he studied them the more convinced he became that they were from some ancient version of a distantly related language he had not yet come across. And it wasn't just the language that was foreign; the device itself bore little resemblance to anything he had ever seen. The color of the brass, the richness of its hue, the way the copper symbols were laid into the wood, everything was completely strange to him. He supposed it could be of Islish make, but he had met Islish scholars and seen the implements they carried, and they looked nothing like this.

Merk shuffled up, almost losing his balance as he

lowered himself into a chair next to Sylvan. He looked drained, suddenly much older than before, and his breath came in loud wheezes. He pulled a skin from his side, took a drink, and coughed a little.

"You're trying to figure out where that comes from, aren't you?" Merk croaked.

"I am. I know several ancient and modern languages, and now a little of your tongue, but this bears only the faintest resemblance to any of them. And the craftsmanship, it's...it's unlike anything I've ever seen."

Merk grunted as his long fingers gently removed the tube from Sylvan's fingers, which felt suddenly empty, useless without it.

"I myself do not know for sure, but I believe it to be ancient, from the time before your civilization came to be. From a time when magics such as this were more commonplace."

Sylvan shook his head. "I know what they say about magic on the Isle, and in the western provinces, and I've read a bit of theory, but if I hadn't seen it with my own eyes, I wouldn't have believed it."

"I expect there's a lot you wouldn't have believed before you came here."

Sylvan nodded, picking at his fingernails. "Like you—how is it no one knows about the *ipsis*?"

Merk's chuckle turned into a dry cough, and he cleared his throat several times and drank from his skin before he spoke.

"Just because you have not heard of something, just because it's not in your books, doesn't mean no one knows about it. Perhaps this Servais, the author of your book, knew more than he let on, but in his wisdom, he chose not to share it." Merk's big eyes looked hard into Sylvan's, with a mysterious flicker.

"But what good is knowledge if it cannot be shared? Surely the more we know, the more we can use that knowledge to improve the world."

Merk blinked, looking out into the misty forest. "I see you know little of politics."

"What about you? How do you know so much about the human world? How did you learn to speak Southish, when none of the other *ipsis* can?"

Merk cleared his throat, stifled a cough, and his head swiveled on his long neck to look at Sylvan.

"That is a rather long story, and not one I think I'd have time to share properly before you leave." He cocked his head toward Sylvan's companions, who stood talking, bags across their shoulders.

Sylvan looked to Temi, who blinked at him, and he held up his index finger toward her, turning back to Merk, his heart suddenly heavy. The world of Anari, his family's sumptuous compound, the sterile halls of the university, seemed like a distant dream, and not one he was eager to return to. The Living Waters was a university, or a universe, unto itself, and there was so much more he needed to know. One thing was sure: if he went back to Anari now, he would never see the Living Waters again.

"We've still got time. Tell me a little bit of your story. I promise to show wisdom and keep your secret."

Merk gripped his cane, pushing it into the floor, though he remained seated. He stared out into the forest for so long Sylvan wondered if he was going to say anything.

"When I was a young *ipsis*, not halfway to maturity, I went out exploring with my playmates, and I became separated from them. Night fell, and I wandered, trying to find my way back, but by morning I was far from anything I recognized. I managed to find the river again, but I was bitten by a crimson horn, a kind of venomous snake—"

"I have read of them. Their poison causes deep hallucinations, does it not?"

"Indeed. If I had been back in the village, they would have had an antidote, but I was alone, and I entered a dream-world, with colors swirling all around. I swam in the colors, and they washed over me, until I fell out of comprehension, out of mind." He paused, turning his neck to spit behind him. "When I awoke, I was laid out on the bottom of a small fishing boat, with two bizarre creatures eyeing me warily. Humans, I now know. They took me to a strange building of white stone, where I met the woman who was to be like a mother to me, for many years. It was she who taught me to speak your language. Because I was young, I picked it up easily enough, though some of the sounds were difficult for me to form. She taught me many other things as well, science, alchemy, and the subtleties of the Endulian practices, which are not unlike our own."

"You were in Endulai?"

"Not in Endulai proper; more of an annex downstream, for study of things not directly related to the main disciplines. They had a wondrous laboratory, and strange forges for making fine pieces out of copper and other precious metals. And a library, such as I expect you have never seen, even in Anari. Books of a mystical nature, some alchemical, others detailing practices and knowledge you would likely see as magical. And some ancient scrolls as well, or copies anyway. I would give anything to go back there, even for a day."

"But it's so close, isn't there some way..."

Merk shook his head. "I am too old, and the risk too great. Not to my life, for the few days I have left are surely not worth much. But the risk to the others, to our life, our secret..." He trailed off as Sadie approached, slinking over with long steps and timid eyes. Merk struggled to his feet, using Sylvan's shoulder and his cane for support.

"I will leave you and Sadie to say your goodbyes." Merk blinked at Sylvan, his mouth twisted in a half-smile.

“Thank you, Merk. For everything. *Hello Sadie,”* he continued in *ipsis, “How are you?”*

She folded her long, soft fingers around Sylvan’s. *“I will miss you.”* He could feel her desire to wrap her arms around him, to hold him tight, to keep him safe. He leaned into her shoulder and her heat enveloped him. He melted against her body as her arms circled around his back. His heart ached at the thought of leaving her behind, leaving this cocoon of safety and calm. He pushed away gently, and she clutched his wrists to her chest, her deep eyes staring into his.

“Stay with us. For a little while longer. Stay with me. Let me be your...” He did not understand the word, and she must have seen it in his eyes. She swiveled her head around and called to Merk, who hovered nearby. He turned and pushed his way toward them, leaning into his cane.

“She’s hoping, we’re both hoping, if you decide to stay with us for a while, you’ll let her be your support, for a time.”

Sylvan looked from Merk to Sadie, then off into the lush forest, the water glimmering in the distance, alive with light and movement.

“I don’t know if I can be everything you need,” Sylvan said, his eyes moving from Sadie to Merk and back again. “But I do have a lot to learn here, if you’ll have me, for a time.” Sadie cocked her head, squinting to understand. *“Yes,”* he said to her in *ipsis*. Sadie’s eyes closed, and she sucked her huge lips inside her mouth, then puckered them as she raised his hands to her mouth to kiss them. His heart caught in his throat at the gentle feel of her lips, and a wave of warmth swept over him. “Yes, I will stay with you, for a while,” he said to Merk in Southish, out of habit. “But I will need some paper and ink, and a desk to write on.”

Merk smiled, murmuring a few words to Sadie, who pulled Sylvan from his chair and nearly dragged him toward their hut. Temi flashed him an odd look, which he tried to deflect with a smile.

"I'm staying," he said. Temi gasped, Gilea remained impassive, and Leo's face broke out into a grin. "But I have several letters to write first. Do you think you can deliver them for me?"

When Sylvan emerged from the hut, Leo was walking on his hands, entertaining the children, while Gilea and Temi stood almost touching, watching with bemused smiles. The skin on Temi's face and hands was blistered and peeling, and she seemed to take no notice of it whatsoever. She had stopped painting her face, or any other part of her, and the forest canopy only offered so much protection. Sylvan wondered if there were enough ointment in all of Anari to bring back her shade seven tone.

Temi smiled as he approached, letters neatly rolled and tied with the rough string the *ipsis* used. The paper must have come from a human source, and though it was old, it was of good enough quality it had survived without becoming too brittle.

"Here's one for my parents, and this one's for the university. I've asked for a year sabbatical, and though it's out of the ordinary, my father will probably pull some strings."

"Aren't you worried they'll send someone out here to find you?" Temi asked.

"I expect they will send an investigator to Guluch, where I told them I intend to take up the study of alchemy. On a purely academic level, of course." He glanced at Gilea, hoping she would take the hint, or at least know better than to tell his family the truth.

"Guluch is a big place," Gilea said with the hint of a smirk. "They might not be able to track you down. I've heard alchemists can be a secretive bunch."

"Indeed they can, and I'll be back in a year's time, just like I said. I also wrote this for you, officially releasing you from your contract to return me to Anari. If you could just sign here, saying I was of sound mind and body when I made this decision..."

Gilea unrolled the contract on the table as she straddled the log bench, taking the inked quill Sadie held out and signing without a second look.

"It's been a pleasure getting to know you, Sylvan." Gilea held out her hand and shook Sylvan's hard enough he almost cried out.

"Likewise. And Leo, I want to thank you for all you've taught me. And for saving my life."

Leo grinned, glancing around the village with what looked like envy. He would have fit right in, but Sylvan doubted he'd want to stay in any one place very long.

"You even managed to teach me a thing or two. Nice to know you, Sylvan." They shook hands, and Leo pulled him in for a powerful hug.

Temi's shoulders shifted as she stepped to Sylvan and wrapped gentle arms around him, holding him for a long moment before pulling back, wiping tears from her eyes.

"I'll see you back in Anari in a year," he said. "My family will throw a big party, I'm sure of it, and you'll be the first person on the guest list."

Temi blinked at him, then turned to Gilea and Leo, and they all seemed to nod at the same time.

Sylvan stood next to Merk and Sadie as Ranger led his friends off the platform and into the marshy forest.

"I'll see you soon," Sylvan said under his breath as Sadie's long fingers found his waist and pulled him into her warmth.

Chapter Thirty Six

Leo crossed his arms to say goodbye to Ranger, who smiled and pulled him in for a long, warm hug. Leo would miss Ranger most of all, and he wasn't sure how the whole mindshare thing worked, but he felt like Ranger was sending him the same vibe as they held each other. When at last Ranger let him go and turned away, Leo joined Gilea and Temi in the canoe, which the *ipsis* had pulled through the maze of channels to the edge of the lake where they had first entered. He picked up the paddle, nodding to Temi, who had wrestled the other paddle from Gilea and was sitting in the front. Temi smiled, her face red and peeling. Leo hoped Gilea didn't lose her bonus over it, but that was her problem, not his. Temi stuck her paddle into a clump of bladegrass and started to push.

"Wait," Gilea said, pointing at a wide crescent-shaped disturbance in the water, like a slow-moving wave. It separated into a dozen individual *sitri*, which rose into their humanoid form. They stood perfectly still, then the one in the middle flashed a pattern of circles, which was repeated by the adjacent *sitri*, on down the line and back in less than a second. The pattern changed, becoming more angular, and was broadcast out and back again, with the same dazzling speed and effect. The *sitri* each began flashing different patterns and changing their shapes, growing taller, shorter, wider, narrower, or growing dozens of watery appendages. They moved and undulated and flashed shapes, pictures, something that looked like ancient lettering, and all manner of fractal patterns, in a dance that was equal parts coordinated and chaotic. Each movement, shape, or pattern from one was echoed by another as if they were tossing a ball back and forth, and each movement brought a new dimension to the dance. The speed and energy of their performance intensified, until they began to merge, growing into one tall pyramid shape made up of a dozen smaller pyramids. This watery structure grew suddenly still and glittered in the sun like an enormous crystal, then collapsed with a thunderous splash. A dozen humps rose up slowly and filed back across the lake as a group of lavender breathfins leaped and cavorted over and around them.

"Those *sitri* really know how to say goodbye," Leo said, suddenly close to tears. Part of him wanted to leap into the water and swim after them; he doubted he'd ever again see such wonders. But he had seen what there was to see in the Living Waters, and he needed to keep moving forward, not back.

Everyone was quiet in the canoe as they paddled along the bank toward the raft. Sylvan's absence seemed to have sucked the breath out of everyone's lungs, and whatever was going on between Gilea and Temi didn't seem to require a lot of talking. He had seen Gilea cut loose on leave, having her share of amorous adventures, but he had never seen her like this. All her strength, her centeredness, her drive, everything she had, was all focused on Temi, and she only looked away when they heard Sea Wolf barking and whining with joy. Leo steered them alongside the raft, which was right where they'd left it, and tied off the canoe to the cleats as Sea Wolf licked him from head to toe. Leo gave as good as he got, rolling on top of Sea Wolf and licking his nose and face.

"Who's a good boy took care of my boat?" As Sea Wolf licked his nose and mouth, Leo smelled fish, and he wondered how the dog had managed to feed himself for several full weeks on the raft. Had the *ipsis* been bringing him fish? He could think of no other explanation. Temi knelt next to him, and Sea Wolf jumped up and put his paws on her shoulders, nearly knocking her down with a ferocious barrage of licks. Temi pushed him away from her face, pinning his snout on her knee and scratching him behind the ears, which he quickly accepted, though the rear end of his body wouldn't stop moving.

"I'm going to go inside and get some salve for your face," Gilea said, touching Temi on the shoulder as she passed.

"I'll join you." Temi grabbed Sea Wolf's snout playfully, then let go, sprang up, and followed Gilea into the cabin.

Leo let them have their space and moved to the front end of the raft, where he threw out the cast net a few times until he had a dozen baits, including one of the baby thinkfins Sylvan had pointed out. He smiled at the pearly white fish flopping in his hand, its big eyes seeming locked on his as its tiny mouth opened and closed, sucking useless air. He cupped it in his hand and lowered it over the side of the raft, then watched it wriggle free and disappear into the muddy water. He baited the trotline with the other minnows, dropped his pants, and swam the weighted end downstream, finding a bit of a dropoff and letting it sink.

He saw no movement from the raft; Temi and Gilea were inside the cabin, he thought. He gazed out over the golden-brown river, feeling the eager strength in his muscles as he treaded water just beyond the dropoff. He figured Temi and Gilea could use some privacy, and the river's wide expanse was calling to him, so he lowered his head and pushed his arms forward as his legs propelled him with a powerful kick. He started in breaststroke to warm up, but he soon switched to a fast crawl, pushing his body to its limit, then pulling back just a hair, for good measure. He gulped air between strokes, blowing turbulent bubbles out when his face was beneath the water. He fell into a rhythm with his breath and his movements, and as he approached the opposite shore, he turned quickly upstream so he wouldn't lose his momentum. He plowed straight into the current, which was slow, but the weight of the whole river pushed against him, putting him at a breath deficit. He powered through until he was far enough upstream, then turned abruptly left toward the opposite shore, maintaining the same speed but getting some of his breath back, as he was no longer fighting the current.

He stopped in the middle of the river, treading water for a moment and scanning the surface of the water for swirls. He looked behind him and there he saw two of them, spinning side by side not twenty feet away. He kicked gently toward them, and they moved in unison away from him in an arc, so they stayed the same distance no matter which way he swam. Leo's chest tightened, and the tightness spread up to his face, bringing a painful tingling sensation around his eyes. Tears began to flow, surprising him at first, then his chest began heaving as sobs burst forth. He flipped over on his back, half-closing his eyes to shield them from the sun, and floated, his midsection dipping below the water and floating back up with each sob. Images flashed in his head, of yellow powder flying by starlight and scattering into dark waters. Of swirls thrashing and roiling, wobbling as they spun out of control, then dissipated, leaving only feeble waves in the squares they each occupied in the nursery, which he had turned into a graveyard.

The *duni* shadowing him maintained their distance, and Leo's sobs became more sporadic. At last, his breathing returned to normal and his tears dried, and he rolled over onto his stomach, treading water again. He wished he could flash patterns to the *duni*, as the *sitri* did to each other, tell them why he had to do what he'd done, how sorry he was, how he wished he could make it right. He wondered if they even knew, if they understood, if they were capable of knowing or understanding. He scrunched his face a few times to get rid of the tingling feeling left by the crying bout, then took in a few deep breaths through his nose. He swam off with a strong kick, angling upstream a bit since he had drifted down during his brief float. The water did not wash away the heartache, but by the time he reached the raft, he was tired enough that the sadness was harder to feel. He watched the two swirls edge close to the bank and move downstream, side by side, back toward the Living Waters.

Leo slept on the roof that night with Sea Wolf, who stretched along his leg, snoring contentedly. He could almost feel the starlight bathing his body like a million cooling suns. As he stared up into the infinite spiderweb of the heavens, he was struck by his own insignificance, a feeling he knew all too well. But if his life was small and meaningless, that meant his actions too, however horrible they might seem in hindsight, were inconsequential, in the cosmic scheme. They had already flowed beyond his control, and he would make peace with them, given sufficient time and sweat. The only thing yet in his power to influence was where to go next, what to see, what to do. For do he must, or perish from lack of trying.

After his morning swim, Leo tended the fire and set water to boil as quietly as he could. Gilea emerged from the cabin, walking on quiet feet across the logs to crouch down by Leo and hold her hands in front of the fire, though the morning was already warm and muggy. Sea Wolf nosed her hand gently, and she grabbed him by the ears and gave his head a good shake.

"If you can help us paddle to Endulai, I'll sign off on your contract," she said, ruffling Sea Wolf's fur as she stared into the fire.

"You sure? I'm happy to head back up to Anari with you. I could check in with the bureau there, maybe pitch a winter roughabout in the southern seas. I was thinking a deserted island type of thing, maybe someplace with some sea caves to poke around in. What do you think? You feel like tasting the salt air again? I know Wolfie does, don't you boy?" Sea Wolf darted over, his posture alert, then licked Leo's face three times in rapid succession.

"I'm going to have to think about it, okay? This trip was...a lot. Give me some time, and I'll send word to... Rontaia, I assume?"

Leo scratched his beard, squinting at the rising sun. "Makes the most sense, doesn't it? I'll need to scout out some options, find a boat, some maps, so yeah. I'll make my way down there and wait for your letter."

"You'll hear from me one way or another in two months."

Leo nodded. "Sounds about right."

They made tea and stood watching the circles from the fish surfacing and the V-lines from a pair of *chukin* swimming by. Leo looked for swirls but saw nothing except those made by a few larger whiskers. Gilea turned to him after a while, her mouth twisted in a crooked smile.

"How exactly are you planning to get the raft down to Rontaia all by yourself"

Temi wore her hat and veil the next day, and the oversized gloves Leo had bought her in Guluch. Gilea had applied some sort of ointment to Temi's face, a thick coating of bluish-white that smelled like it might have had medic's balm mixed into it. Her face glowed ghostly white beneath the veil, and Leo realized that of all the painted faces he'd seen on his tours, not one of them had worn white paint. When they pulled up to the dock, Temi stood up and grabbed hold of the ladder, then tied the front rope off to a cleat on one of the support poles. She shouldered her bag, then lifted her veil, blinking against the sun.

"Thank you, Captain Leo," she said, "for everything."

"Well, we got you back in one piece, though it was a bit closer than I generally aim for."

"It was perfect." She leaned forward, extending her arms, and Leo stepped over the canoe's support beam and gave her an awkward shoulder hug.

"You were amazing," he said. "I hope we meet again someday." Knowing they wouldn't.

Temi smiled, lowered her veil, and climbed up the ladder.

"See you in a few months, I hope?" he said to Gilea. She turned and gave a weary smile.

"For a beer at least," she said, pressing her hands together at her forehead and bowing to him. He repeated her gesture, though it felt a little odd since her usual goodbye was her hands pressed together at heart level. She stepped onto the ladder, untied the rope, and tossed it into the front of the canoe.

"Have a nice float."

Leo's heart leaped at the sight of Max and Zander's little encampment. He was exhausted from two days of hard upstream paddling, and he kept looking over his shoulder at some gray clouds that had not yet made their intentions clear. Max and Zander walked to the water's edge to greet him, waving when he got close enough to meet their eyes.

"Where's the rest of your crew?" Zander said, glancing from Leo to the bank of approaching clouds.

"They got off at Endulai. Gilea has some kind of connection there, I think. Anyway, my contract is up, so I'm a free man. Thought I'd stop by and see how you all were doing."

"Working on that paddlewheel mostly," Max said, meeting Leo's eye for the briefest moment before looking back down. "Need a few more boards and a couple pieces of iron, but we'll get there. We'll get there."

"That we will." Zander put his hand on his brother's shoulder. "It's quite a long paddle from Endulai. I see you brought your dog."

Leo reached behind him to tousle Sea Wolf's ears. "Yeah, I didn't want to leave him behind all by his lonesome on the raft again."

Max smiled, gazing at the dog, who moved to the front of the canoe, wagging his tail. "I miss having a dog. We used to have a dog, but he ran off on us one morning and never came back. Otto was his name, wasn't it Zander?"

"Otto was a good dog," Zander said with a wistful smile. "Well come on in and have some tea, sit out the storm."

Leo looked over his shoulder at the clouds, which were approaching more quickly than he'd thought, with a darkness behind them.

“I’d appreciate that, and a bite to eat if you’ve got anything.”

“What’s ours is yours,” Zander said. Leo loved that about river folk, their willingness to share what little they had.

Leo nosed the canoe up to the bank, hopped out, and Zander helped him pull it up on shore. Sea Wolf leaped out and ran to Max, who crouched and let the dog lick his face up and down.

They sat under the tarp on Zander and Max’s little floating house, drinking tea and eating knotted, unleavened bread so hard Leo had to dunk it in the tea before he could chew it.

“I’m glad you came all the way up here to see us,” Zander said once they had finished their bread and tea. Something in his tone made Leo wonder if he had sniffed out the reason for his visit. “Where you off to next?”

Leo looked from Zander to Max, who was staring up at him from under the brim of his hat.

“I was thinking of floating the raft down to Rontaia.”

“You can’t work those sweeps with only one person.” Max shook his finger. “It takes two.”

“Either of you ever been to Rontaia?”

Zander waved him off, but Max’s eyes burned into Leo’s.

“I’ve always wanted to go, see the shipyards. I heard they got all kind of ships, for river and sea.”

“Every kind of boat you ever imagined, and some you wouldn’t believe unless you saw them.”

Max stared off at the river for a moment, then looked back to Zander, whose eyebrows were raised almost to the top of his head. Max turned to Leo, staring at him like he was on fire.

“Max, why don’t you go get some more tea going. We can sit a spell and catch up, and maybe Leo can tell us a bit about some of those ships he mentioned, the ones so fancy we wouldn’t believe them unless we saw them with our very own eyes.”

Chapter Thirty Seven

Temi stood next to Gilea on the deck as the twisting spires of Anari came into view. Their construction was a marvel she rarely saw from this perspective, and when in the city she seldom looked up, due to her sensitive eyes. The three towers dominated the skyline, flying their silver flags with the red star in the center. Temi's father had taken her to the top of one of the towers for her thirteenth birthday, and she had gazed down at the city's rings, the inner ones white and green with marble and trees, the middle ones mostly gray, and the outer ones brown. She had always wondered what it was like in the brown circles, but she had never been allowed to go outside the fourth, except by the port road, which was walled from the fourth circle outward.

Temi felt the warmth of Gilea's fingers a hair's breadth from hers, and she inched her pinky finger over to rest atop Gilea's. A tingle ran from her pinky, up her arm and into her chest, pulling her ribcage tighter and enveloping her heart like an oven-warmed mitten. She moved her fingers to interlock with Gilea's, and Gilea clasped hers tightly, then relaxed a little so as not to bruise Temi. Gilea leaned into her so their arms touched, heat flowing between them through the thick fabric of Temi's sleeve.

"Are you sure you won't come stay with us for a few days? I'm sure my mother would greet you with her waxiest smile, but she would never turn away a guest."

Gilea turned to face Temi, taking hold of both her hands. She looked into Temi's eyes, and Temi could feel the 'no' before Gilea opened her mouth.

"I'm going back to Endulai."

Temi bit her lip as if that would stop the sudden tears rising behind her eyes. "I know, I just..."

Gilea lifted Temi's veil with gentle fingers, and Temi grew dizzy with the thought of Gilea kissing her, half-wishing she would, but unsure if her heart could take it. Gilea leaned in with her forehead, pressing it against Temi's. Temi almost expected her mind to open up, but she felt nothing other than Gilea's hot skin against hers.

"You have things to do," Gilea murmured. "I can feel that, and I would only get in the way. Besides, I have things to do too."

"In Endulai, of course." Temi let go of Gilea's hands, turning toward Anari, which was approaching faster than she was prepared for.

"Yeah." Gilea moved toward her, brushing the back of her hand against Temi's. "I think it's past time. There's someone there I need to see. And I'm not the biggest fan of the waxy smile, to be totally honest."

Temi covered her laugh, trying to mask the fact she was wiping her eyes. "Well, I aim to melt that wax and find out what's underneath. It could get a little ugly. You probably wouldn't want to see that anyway."

Gilea gave a tight smile and shook her head. "But look, I'll be coming back this way in the fall. I'll send word to let you know for sure when." She took Temi's hand and lifted it toward her chest, raising her own hand toward Temi's and looking her in the eyes. Temi nodded, pressing her hand into Gilea's chest as Gilea's pressed into hers.

"Promise?" Temi said, struggling to see Gilea through her tears. Her heart was raw, but it didn't feel broken. The bond they shared was unlike anything she'd felt before, rooted deeper than their physical presence, woven into her mind and heart. She wondered if this is what everyone referred to when they spoke of love. She carried a part of Gilea within herself, from when their minds had intertwined in the Living Waters, and that part would remain intact until they met again. She smiled as she realized with perfect certainty that they would.

"Promise," Gilea said.

Temi threw her arms around her, feeling Gilea's muscles close around her shoulders, and she closed her eyes. They stayed locked together, unmoving, for a long moment, until Gilea slowly relaxed, and Temi slid out of the embrace, feeling a little unsteady on her feet. She pulled out her handkerchief and dabbed around her eyes, breathing a small laugh as she saw the yellow on the cloth where some of her paint had come off. Her laughter grew into a snort when she looked up and saw the yellow smudge on Gilea's forehead. Temi reached the handkerchief up to wipe it away, but Gilea caught her wrist and lowered it.

"Leave it," she said with a sly smile.

Temi checked her paint in her battered little mirror as the carriage waited for traffic to clear so it could pass through the gate into the third ring. In the smudged reflection, she could see her skin had mostly returned to its usual smoothness, thanks in large part to Gilea's attentive care and ointments, but she wasn't sure if she would retain her shade seven at her next ceremony. She almost hoped she didn't, despite the advantages it brought.

When the carriage finally stopped in front of her house, she dropped the rest of her coins into the driver's outstretched hand, a bigger tip than she would normally have given, though perhaps less than he might have received from someone of Sylvan's status. These were the coins she had intended as her seed money for Rontaia, but she had abandoned that plan for now. She would see Rontaia, that much was certain, but it would be on her own terms, with Gilea to show her around, once she had accomplished what she set out to do back home.

The gate squealed its complaint as she wrenched it open and leaned into it to close it tight. She steeled herself with a deep breath and walked through the dusty courtyard, removing her hat as she reached the portico and opened the door. The house had an air of emptiness, and a stale, melancholy smell greeted her as she set down her bag at the foot of the stairs and wandered into the kitchen. She heard the back door open and close, and her mother's measured footsteps approaching.

"Temithea," her mother said from the kitchen doorway, her smile almost genuine beneath her mask of lavender paint.

"Mother." Temi took a tentative step toward her mother, who crossed the room and took her in a gentle embrace, holding her for longer than usual. When she pulled back, she looked Temi up and down, her gaze lingering on Temi's face.

"We'll have to burn that dress," she said, though Temi was sure she was studying her face for remnants of sunburn. It was just like her to avoid saying the main thing on her mind. "I'll send word to Gallitin to come fit you for a new one for your Rising."

"There's no need, mother. I have that beautiful pale blue one from last year. I've hardly worn it."

"Nonsense. You only Rise once, and we haven't lost any contracts since you left, though it's been a tough summer." She turned and retrieved the etched glass decanter from the shelf, with about three fingers left of her father's favorite redfruit brandy, which they drank on special occasions in tiny amounts. She poured a mouthful into each of the two tasting glasses, swirling both around and handing one to Temi. She raised her glass to her nose, locking eyes with Temi as they both sniffed the sharp, musky fumes.

"To his name," her mother murmured.

"To his name." Temi closed her eyes and let the brandy slide down onto her tongue, equal parts fire and tang, opening her senses as it burned its way down to her stomach. The alcohol's bite masked the sudden shock of sadness at the memory of losing him, which she saw in her mother's eye for the briefest moment.

Her mother cleared her throat, blinking and dabbing at her eyes with a handkerchief. "Speaking of names, how did you get along with that Kirin boy?"

"He's not a boy, mother. He's a Doctor of Life Science at the Great University."

"Sounds like quite a catch." Her mother's eyes twinkled with something like mischief.

"Well yes, he would be, but no, it's not like that, and anyway he's decided he's staying in...Guluch to... study alchemy, I guess?" Temi tried to play it off, but her mother's single raised eyebrow showed she'd sussed something was amiss.

"His parents are going to paint their faces red," her mother remarked drily.

"He sent a letter, which I have to deliver—"

"Later. Ciro is coming with a fruit delivery this afternoon. He can take care of it for you."

Temi looked down at her glass, then tipped it to let the last burning drops roll onto her tongue. "So, you said it's been a tough summer?"

Her mother sighed, replacing the glass decanter and picking up the pewter one and two larger glasses, which she filled rather full of red wine.

"The western traders brought in a new design set, some kind of mountain rune theme, which for some reason has caught on. We've had to drop prices and boost production of the fruit tree line, which hasn't been easy." *With you gone*, Temi could feel her not saying, almost as if she had heard the words.

"I'm ready to get back to work," Temi said, swinging her shoulder bag around front and opening the flap.

"After your Rising, of course, what..." Her mother trailed off as Temi opened her sketchbook, showing the pages of swirls, turning them one at a time until her mother stopped her by pressing her finger onto the drawing of a plate with a swirl in the center and breath-fins around the edges.

"This one I like. I like it a lot..." She turned the pages, stopping on the *chukin* close-up, the speckles, Max and Zander's crazy boats, the swirls outside the alchemist's hut, nodding her head as she touched each one with her finger. She inhaled audibly when she saw the sketch of the *ipsis,* her brows furrowing as she shot Temi a hard glance.

"What on earth is this supposed to be?"

"Nothing mother, just a little fantasy sketch, for a side project. Look at these here." She flipped to the drawings of the stickbirds, the bladegrass, the snakes, and all the other creatures she'd seen in the Living Waters.

"Temithea, these are extraordinary, and with the little waves, really, I—" Temi's throat swelled up in a lump as she heard the tone of her mother's voice, the unadulterated praise she had so seldom heard before. "Another one for your side project?" she asked, studying the drawings of the Seeing Tube, the *sitri* flashing patterns, the *ipsis* and their tree trunk canoe.

Temi bobbed her head, unable to hide her growing smile. "Sylvan gave me the idea, to do some illustrations for a river fables book, which we would work on together when he returns. He'll write summaries of the fables, and I'll do drawings of the monsters and fairies and what-not. He'll come up with plausible explanations for the natural phenomena behind them, and I'll illustrate those too. With his University connections..."

"Not to mention family connections, yes, this is an excellent idea Temi. And who knows? Maybe we could do a special series of fantasy plates." She flipped back to the animal drawings, sipping her wine as she turned the pages and studied them, moving the book into a slanted rectangle of light reflected off the stucco wall opposite the open window. "I think I like these breathfins most of all. I hadn't realized there were breathfins in the Agra."

"There's a lot more out there than you'd think," Temi replied.

Her mother closed the book and looked up at Temi, studying her face again. "A lot of sun out there too, from the look of things." Her brow furrowed as she raised her hand toward Temi's cheek. Temi pulled back, and her mother's hand returned to her glass.

"My paint dried up and I had to make do. But Gilea gave me some ointments, and I think it will clear up in the end."

Her mother raised her glass to her lips, eyeing Temi over the rim. "I hope so. I've always been a little jealous of your tone, and it would be a shame—"

"What would be a shame is for me to live in fear of how people perceive me, or to marry someone who only valued me as a shade seven." Temi lowered her eyes and her voice, which had grown unexpectedly loud. "I'll be fine, mother."

"I'm sure you will," her mother said, her voice rising in something like admiration. "Still, I'd like to make an appointment with Doctor Gineli, just to be on the safe side. If you have no objections, of course."

Temi cracked a smile. Gineli had been the family skin doctor for Temi's whole life, and he didn't have a judgmental bone in his body.

"Sounds perfect. Thank you."

They sipped their wine in silence, her mother filling both glasses once her own was empty, though Temi's was still half full.

"Come, let's have a sit in the back garden under the featherpine. The sun has dipped below the wall, so we can go without our hats, I think. I want to hear all about your little raft adventure. I'm sure you have some interesting stories to share."

Temi hid behind her glass and took rather a larger gulp than she was used to.

"There's not much to tell beyond eating muddy fish and swatting suckflies."

"I very much doubt that."

"Well, there may be one or two things," Temi said as she rounded the table. She took her mother's outstretched hand and walked with her out the back door into the garden.

"I've missed our little oasis," Temi said as they sat on the bench under the featherpine, staring at the fountain, which burbled and splashed into the stone basin. Something deep inside her stirred as she watched the morphing and overlapping circles and ripples of the water, suffusing her with a sense of wonder and calm.

"So," her mother said, placing her hand atop Temi's. "Tell me everything."

Chapter Thirty Eight

Gilea sat on a stone bench in a circle formed by hedges with glassy reddish-green leaves. The pond in the middle of the circle had clumps of round-leafed aquatic plants with sinuous flowers in shades from lavender to royal purple. Two large white fish drifted around and between the vegetation, with filmy white discs where their eyes should have been. Thinkfins, Leo and Sylvan had called them. Bubbles rose up from the bottom at regular intervals, bursting on the surface and scattering ripples across the pond. The noise from the docks did not carry here; Endulai itself was as silent as its reputation suggested.

The acolyte who had brought her into the circle reappeared, emerging from a break in the hedge Gilea hadn't noticed before. She was followed by an older woman, whose stately bearing and pacific smile Gilea recognized instantly, even before the mottled brown and white skin on the left side of her face registered.

Gilea resisted the urge to stand, to call out, to rush to Amini and take her in her arms. She pressed her hands together against her chest and closed her eyes, breathing in through her nose and letting it out slowly through her mouth. When she opened her eyes again, Amini and the acolyte had approached to within about ten feet and crossed their arms toward Gilea, who stood and repeated their gesture.

"My lady," said the acolyte in a hushed voice, "She says her name is Gilea, and she—"

"Is welcome here." Amini blinked, and a wave of warmth and invitation flowed through Gilea, who gasped, touching her chest and looking into Amini's kind eyes. "If she comes with an open mind."

Gilea covered her mouth, nodding, and floated gratitude toward her former teacher, whose smile stretched a little wider. Had this been the silent interview she had been fearing all these years? Was it already over?

"I do," Gilea said. "I look forward to sharing minds with you again. It has been far too long, Amini."

"It has been just as long as it needed to be." She stepped forward to meet Gilea and clasped hands with her. "You may go now," she said without looking at the acolyte, who gave them each a modest bow and disappeared into the hedge.

"The years have been kind." Gilea looked up at Amini's wrinkles, which had deepened and softened in the ten years since they'd last met.

"They have moved me along my path, just as yours have brought you here, at long last. I am pleased to see you've kept up your practice."

"I have, as best I can, but how could you—" Gilea stopped herself, shaking her head. Amini's ability to read auras had always been without equal.

"Don't worry, I've not read your mind. I know you'll share with me later. I can feel it, see it almost, in the air around you." Her fingers fluttered as she moved her hands in a circle framing Gilea's head. "Something's changed."

"It has," Gilea replied, looking over at the pond, watching the thinkfins brush up against each other, shimmying their bodies together before curving off in opposite directions. "I want to know what it means."

As Amini led her through the curving hallways, Gilea peeked through an open doorway into a long meditation room, where several dozen students sat staring into their cupped hands. Gilea tended to use movement in her meditation, and this motionless form was going to take some getting used to. A brazier in the center of the room gave off thin streams of purplish-gray smoke, which rose into the high, arched ceiling, merging to form a nebulous haze. Amini stopped, returning to stand beside Gilea in the doorway. One wall of the room had a row of bookshelves, and one student sat apart from the rest, staring at a blank patch of wall at the end of the row.

"What is that one doing?" Gilea whispered.

"Rin is reading," Amini said with a slightly indulgent tone. "They can self-segregate any time if they're struggling to find their center, and read one of the books on philosophy and meditation."

"But...she's just staring at the wall."

"She's reading the thirteenth shelf. It's where we keep all the books that have yet to be written. Come, let's leave them to their practice. I'll show you to your quarters, and then we'll see what you're ready for."

Gilea knelt on a cushion next to Amini, facing a small round pool lined with glittering quartz. Amini picked up a large wooden spoon and ran it along the edge of the pool in one slow stroke, then removed it and laid it back on the ground. The surface of the water turned and swirled enough that the glints from the quartz danced and shimmered in a dizzying yet soothing way.

They knelt and stared at the water, lost in its gentle fluctuations, almost predictable in their randomness. Every now and then Amini stirred the water again, and the patterns sped up, then wound their way slowly back down. Gilea sank into the larger rhythm, her breath and mind moving and slowing along with the water, which Amini eventually allowed to come to stillness. Gilea felt something release inside her, and a space opened like a bubble surrounding them, and Gilea's awareness filled the bubble.

I would not have thought it possible. Amini's thoughts came to her like a murmur of wind among leaves. *To achieve such a state on your own.*

Not on my own. Gilea felt the part of Sage inside her giving her strength, like the ribs on a parasol. Before merging with Sage, she had never before been able to receive and share thoughts so clearly, but in this moment it came almost without effort. *I have been to the Living Waters.*

Amini radiated surprise, laced with concern. *Things have not been right there for some time. We sought to increase our offerings, but it did no good.*

Things are better now. Gilea believed it was true, though she had many doubts, which she allowed to flavor her message. *I think.*

Your coming is fortuitous, then, in more ways than one. Amini's thoughts paused, and Gilea's gaze was drawn down into the pool again, to the glimmering rainbows beneath the surface.

How?

The Caravan has a new crossroad, in the mountains to the north, among a tribe who call themselves the Maer. Its breadth and clarity are unparalleled. We think they must have a new source of sunstone. We are short on travelers as it is. We could use your help.

*But I've never...*She knew of the Caravan and had

even seen the cradles in Rontaia, but it was always spoken of as the province of only the highest masters.

We will teach you. With your talent, it will not be hard. And your coming from without, rather than within, may be to our advantage.

Gilea let her doubt flow toward Amini, who sent it back as calm.

We will take all the time you need.

Gilea's awareness shrank back inside her body, landing gently inside it, but not enclosed, like riding in an open-topped carriage. Amini took her hand, her face crinkling into a warm smile.

The days flowed together like water, an endless cycle of meditation, poses, reading, and games. Endulians were surprisingly enthusiastic about their ball sports, releasing their pent-up energy in bruising competitions each day before dinner. Even Amini joined in; frail though she appeared, she had a light step that allowed her to avoid physical contact with uncanny ease. Once dinner had settled, everyone paired off under the stars to share minds, and sometimes bodies. Gilea had heard that true Endulian practice held bodily and mental unions as equally important, though the physical side was not always sexual; sometimes it took the form of lying back to back in perfect stillness. She preferred this method of touch, as she was still raw from Temi's absence and not ready for greater intimacy quite yet. Gilea still felt Temi's spark in her forehead, long after the paint had washed away, which was a comfort at times when it was not an insatiable itch she could never scratch.

Gilea lost track of days and weeks, but the sun began to weaken, and the nights grew cool enough to sleep with a light blanket. One evening after dinner, before the pairings, Amini found her standing by one of the fountains. She did not speak, or even push a thought into

Gilea's head, but Gilea knew. It was time. She followed Amini back inside, through a series of twisted hallways to a round, domed room with a bronze door covered in strange symbols that reminded her of some of the alchemy books in Wulif's library. The floor around the door was inlaid with similar symbols, and in the center of the outer rim, a black stone knob protruded from the floor. Amini knelt by the knob, pulled it out, and a shaft of bright light pierced the air, casting an almost hexagonal shape on the ceiling. Amini retrieved another knob from a pocket, this one made of shining bronze. She inserted the bronze knob into the hole, blocking the light in an instant, and the door swung open without a sound.

Amini gestured Gilea through the doorway, with Amini following close behind her. A similar arc of bronze runes lay in the floor on this side of the door, and Amini removed the bronze knob from the floor, replacing it with the stone one from the other side, and the door swung closed. They stood in another round room, with six elaborate bronze structures like no cradle Gilea had ever seen. They were shaped like giant eggs, but the sides were made of burnished bronze latticework in a dizzying array of symbols and patterns. Four of the cradles had people reclined inside them, their bodies covered in heavy blankets, their heads fitted with copper circlets like Gilea had seen in the cradles in Rontaia. Their eyes were closed, and an acolyte stood next to each of them, watching their faces. The acolytes did not even look up when Gilea and Amini walked through the room.

I've never seen such cradles, Gilea thought. The ones in Rontaia were wooden, with only the headpieces in copper.

They are from the Time Before, Amini replied. *They have been here for millennia.*

Where is the furnace? The room was cool, not hot, and Gilea knew a large amount of heat was required for the energy to power a crossroad.

That is what makes this crossroad special. She pointed up to the ceiling, where a bronze sphere about a foot in diameter was affixed to the ceiling, with thick bronze pipes running from the sphere to the six cradles. *Sunstone. We have an auxiliary furnace we can use in emergencies, but we have enough sunstone to last us another two or three years. After that, it may get complicated. The Timon claim to have exhausted their mine and are searching for an alternate source, and in the meantime, they have tripled their prices.*

And that's where this mountain tribe from the north comes in, thought Gilea, wondering who the Timon were, what her role in the Caravan would be. What the Caravan even was. A thousand doubts flooded her mind as she realized the goal she had focused on for so long was no more than the starting point of a new journey she had hardly dared to dream of. She doubted that she was ready, that she'd ever be ready, but if Amini was showing her all of this, she had to believe there was a reason.

Amini smiled and squeezed Gilea's bicep. *Enough about these menial matters. We will teach you everything you need to know, if you decide you are ready to begin this next journey.*

I place myself in your hands, Amini.

Amini took Gilea by the shoulders and stared deep into her eyes.

You've followed the Lonely Way, but you've never managed to fully trust yourself. Now comes the part where you learn to fly on your own.

She picked up a honeypot and took a spoonful into her mouth, then passed the spoon to Gilea, who coated her own tongue. Amini then produced two glass vials, containing a thick, reddish liquid, and handed one to Gilea. She unstoppered her vial and drank the tincture in time with Amini, scrunching her face against the metallic tang. Its taste was similar to the meditation tinctures she had used before, but it went to her head almost instantly. Amini pocketed the two vials, then reached over, turned a handle on the cradle, and a door opened, revealing a cushioned seat that reclined at a forty-five-degree angle. Gilea looked into Amini's eyes and felt nothing but kindness and encouragement. She eased herself onto the seat and lay back, feeling a little claustrophobic as Amini lay the weighted blanket over her, fitted the cold copper circlet on her head, and closed the door.

I'll be joining from the next cradle over. Just close your eyes and wait for my invitation.

Gilea closed her eyes but struggled to control her breathing and heartbeat, which were fast and uneven. She felt the panic of a child thrown into deep water for the first time, and her mind flailed about for something to ground into. A wave of calm rolled over her as if her consciousness were being cradled by a great, gentle hand. Her fear and doubt melted away, and she saw only darkness, with a great orange-golden light speeding toward her. The light stopped suddenly just as she was sure it was going to hit her, and she was pulled toward it like a lodestone to iron. The light formed into a shell that extended around her, then began to move as a streak of coppery light appeared in the darkness, pulling her forward along its length. The shell around her began to distend, forming a long tunnel, and she hurtled through it, streaks of copper extending from the edges of her vision through the blackness. Soon the sensation of movement slowed, and she saw a warm, orange-golden light at the end of the tunnel. She drifted with infinite slowness toward the light, which was shaped like an arched doorway. The blackness retreated behind her as she approached, her vision filling with a light of unimaginable purity and warmth.

Amini's thoughts reached her like the whisper of the

sea at night.

Welcome to the Caravan.

Acknowledgments

This book would not have been possible without the efforts and support of too many to count, but I would like to thank a few of them specifically:

Phil Babiak, may he rest in peace, to whom this book is dedicated, for showing me the wonders of nature and the human spirit, and for taking me on the real-life raft adventure that inspired this story;

Demetrius Babiak, may he rest in peace, Phil's father, who told me stories and sent me precious materials that helped inspire my writing;

Madelaine Robinson, a dear family friend, who was eager to share stories of Phil and the raft and encouraged me to pursue this story;

My wife **Sarah**, my biggest supporter;

My longtime critique partner **Beth Blaufuss**, who helped guide and shape the book from its very first draft;

My father-in-law and fellow writer **Tom Zaniello**, my most faithful beta reader;

Jessica Moon and **Mandy Russell** of Shadow Spark Pub, whose editing, cover design, formatting, and general guidance and cheerleading have pushed me to become a better writer than I ever could have become on my own;

My **Shadow Spark family** of writers, whose constant encouragement and suggestions help me stay on track and never lose sight of the end goal;

My sensitivity reader **Arina Nabais**, whose keen eye and gentle hand helped me find my characters' true selves, and avoid some pitfalls I might have missed on my own. Wherever I may have stumbled, it is through my own fault, not theirs.

Erika McCorkle and **Anny**, who were kind enough to answer some of my questions about asexuality;

Karkki, whose amazing cover art helped bring the spirit of the book to life;

Kriti Khare, whose inspired art piece graces the interior, as well as the naked hardcover;

The **many book bloggers** who agreed to read ARCs, and whose honest feedback always makes me a better writer;

And as always, the glittering hordes of the **#amwriting** and **#amwritingfantasy** Twitter community, who are a daily source of inspiration, information, and joy.

Dan Fitzgerald is the fantasy author of the Maer Cycle trilogy (character-driven low-magic fantasy) and the Weirdwater Confluence duology (sword-free fantasy with unusual love stories).

He lives in Washington, DC with his wife, twin boys, and two cats. When not writing he might be found doing yoga, gardening, cooking, or listening to French music.

Find out more about Dan and his books at
http://www.danfitzwrites.com,

or look him up on Twitter or Instagram, under the name danfitzwrites.

Also By Dan Fitzgerald

The Maer Cycle Trilogy:

Hollow Road

The Archive

The Place Below

The Weirdwater Confluence:

The Living Waters

The Isle of a Thousand Words (coming January 2022)

CPSIA information can be obtained
at www.ICGtesting.com
Printed in the USA
BVHW050450061121
620874BV00007B/72

9 781956 883008